Global Perspectives on Orhan Pamuk

Literatures and Cultures of the Islamic World

Edited by Hamid Dabashi

Hamid Dabashi is Hagop Kevorkian Professor of Iranian Studies and Comparative Literature at Columbia University. Hamid chaired the Department of Middle East and Asian Languages and Cultures from 2000 to 2005 and was a founding member of the Institute for Comparative Literature and Society. His most recent books include *Islamic Liberation Theology: Resisting the Empire*; *Makhmalbaf at Large: The Making of a Rebel Filmmaker*; *Iran: A People Interrupted*; and an edited volume, *Dreams of a Nation: On Palestinian Cinema*.

Published by Palgrave Macmillan:

Global Perspectives on Orhan Pamuk
Existentialism and Politics

Edited by
Mehnaz M. Afridi
and
David M. Buyze

palgrave
macmillan

First published in 2012 by
PALGRAVE MACMILLAN®
in the United States—a division of St. Martin's Press LLC,
175 Fifth Avenue, New York, NY 10010.

Where this book is distributed in the UK, Europe and the rest of the world,
this is by Palgrave Macmillan, a division of Macmillan Publishers Limited,
registered in England, company number 785998, of Houndmills,
Basingstoke, Hampshire RG21 6XS.

Palgrave Macmillan is the global academic imprint of the above companies
and has companies and representatives throughout the world.

Palgrave® and Macmillan® are registered trademarks in the United States,
the United Kingdom, Europe and other countries.

ISBN: 978–0–230–11411–1

Library of Congress Cataloging-in-Publication Data

Afridi, Mehnaz Mona
    Global perspectives on Orhan Pamuk : existentialism and
    politics / Mehnaz M. Afridi & David M. Buyze
        p. cm.—(Literatures and cultures of the Islamic world)
        ISBN 978–0–230–11411–1 (hardback)
        1. Pamuk, Orhan, 1952——Criticism and interpretation. 2. Politics and
    literature. 3. Existentialism in literature. I. Buyze, David M. II. Title.

PL248.P34Z53 2012
894'.3533—dc23   2011042942

A catalogue record of the book is available from the British Library.

Design by Newgen Imaging Systems (P) Ltd., Chennai, India.

First edition: May 2012

10 9 8 7 6 5 4 3 2 1

Printed in the United States of America.

In memory of Aijaz Afridi and Jaspert Buyze
and
Charles E. Winquist—"in thinking otherwise."

Contents

Note from the Editor

The Islamic world is home to a vast body of literary production in multiple languages over the last 1,400 years. To be sure, long before the advent of Islam, multiple sites of significant literary and cultural productions existed from India to Iran to the Fertile Crescent to North Africa. After the advent of Islam in the mid-seventh century CE, Arabic, Persian, Urdu, and Turkish authors in particular produced some of the most glorious manifestations of world literature. From prose to poetry, modern to medieval, elitist to popular, oral to literary, this body of literature is in much need of a wide range of renewed scholarly investigation and lucid presentation.

The purpose of this series is to take advantage of the most recent advances in literary studies, textual hermeneutics, critical theory, feminism, postcolonialism, and comparative literature to bring the spectrum of literatures and cultures of the Islamic world to a wider audience and appreciation. Usually the study of these literatures and cultures is divided between classical and modern periods. A central objective of this series is to cross over this artificial and inapplicable bifurcation and abandon the anxiety of periodization altogether. Much of what we understand today from this rich body of literary and cultural production is still under the influence of old-fashioned Orientalism or post–World War II area studies perspectives. Our hope is to bring together a body of scholarship that connects the vast arena of literary and cultural production in the Islamic world without the prejudices of outmoded perspectives. Toward this end, we are committed to pathbreaking strategies of reading that collectively renew our awareness of the literary cosmopolitanism and cultural criticism in which these works of creative imagination were conceived in the first place.

HAMID DABASHI

Acknowledgments

It has been a wonderful experience to work on this book as old friends. Writing and coediting a book can be difficult; however, because of our shared training in critical and theoretical approaches we were able to write and work with one another with ease and delight. It was pleasurable, challenging, and constructive. However, we would not have had the opportunity of editing this volume without the hard work and tenacity of the contributors and their continued work and support of this project. Thank you!

Finally, we would like to extend our gratitude to our mothers, Zwaantien and Nasreen, and to our loved ones, Sandra, Scott, Alex, and Rüya.

Foreword: Pamuk and No End

Sander L. Gilman

As I write this, we are deep into the summer following the Arab Spring of 2011—riots and sit-ins are followed by regimes falling, collapsing, resisting; nonviolence meets with violence; and constitutional changes, some voluntary and some dictated by totalitarian regimes, followed by more riots and sit-ins, and still no clarity. But what will be the outcome? Some have suggested that a new model is needed: the ideas of a new definition of "democracy" with a Muslim turning or a return to the old notion of the Caliphate—now reborn as a type of pan-Muslim cultural rather than political realm—have surfaced. But over and over again, a pragmatic, empirical model has been proposed for the shape of the nation-states of the Arab Spring. The American secretary of state Hillary Clinton stated it most clearly in July 2011:

> Across the region, people from the Middle East and North Africa particularly are seeking to draw lessons from Turkey's experience. It is vital that they learn the lessons that Turkey has learned and is putting into practice every single day. Turkey's history serves as a reminder that democratic development depends on responsible leadership, and it's important that that responsible leadership help to mentor the next generation of leaders in these other countries.[1]

It seems improbable that Turkey, having evolved from a radical secularism of Ataturk "guaranteed" by a military quite willing to intercede in democratic processes to a state with a strong and popular Islamic party and a sense of democratic institutions honed by a (unrealistic?) desire to join the European Union (EU) with its army in check, has become a model for the

Arab Spring. Especially when Clinton followed her comments noting that, with all the positive changes under Prime Minister Recep Tayyip Erdogan (his "responsible leadership"), there still persists one problem area:

> Turkey's upcoming constitutional reform process presents an opportunity to address concerns about recent restrictions that I heard about today from young Turks about the freedom of expression and religion, to bolster protections for minority rights, and advance the prospects for EU membership, which we wholly and enthusiastically support.

She was more candid in a closed news conference:

> Well, first of all, if there is an area that I am concerned about with recent actions in Turkey, it is this area that you have raised. It's the area of freedom of expression and freedom of the media. I do not think it's necessary or in Turkey's interest to be cracking down on journalists and bloggers and the internet, because I think Turkey is strong enough and dynamic enough with enough voices that if there are differences of opinion, those will be drowned out by others who can debate it in the marketplace of ideas.... I come from a country that has very, very broad protections for the media. And I know that a lot of times people on the outside do not understand that, because people say or do things in my country that personally I find just offensive and unpatriotic and anti-American, and it makes my blood boil. But we know that over time that basically gets overwhelmed by other opinions, and so you then get to a point where you've got a much clearer idea of what the basis of opinion and change might be. So I would, if I were in the Turkish Government, which I am not—and I say this very respectfully—I would be standing up for freedom of expression and freedom of journalism—(applause)—and freedom of bloggers and freedom of the internet, because I think in today's world information is so broadly available that it's going to get out there anyway.[2]

Kemal Ataturk founded modern Turkey in 1923 as a Western, secular nation with a firm orientation to the West. As a result, it quickly became a haven for Jewish scholars from Germany after 1933—for scholars such as Erich Auerbach whose *Mimesis* was written there. Today, in 2011, Turkey has become *the* model "Middle Eastern Country" under the present government with its new political tilt toward the East (including non-Arab [Persian] Iran) and its new (but ambivalent) anti-Israel and anti-Zionist position. Turkey is in the same position as American Mormons in the summer of 2011, who, with two leading candidates running for the Republican nomination for president, have suddenly become mainstream Christians in their public rhetoric—at least in part out of their political desire to fit into the Evangelical tilt of the Republican Party. Middle Eastern Arabs (and Persians) and American Evangelicals are not quite convinced by the conversion.

Yet, the conversion to the model Middle Eastern state does seem to have a serious problem in the realm of freedom of expression, what in the United States is usually referred to in the shorthand of American politics as "First Amendment Rights." This seems to be a problem for the new Muslim model state (and for many of those in the Arab Spring) with regard to "journalists and bloggers and the internet." As Hillary Clinton notes, this is not a trivial omission, and yet her seeming reluctance to note that this model also (if not primarily) impacts on the world of letters and high culture is noteworthy. Indeed, her notion that opinions that are "just offensive and unpatriotic and anti-American" will eventually vanish rather than dominate in public discourse is one that seems to argue for a rational flow to the course of history, a sort of public sphere Gresham's Law, in which bad ideas are driven out by good ideas—but whose good ideas? In a world in which it is claimed that Facebook generates revolutions, the notion of the Hegelian *epopee,* the modern novel, putting the status quo at risk because of repressive politics seems quaint at best.

Yet, the work of (Ferit) Orhan Pamuk, the Nobel Laureate of 2006 in Literature, is more than a major voice in the globalized world of modern letters (his work has sold over 7 million books in more than 50 languages); he is also a central figure in any understanding of the "new" Turkey, and through this understanding the desires and aims of a large swath of North Africa and Middle East. Mehnaz Afridi points out how complicated such a position is in her chapter in this volume looking at the Egyptian novelist Naguib Mahfouz and the much younger Pakistani writer Mohsin Hamid. Mahfouz having survived the experience of military dictatorships with secular coloration in Egypt after the fall of Farouk thus has much the same position as that of Pamuk—surviving an attempted assassination because of his insider/outsider status.

Like Mahfouz, Pamuk is a "cultural" Muslim rather than a religious one. Educated at Roberts College, the elite, secular American high school, in Istanbul in the 1970s, with a further long exposure to American (or at least to urban New York) culture in the 1980s, Pamuk's orientation is Western and secular—thus a representative of the "Old" (Ataturk's) Turkey, but, of course, with radical differences to that tradition and with equally uncomfortable relations to the "new" (Erdogan's) Turkey.

What the present volume elegantly edited by Mehnaz Afridi and David Buyze has quite successfully undertaken is the tracing of such cultural and literary webs in which Pamuk and his works—not only read in Turkish but also in English, Arabic, and Japanese—are believed to be found. Pamuk is a "Turkish" author, but he is also a celebrity modern writer whose postmodernity is very American. (On the American quality of Pamuk's writing, see the chapter by Fran Hassencahl.) Like his contemporary Haruki Murakami, whose American experience was Princeton University rather than Columbia, and is "Japanese" modern suspended halfway on the spectrum between Kenzaburo Oe (the Japanese faux existentialist Nobel Laureate) and Banana Yoshimoto (the Japanese global exponent of modernist kitsch à la Bret Easton Ellis), Pamuk is too postmodern to be Turkish and too Turkish not to be postmodern. (David Buyze gestures toward this position in the literature of postmodernism in his contrast of Pamuk with Italo Svevo, who felt himself suspended between futurists like Filippo Marinetti on the one hand and modernists like James Joyce on the other.)

Pamuk was a global celebrity early on, beginning with winning the 1991 Prix de la Découverte Européenne for the French translation of his second novel *Sessiz Ev* (*The Silent House*). *Beyaz Kale* (*The White Castle*) was awarded the 1990 Independent Award for Foreign Fiction and extended his reputation abroad. (Michael Pittman's reading of this novel points toward why it translated so easily and found a critical audience with alacrity, and Erdağ Göknar's chapter on Pamuk's untranslated novels illustrates what travels abroad and what does not, as well as why Pamuk makes the choices he does.)

Pamuk's global celebrity status was both acknowledged and unpinned by his Nobel Prize of 2006, given, as many have been recently awarded, more for clearly political rather than literary concerns. (To mention, only recently, Gao Xingjian in 2000, but the list is much, much longer, perhaps beginning with Carl von Ossietzky in 1935.) For as early as 1995, Pamuk had been among a group of authors tried for writing essays that criticized Turkey's treatment of the Kurds and Turkey's official denial of the Armenian genocide, as well as the question of political repression in contemporary Turkey. Pamuk's outspokenness on these issues culminated in 2005 when he was indicted for his comments about the Armenian genocide and became the international focus of the debate about freedom of expression, which certainly made it to the floor of the US Congress. The political realities in Turkey were such that Pamuk fled the country but returned to face trial (which was dismissed on a political technicality as the government did not want this type of exposure on a human rights issue during the lead-up to the EU discussions about membership for Turkey). Pamuk was put very much in the position of Salman Rushdie in 1989 when Khomeini issued a fatwa against him for the publication of *The Satanic Verses*. Having written widely on the political issues of the day concerning Islam and the Middle East (including op-ed pieces in the *New York Times*), Rushdie suddenly claimed to be merely a novelist with the innate freedom to imagine the world as he would like to have had it—not a politician. Pamuk's response to the Turkish media about the Armenian genocide was similar. When Turkish television CNN TURK asked Pamuk about his comment on the Armenian genocide, he admitted that he said that "Armenians were killed," but he rejected that he said "Turks killed Armenians."[3] A subtle use of the passive, but a real difference in the *realpolitik* of the day.

Pamuk is an example of an oppositional writer, not a dissident. A dissident (Aleksandr Solzhenitsyn is a good example) confronts the system under which he must write to overthrow it; an oppositional writer finds the spaces within the system to function (take Ovid in Imperial Rome or Jurek Becker in the German Democratic Republic). That dissidents can be used by the system as weapons within the system is clear. The publication of *One Day in the Life of Ivan Denisovich* was used as a blast against Stalin after his degradation, while Ovid and Becker were forced into exile when the hole in the system they wrote within closed their possibilities to function within the world of high culture. Pamuk too is both a Turkish writer and a *Poeta en Nueva York* (remember Federico García Lorca so suspended), both postmodern and Turkish national in a global sense, as noted in his Nobel speech: "My world is a mixture of the local—the national—and the West."[4]

Pamuk sees himself as BOTH Turkish (which means writing in a "minor literature" as Deleuze and Guattari stated that Kafka did) and Western, that is, global and postmodern. But the question of what Turkish box he needs to check is always problematic:

> As for my place in the world—in life, as in literature, my basic feeling was that I was "not in the centre." In the centre of the world, there was a life richer and more exciting than our own, and with all of Istanbul, all of Turkey, I was outside it. Today I think that I share this feeling with most people in the world. In the same way, there was a world literature, and its centre, too, was very far away from me. Actually what I had in mind was Western, not world, literature, and we Turks were outside it. My father's library was evidence of this. At one end, there were Istanbul's books—our literature, our local world, in all its beloved detail—and at

the other end were the books from this other, Western, world, to which our own bore no resemblance, to which our lack of resemblance gave us both pain and hope.[5]

Yet, Pamuk, unlike Rushdie after the fatwa affair, is quite willing to put this ambivalence into his best literary work. Certainly his novel *Kar* (*Snow*) (2002) presents the tension between the inner conflicts within the complexity of Turkish identity from the radicals of the Kemalists to the reactionaries of the Islamists (and vice versa). (Thomas Cartelli, Hülya Yilmaz, and Esra Santesso elegantly illustrate this in their chapters in this volume.) But he is also more than willing to place himself (or at least his narrative doubles) clearly in the world of the oppositional, if not always transparent as to what world—the West or modern Turkey—he stands in opposition to. (Sevinç Türkkan and Hande Gurses show how complex this *Dance to the Music of Time* [with apologies to Anthony Powell] really is.)

Thus, the chapters in this volume provide not only a literary but also a political stocktaking of a prolific and widely read writer, whose works, like those of his contemporary Rushdie and Murakami, may well be better known outside their "native land" than within it, and for good reason, but whose persona is of enormous importance to the modern states out of which these writers came. The chapters in this volume comprise the most important collection of essays by far on Pamuk to have appeared in English. It is a vital contribution to our global and local conversation about letters and history, ideology and politics, reading and its consequences, and between Facebook, blogs, and journalism in the twenty-first century.

Notes

1. "07/16/11 Joint Press Availability With Turkish Foreign Minister Ahmet Davutoglu; Secretary of State Hillary Rodham Clinton; Istanbul, Turkey," http://www.state.gov/secretary/rm/2011/07/168665.htm
2. "07/16/11 Coffee Break with Hillary Clinton Hosted by CNN-Turk and Moderated by Sirin Payzin; Secretary of State Hillary Rodham Clinton; Istanbul, Turkey," http://www.state.gov/secretary/rm/2011/07/168667.htm
3. Gergin Bir Mülakatti, "Kişkirtildim," Haberpan.com. October 16, 2005.
4. http://nobelprize.org/nobel_prizes/literature/laureates/2006/pamuk-lecture_en.html
5. http://nobelprize.org/nobel_prizes/literature/laureates/2006/pamuk-lecture_en.html

Introduction

Mehnaz M. Afridi and David M. Buyze

I have sometimes even entertained the thought that I was fully dead and
trying to breathe life back into my corpse with literature.[1]
—Orhan Pamuk, "The Implied Author"

Global Perspectives on Orhan Pamuk: Existentialism and Politics
vitalizes and proposes nuanced and different considerations
of the study of literature in a cross-disciplinary manner with
an array of uncharacteristically academic essays that form the chapters of this volume. These essays illuminate a study of Orhan Pamuk's
literature into an intellectual and humanistic light. Our decision to
coedit this book on Pamuk evolved from many intellectual discussions
as friends, and as colleagues, who share a common academic field of
religion and a deep interest in modern comparative literature. Our
shared commitment to literature over many years brought us to deliberate upon Pamuk, who represents a mélange of voices in his complicated and multifaceted existential and political narratives of ordinary
lives. Typically, academia is separated into areas of study with little
room for multiple disciplines to speak as a singular voice, or, as Gilles
Deleuze[2] would put it, the "singularity" is a new way or exigency of
posing a problem, or a way of thinking by looking at different results.
In this vein, certain academic categories tend to constrict the singularity of the narrative rather than release the multiple facets of the
experience(s), or, as Edward W. Said has expressed, experience must
come to be considered as irresolute, as meaning cannot be found in one
singular societal facet of identification that creates a narration of how
life is lived.[3] Academic and historical systems of ordering narratives and
things tend to empty meaning of its worth, and as Michel Foucault has
thoroughly suggested in *The Order of Things*,[4] the narratives of naming are invented and not given. The exact incisiveness and brilliance of

literature relies on a lever of intervention in how it upsets and sets adrift what is taken as *given* in this world, and in the particular sense of how language can be excavated. We feel that it is highly crucial to stress the novel that can perhaps simultaneously undo or rather incite consciousness to reimagine what is the seemingly *given* sense of how one's life seems to be constructed and intuited by society. Narratives can explore every dimension of life from art to science, to religion, to war, and we view the novel as an essential map of all disciplines in multiple dimensions. Pamuk's writing embarks on an imaginative canvas that invites the reader to wander in psychological and historical descriptive dimensions of literature that rethink subjectivity amid multicultural and societal characterizations that disrupt language and human ways of knowing. As he writes in *Snow*:

> **Snow:** The solid form taken by water when falling, crossing, or rising through the atmosphere. Each crystal snowflake forms its own unique hexagon. Since ancient times, mankind has been awed and mystified by the secrets of snow. In 1555, a priest named Olaus Magnus in Uppsala, Sweden, discovered each snowflake, as indicated in the diagram, has six corners.[5]

This atmospheric transmission from liquid to solid creates an utter uniqueness in a snowflake never to be replicated, which can certainly be taken metaphorically in considering human experience in how each seemingly insignificant episode of narration can never be captured or told the same way; yet this is what Pamuk, in a manner of speaking, seeks to capture in narrating human experience—that which can never be captured or perhaps told.

Pamuk is an author whose novels we have taught in varied classes on religion, Islam, and postcolonialism. In the classroom, and as an intellectual undertaking, we ask the question: What is the place of literature and religion? Do the two fields collide and clash with one another? Why is there a tendency in the humanities to separate the different types of criticism? Do novelists think categorically about the fields of study? Pamuk would respond and say: No. Clearly, Pamuk's novels and trajectory express a complicated fabric of today's global citizenry with nuances of religion, secularity, existentialism, nationalism, and violence. There is an urgency that beckons in our globalized world that the novel should be taken with much more seriousness as it is a vehicle that propagates a revisioning of one's imagination in how the self and world can be considered anew. Pamuk's work takes categorical understanding of well-worn binaries such as East/West, religion/secularity, and traditional/modern into areas of thinking that we feel still need more profound exploration and openness in the fields of religion and comparative literature. Pamuk's novels, in a similar fashion to those by Naguib Mahfouz (Nobel Laureate 1988), were never meant to be strictly religious or political in ambition, but rather they unfold a stunning oeuvre on their own lives and the family drama that surrounds personal experiences in their respective countries. This regional sense of, respectively, narrating Egypt or Turkey can be reflected to the global, when, for example, Pamuk is surprised to discover that his novels will be translated into several languages:

> My books have been translated into 46 languages. I have won the Nobel Prize! And since (the announcement of) the Nobel, my books are being translated in Vietnam, Bangladesh, and the Spanish Basque country... It's weird, it gives me goose bumps that it's being read all over the world.[6]

Pamuk, who has been writing for around 30 years, is a prominent voice in global literature that speaks to Turkey's history alongside timeless reflections of the world, and how humans make sense of existence. In 2006, he became the first Turkish writer to receive the Nobel Prize for Literature. Pamuk's critique of the Turkish government and the acceptance of the Armenian genocide also created quite a sensation by the complicated series of events that led up to Pamuk's highly publicized trial on charges of denigrating Turkish national identity in 2005–2006. However, his voice is still very strong, and his writing expresses the timeless historical, cross-cultural, and literary influences that speak to the idea of this book on global perspectives that resonate on existentialism and politics. In this epoch of globalization, it can be suggested that the personal and the political, and the intimate and the foreign, are so enmeshed and entwined with one another that it is not possible any longer to know what is Eastern or Western. As he writes in *The Black Book*:

> Whenever I venture into the endless saga about what the West stole from the East and East from the West, I think this: If this realm of dreams we call the world is but a house we roam like sleepwalkers, then our literary traditions are like wall clocks, there to make us feel at home. So:
>
> 1. To say that one of these wall clocks is right and another wrong is utter nonsense.

2. To say that one is five hours ahead of the other is also nonsense; by using the same logic you could just as easily say that it's seven hours behind.

3. For much the same reason, it is 9:35 according to one clock and it just so happens that another clock also says its 9:35, anyone who claims that second clock is imitating the first is spouting nonsense.[7]

The relentless contact and exchange between these supposed opposing orientations have blended and saturated into the same, to the degree that difference is no longer recognizable. Pamuk puts it this way in "The *Paris Review* Interview": "Everyone is sometimes a Westerner and sometimes an Easterner—in fact a constant combination of the two."[8] Continued claims that see the world through a lens that bifurcates to the degrees of East/West have to bear witness to the sensitivity and finesse that a writer such as Pamuk is addressing within his novels.

We decided to begin the first section of this book with the section entitled "Pamuk between Worlds," because it stresses upon comparative readings of Pamuk alongside those of Mahfouz, Mohsin Hamid, and Italo Svevo. The two chapters in this section establish global postcolonial and postnational readings of Pamuk that place some of his novels and his memoir into a larger arena in thinking through issues such as religion/secularity, modern/traditional, self/nation, and existentialism. We wanted to stress upon Pamuk's work alongside that of other contemporary novelists to show the similarities, subtle differences, and to significantly suggest a collapsing of the borders of nationalism, East/West, and regional/global. Afridi's chapter puts Pamuk in conversation with other culturally Muslim writers in demonstrating how religion can be deconstructed through literature in a manner that allows for many leakages and doors to open, close, and remain ajar. In this sense, her chapter figures innovative rereadings of Mahfouz and Hamid that place Pamuk on a very different platform of conversation, which shifts geographical comfort zones of how the world is designated, and how it seems to be known. Buyze's chapter focuses on local and global tensions of the individual in regard to society and the nation, from two seemingly diverse yet very similar authors, in regard to the specificity of Pamuk's *Museum of Innocence* and Svevo's *Zeno's Conscience*. His comparative essay incisively reads Muslim/Jewish and Turkish/Italian identity in regard to issues of secularity, nation, and existentialism while being immersed within the perils of love and a fall from society.

In the second section, "Pamuk's Textual Diversity," four individual authors focus their chapters on close readings of one text by Pamuk that includes *Istanbul: Memories of a City*, *The White Castle*, *My Name Is Red*, and *The New Life*. The four very unique approaches by these authors create manners by which to explore and contemplate the spectrum of Pamuk's oeuvre, and which exemplifies the diverse manner in which Pamuk can be read. The chapter by Hande Gurses is a striking reading of Pamuk's memoir, his life/context, and Istanbul, which, as Pamuk would say, is the "center of writing" for him. Gurses further places her chapter in relation to Edward W. Said's memoir, *Out of Place*. Pittman's chapter utilizes the theory of Michel Foucault as a foil to consider Pamuk's biographical life vis-à-vis the novel *White Castle*. His discussion revolves around the reading of East/West as a conflicting yet reconciling aspect in Pamuk's work. Esra Almas looks at Pamuk and the idea of the masterpiece; she asks the question and perhaps at times puts Pamuk in a category that he may want to resist, as an author who simply writes from, as he puts it, "familiar stories." As Almas identifies what a masterpiece is, and what it may be for Pamuk, her chapter in turn challenges the categories of classical literature. Finally, in this section Fran Hassencahl presents another innovative way to read Pamuk and his work through the idea of a journey. A journey that she claims is in every author from Kerouac to Pamuk in illustrating the psychological transformation of journey and author.

The third section focuses on Pamuk's novel *Snow*, where the varied valences of three very different approaches to reading this novel allow for a distinctive contemplation of how one of Pamuk's novels can be read and interpreted from three very different perspectives. Hülya Yılmaz's chapter distinctly reads Pamuk's identity alongside that of Joseph Conrad's in a moving reading of *Snow* that is situated on the trope of exile. Esra Santesso provides a dynamic reading of the themes of secularism and Islamism in *Snow* vis-à-vis a textual analysis that places the novel into an even further level of political consideration. Thomas Cartelli's chapter incorporates the theory of Slavoj Zizek that provides a very compelling way to consider *Snow* in a comparative reading of Amitav Ghosh's *In an Antique Land*.

The last section of this book, "Pamuk and Translation/Untranslation," deliberates the complexity of the issue of translation through two chapters. Sevinç Türkkan assiduously situates the dynamic of how *The Black Book* is placed in Turkish and English, and what this signifies in the reception and interpretation of this novel. She sets the stage of her chapter through the lens of Walter Benjamin in setting translation as transformation. Erdağ Göknar's terse chapter illuminates the significance of Pamuk the writer and his placement on the stage of world literatures, in focusing on Pamuk's two untranslated novels *Cevdet Bey and Sons* and *The Silent House*.

It has been a passion for us to edit this book together, and we are so very thankful to the contributors for their collaboration and to Sander L. Gilman for writing the foreword and helping to place this work on Pamuk in a larger arena of contemplation. We hope that teachers, professors, and students will see literature as a vehicle of teaching and an essential part of an interdisciplinary education. With this thought in mind we will let the following chapters on Pamuk speak for themselves.

Notes

1. Orhan Pamuk, *Other Colors: Essays and a Story*, trans. Maureen Freely (New York: Alfred A. Knopf, 2007), p. 3.
2. Gilles Deleuze, *Capitalism and Schizophrenia* (Minnesota: University of Minnesota Press, 1987).
3. See Edward W. Said, *Freud and the Non-European* (New York: Verso, 2003).
4. Michel Foucault, *The Order of Things*, translated from French (New York: Routledge, 2001).
5. Orhan Pamuk, *Snow*, trans. Maureen Freely (New York: Alfred A. Knopf, 2004), p. 214.
6. Michael McGaha, *Autobiographies of Orhan Pamuk: The Writer in His Novels, "Uluengin, Nobel Konusmasini,"* trans. Michael McGaha (Salt Lake City: University of Utah, 2008), p. 44.
7. Orhan Pamuk, *The Black Book*, trans. Maureen Freely (New York: Vintage, 2006), p. 154.
8. Pamuk, *Other Colors*, p. 370.

PART I

Pamuk between Worlds

CHAPTER 1

Modern Postcolonial Intersections: Hamid, Mahfouz, and Pamuk

Mehnaz M. Afridi

Some of the overarching literary theories that stem from postcolonial theory spearheaded by Edward Said[1] and Gayatri Spivak[2] call into question the underlying assumptions that form the foundation of Orientalist thinking. Said's[3] thesis states that there is a need to revise and reject old and new Oriental perceptions, generalizations, cultural constructions, and racial and religious prejudices. Said asserts that there should be a conscious understanding of the line between "the West" and "the other." Naguib Mahfouz, Orhan Pamuk, and Mohsin Hamid demonstrate this understanding in their work. Said argues for the use of "narrative" rather than "vision" in interpreting the landscape known as the Orient. In other words, a scholar or interpreter would need to focus on a complex history that allows space for a variety of local human experiences. Mahfouz provides this type of complexity in his writings, as does Pamuk,[4] who describes his own oscillation between East and West in Turkey. Hamid[5] asserts his own ideas on what might be considered exemplary of Orientalism and, more importantly, on the transformation that occurs when the lines between the Orient and the Occident are diminished, as he writes:

> But as I reacclimatized and my surroundings once again became familiar, it occurred to me that the house had not changed in my absence. *I* had changed; I was looking about me with the eyes of a foreigner, and not just any foreigner, but that particular type of entitled and unsympathetic American who so annoyed me when I encountered him in the classrooms and workplaces of your country's elite. This realization angered

me; staring at my reflection in the specked glass of my bathroom mirror I resolved to exorcise the unwelcome sensibility by which I had become possessed.[6]

Mahfouz's writing is an exemplary testimony of Muslims living in Cairo, which is full of turmoil and undergoing many changes in response to a loss of old Cairene culture, the presence of colonizers, and the loss of hopes and dreams for the future. Mahfouz's characters illustrate the emergence of modern or Western influences in an already old Islamic—Egyptian Muslim—culture. Mahfouz's Egypt comprises multiple cultures with multiple languages and religions. His depiction of the climate in Cairo encompasses the Christian, Jewish, Pharaonic, and African cultures. As such, it can be compared to Clifford Geertz's ethnographical analysis of Indonesia and Morocco, which, he states in *Islam Observed*,[7] were colonized, resulting in a syncretism of many aspects of their countries' histories and cultures:

> It is the tension between these two necessities, growing progressively greater as, first gradually and then expressively, the way men and groups of men saw life and assessed it became more and more various and incommensurable under the impress of dissimilar historical experiences, growing social complexity, and heightened self-awareness, that has been the dynamic behind the expansion of Islam in both countries. But it is this tension, too, that has brought Islam in both countries to what may, without any concession to the apocalyptic temper of our time, legitimately be called a crisis.[8]

The tension or crisis to which Geertz refers is also apparent in Mahfouz's writings, as illustrated in *The Trilogy*, especially through Kamal's character as he notes the old disappearing and the new emerging and questions the roles of Islam and modernity. Geertz explains that Morocco and Indonesia had different reactions and responses to similar issues, especially to the secular and the religious, because of the unique culture within each country. He writes, "In one case, science poses no threat to faith because it is seen as religious; in the other, it poses no threat because it is seen as not."[9] This point is significant in considering modern literary writings that discuss similar struggles and the way in which each culture has responded differently to questions of Muslim identity. For example, in *The Trilogy*,[10] Kamal's own struggle revolves around the fact that he is a Muslim questioning his identity through his family life, and, more importantly, his surroundings. Similar experiences can be witnessed in the works of Pamuk and Hamid. The main characters, circumstances, and situations in different places and times provide illustrations of characters who oscillate between Islam, cultural Islam, and the modern dimensions of their identities. In the works of Mahfouz, Pamuk, and Hamid, Islam is always present as a belief or identity, but the local cultural milieus of Muslims who share linguistic, ethnic, and national identities create a sense of tension and flux. Pamuk defines his relationship with religion as one that is based on his imagination of God and one that was ignored in his secular family life in Istanbul. In Pamuk, one can observe that his focus is on Islam as a means to understanding modern Muslim identity, which raises many questions that are analogous to those raised in Mahfouz's writings with regard to literary themes centered on society, morals, and politics. These writers have been instrumental in creating Islamic narrative models and are equally important in demonstrating this new vehicle of expression for Muslims.

Both Hamid and Pamuk left their respective countries and cultures, whereas Mahfouz remained in Cairo until his death. Hamid began publishing in 2000, and Pamuk in the 1980s. Both of these authors are younger than Mahfouz, but are considered his contemporaries from different Muslim cultures. Mahfouz, Pamuk, and Hamid exemplify the tension between modernity and tradition in the context of Islamic culture—Turkey being the threshold of the Ottoman Empire (1922) and at one point the cradle of Islamic civilization, India/Pakistan being the center of the Mughal Empire before its disintegration and the partition of Hindus and Muslims (1947), and finally, Egypt being one of the oldest civilizations.

The advent of Islam and colonization in these different cultures caused similar questions about modern Muslim identity to be raised by these three authors. As they all became well known as Muslim literary writers, Western readers learned from their work that something complex was emerging from the many contested relationships among Muslims and non-Muslims. Even though it is generally through Islamic belief and practice in the *usul al-din* (religious principles) and *ibadat* (acts of worship) that Muslim identities are constructed, I assert that this is only one minor part of Islam. Islam also encompasses the many complex identities formed after colonization, as well as other faiths and ideologies residing in many Muslim cultures. For example, Egypt has a deep African and pre-Islamic culture that carries on a tradition of female circumcision that is un-Islamic, whereas this cultural practice never entered the consciousness or practice of Muslims in Turkey and India or Pakistan. The complexities of the postcolonial identities of these novelists make it possible for their writings to simultaneously accept and recall their native and nonnative influences and heritage as a singular experience.

The cultural identity of Muslims can be characterized as Geertz's[11] formulation of a "simple disjunction," which is the difference between forms of religious life and everyday life involving other cultural practices. Similarly, in Mahfouz's work, the many existential journeys of Omar, the main character in *The Beggar*,[12] and Qindil, the main character in *Ibn Fattouma*,[13] illustrate that Islam can be what one learns from both modernity and tradition at the same time. Mahfouz's depiction of Egyptian Islam is complex in its myriad of identities from the past, present, and future struggles of a Pharaonic, African, Arab, Islamic, and colonial mix including the British and the French.

Islamic identity is discussed with much rumination about the complex relationships between loss, poverty, religion, secularity, memories, and colonization. The writers assert that Islamic identity involves much more than religion—it is the fabric that relates the whole picture of being Muslim, with which one can freely imagine a street in Pamuk's Istanbul or a prostitute in Mahfouz's Cairo.

Pamuk's *Istanbul*,[14] a memoir, but also a historiography of the city, presents descriptive native and historical colonial observations of a destitute city, and the decay that persisted long after the fall of the Ottoman Empire. Pamuk's detailed depiction of Istanbul and his childhood effectively conveys the complex emotions he maintains for Istanbul, his home, which are presented alongside rare and glaring descriptive colonial narratives by Gerard de Nerval (1999), Gustave Flaubert (1987), and Theophile Gautier (1975).[15] Pamuk includes these narratives in a chapter entitled "Under Western Eyes" that presents an image of the native city through the eyes of "the other," or a visitor. These chapters reflect the European gaze at a time when Istanbul was still alive and allowed visitors to observe the exotic times of Ramadan and whirling dervishes, and don themselves "in Muslim dress to stroll about the streets in greater ease."[16] In *Istanbul*, we come to know Pamuk through his childhood memories, the melancholy he relates, and the synergy between the many cultures he describes. Pamuk's identity seems to create tension and, to borrow from Geertz, at times appears to be in "crisis." We witness the melancholy and loss felt for a certain old culture and at the same time a celebration of the nostalgia—much like in Mahfouz's *Midaq Alley*,[17] when old customs are replaced by newer conventions. "In the café entrance a workman is setting up a secondhand radio on the wall." Later the reader encounters the café owner's impression that "[p]eople today don't want a poet. They keep asking me for a radio and there's one over there being installed now."[18] In Pamuk's memoir, Istanbul is already lost, and the decision made by Turkey's governmental officials to Europeanize and secularize in the 1920s transformed the memory of the old sultanate culture. Pamuk observes:

> After the Ottoman Empire collapsed, the world almost forgot that Istanbul existed. The city to which I was born was poorer, shabbier, and more isolated than it had ever been before in its two-thousand year history. For me it has always been a city of ruins and of end-of-empire melancholy. I've spent my life either battling with this melancholy or (like all Istanbullus) making it my own.[19]

The reader witnesses a certain melancholy or *Huzun* as Pamuk recalls his childhood in Istanbul—the loss, despair, and oscillation of his life away from his native identity—and his nostalgia and desire to return to something that was central to his imagination as a child, and, for many Muslims, the cradle of civilization. His book is full of black-and-white photographs that illustrate his personal longing for the revival of Islamic architecture and with it the revival of a culture as well as an aura that he feels has been encapsulated by the loss of heritage, and, most importantly, the people. His insistence on melancholia and feelings of loss reflect the state of Istanbul after the fall of the Ottomans and the departure of the colonizers. The melancholy can be compared with Mahfouz's revelation of the state of modern Islam: "Either one culture will emerge as the most appropriate, or various cultures will coexist. There is always room for a plurality of cultures in art, ideas, and literature."[20] It is in *The Trilogy* that we learn that Kamal's feelings for his father, family, and Islam have decayed not only with the emergence of the new generation but also with the shift in politics. Mahfouz's characterization of Kamal and his loss of feelings for his old generation reveal that culture is shaped by the influences of the external worlds that collide with the old that allows for diversity and plurality. Pamuk began writing amid this plurality, and his work explains how this balance has been superseded by an external disintegration and an internal loss of culture and an old heritage.

Mahfouz challenges one to think about Cairo historically, and to consider how the impact of ancient stories of pharaohs, existential quests, and the tensions of Islam and modernity persist. Similarly, as Pamuk relates in *Snow*,[21] Kars is a place of birth and decay, but it is also a city that has been transformed in response to the influences of colonial rule, and, more importantly, the resurgence of Islam. Pamuk describes Istanbul's disintegration through the demolition of buildings:

> I recall only as dilapidated by bracken and untended fig trees; to remember them is to feel the deep sadness they evoked in me as a young child. By the late fifties, most of them had been burned down or demolished to make way for apartment buildings.[22]

Pamuk and Mahfouz manage to give meaning not only to ordinary life, but also to the personal dramas of Muslims living under colonization, postcolonization, destitution, desperation, and religious fundamentalism. They demonstrate that modern Islamic identity is complex and has a religious, social, and modern role today. As Mahfouz illustrates in *Journey of Ibn Fattouma*, Qindil's quest for a perfect and ideal form of Islam is an adventure through many social ideologies and political systems. Pamuk demonstrates in both his memoir and his novel, *Snow,* that Turkey is experiencing a crisis between the secular and the religious. As Pamuk relates his childhood encounters with religion, he writes:

> According to the first tradition, we experience the thing called *huzun* when we have invested too much in the worldly pleasures and material gain; the implication is, "If you hadn't involved yourself so you wouldn't care so much about your worldly losses." The second tradition, which rises out of Sufi Mysticism, offers a more positive and compassionate meaning of the word and of the place of loss and grief in life. To the Sufis, *huzun* is the spiritual anguish we feel because we cannot be close enough to Allah, because we cannot do enough for Allah in this world .... what I am trying to explain is the *huzun* of an entire city: of Istanbul.[23]

His description of Istanbul relies on Islamic concepts in order to foresee his own tradition, and similarly is the city of Cairo described in *Midaq Alley* by Mahfouz, in its opening chapter, as he writes:

> The dilemma facing Egyptians was clear: either to resign themselves to the slow asphyxiation of the old quarters or to accept assimilation into a way of life brought to them from outside symbolized by the increasing dominance of Western-style buildings, whose spread coincided with the new form of urban development.[24]

The two writers describe their respective cities, yet their personal dilemmas reflect the themes of both, the old and the new, the traditional and the modern, and decay and freshness. Mahfouz and Pamuk take the complexity of these Islamic cultures to a new level that relates another dimension of Muslims living in cultures that have been influenced and lost by others. According to these novelists, Turkish Islam and Egyptian Islam have been tainted by colonization and the impact of transformations of their identities.

In *Istanbul*, Pamuk discusses religion directly in a chapter entitled "Religion," which describes his secular household and the religious nanny who reared him. He finds himself caught between a public insistence on the secular and the spiritual religious underpinning of his culture, as he clearly confesses that

> in the secular fury of Ataturk's new republic, to move away from religion was to be modern and Western; it was the smugness in which there flickered from time to time the flame of idealism. But that was public. In private life, nothing came to fill the spiritual void. Cleansed of religion, home became as empty as the city's ruined yahs and as the fern-darkened gardens surrounding them. [25]

Pamuk's memories depict a nest of emptiness as a result of his father's absence and his mother's unhappiness. He also realizes that Turkey's transformation under Ataturk required a secularization of culture based on a Western model. He decided as a young child that an environment and culture that expressed Western and secular values were in some manner superior and better, as he writes, "And so I looked down on families that were as rich as we were but not as western." [26]

Mahfouz asserts in an interview with Rasheed El-Enany (1993) [27] that he does not want to discuss religion directly, and that his goal and hope for his work is to tell stories that have real historical and social implications for Cairo. Similarly, a search for a meaningful existence and a relationship to the transcendant can also be found in Pamuk's writings. Although he is secular himself, his discussions on religion and the mystical dimensions of Islam remain a major part of his work; as he writes,

> Even if I didn't believe in God as much as I might have wished, part of me still hoped that if God was omniscient, as people said, she must be clever enough to understand why it was that I was incapable of faith . . . . What I feared most was not God but those who believed in Her to excess. [28]

Mahfouz describes Cairo in detail in the opening pages of *Palace Walk*, both as a legacy and also as a deteriorating city that holds special meaning for the natives:

> He headed towards the Goldsmiths bazaar and then to al-Guriya. He turned into al-Sayyid Ali's coffee shop on the corner of al-Sanadiqiya. It

resembled a store of medium size and had a door on al-Sanadiqiya and a window with bars overlooking al-Ghuriya.[29]

These small descriptive details transport one to a neighborhood that typifies the local culture that existed in Cairo at the time and that still exists in some instances today. Pamuk's descriptions of architecture and neighborhoods transport readers to Istanbul. He recreates typical images of sultans and the Ottoman era of old Istanbul, shares vivid memories of his childhood, and details Istanbul in the present. These generational writings of Istanbul render an identity and culture similar to Mahfouz's Cairene identity and culture. Pamuk writes:

> While I was looking at the Bosphorus through the gaps between the apartment buildings of Cihangir, I learned something else about neighborhood life: There must always be a center (usually a shop) where all the gossip is gathered and interpreted, and assessed. In Cihangir this center was the grocery store on the ground floor of our apartment building.[30]

The literary depictions and nuances of the two cities, Cairo and Istanbul, provide the reader with a certain understanding of local culture; however, the reader is also confronted with deterioration that symbolizes the loss of the old neighborhoods overcome by generational and Western influences. For example, in Mahfouz's *Sugar Street,* Kamal mourns the fact that his father's illness and death will end an era not only for him, but also for an entire generation. Visits to the coffee shop and seeing the shaykh in the streets will all come to an end, and his friend's store will close:

> Kamal looked fondly at the shaykh, who made him think of his father. He had once considered this man a landmark of the neighborhood—like an ancient fountain building, the mosque of the Qala'un and the vault of Qirmiz Alley. The shaykh still encountered many who were sympathetic to him, but there were always boys to plague him by whistling at him or by following him and imitating his gestures.[31]

A lost time and a new generation unfold in Pamuk's work, *Istanbul;* however, his nostalgia or longing remains unclear as he recounts his childhood fears of loss and sadness. The loss that he encounters is presented through the eyes of others:

> Even Tanpinar—whose books offer the deepest understanding of what it means to live in a rapidly westernizing country among the ruins of

the Ottoman culture, and who shows how it is, in the end, the people themselves who, through ignorance and despair, end up severing up their country their every link with the past—admits to taking pleasure from the sight of an old wooden mansion burning itself to the ground.[32]

Mahfouz and Pamuk witness the deterioration of their cities in different ways; however, they both express how their respective cultures have been transformed and how the change that takes place is multifaceted and includes external changes in the architecture, neighborhoods, and everyday life, and internal changes in the authority structures of the cultures, which have been split up into different forms. For example, in Pamuk's novel *Snow*, the main character Ka returns to Istanbul after being exiled to Germany. He returns because he has learned of a wave of suicides among girls forbidden to wear headscarves at school. He is struck by the condition of Kars; a city that was once a province of the Ottoman Empire and Russia's glory is now a zone of poverty and destitution. His journey motivates him to examine and evaluate Turkey's crisis as a result of Islamic radicals and the debate about the secular. *Snow* is an important novel in relation to *Children of Gebalaawi*[33] and *Midaq Alley*. All three novels reveal a relationship between fanaticism and Islam and the need for change within Islam, although this change relies upon the interpretation of Islam. Pamuk and Mahfouz foreshadow the doom of religious fervor by questioning the religion itself, both existentially and spiritually. In *Snow*, Ka is vulnerable, yet a strong believer in love and faith, which he justifies through his encounter with his long-lost love, Ipek. In Mahfouz's *Children of Gebalaawi*, women represent lust, as does Hamida in *Midaq Alley*. She never experiences love in the alley, and leaves her neighborhood to make money from the British. Mahfouz's *Children of Gebalaawi* is a controversial novel that discusses the dialectic between religious extremism and justice. It relies upon all three monotheistic traditions. Similarly, in *Snow*, justice and equality prevail in the nexus between faith and fanaticism. The parallel themes of the novels rely on how the main characters point out that there is a certain lack of understanding of Islam. For example, in *Snow*, Ka is already a secular, Westernized character who discovers the enigma of fanaticism, and in *Children of Gebalaawi*, Gebel is an authoritarian figure who loses his power and gift of prophecy through his abuse of power and faith. Additional examples can be found in these novels that illustrate Turkish and Egyptian Islam confronted with extreme and violent Islamic fanaticism.

In *Snow,* Ka returns to Kars looking for a story about the girls who have been committing suicide, and finds himself turning to religion when he encounters a shaykh:

> A feeling of peace spread through me; I had not felt this way for years. I immediately understood that I could talk to him about anything, tell him about my life, and he would bring me back to the path I had always believed in, deep down inside, even as an atheist: the road to God Almighty. I was joyous at the mere expectation of this salvation.[34]

Ka's character and inner struggle bring up the dialectic of religion and extremism, which is echoed not only in his writings, but also in Turkey. Pamuk's novel serves as an introspective look at what takes place in a country as it confronts the secular, the West, and the extremity of religious fanaticism. Similarly, Mahfouz relates this message in *Children of Gebalaawi* when he depicts religious prophets and the authoritarian Gebel as corrupt and hypocritical within a religious framework. What Mahfouz depicts as anti-Islamic to the many who read his work as blasphemous, he also characterizes the prophets and Gebel as those who strayed from the right path of faith; in other words his depictions of sacred characters as corrupt or hypocritical are a reflection of human beings and the way in which they become corrupt even though they proclaim a religious or moral standing. In Mahfouz's novels, his portrayal of religious figures stays out of the realm of a direct critique or commentary on Islam as he himself states: "The problem with this work from the beginning was that I wrote it as a novel and it was read by some as a book."[35]

More importantly, the struggle that Pamuk and Mahfouz depict mirrors the political and social struggles of many Muslims today. It is not the approach of those who attempted to live by Gebalaawi's guidelines. *Jihad* (a holy war) has no roots in those guidelines of true faith. Similarly, Pamuk's main character Ka returns to religion in a spiritual manner that requires a personal struggle, rather than in the fanatic manner of the individuals he encounters in his journey back to Kars. The poetry he presents in the local theater in Kars disturbs the general public, and he is accused of being an atheist and a spy from Europe. The newspaper reads, "A Godless man in Kars asked about Ka, the so-called poet, why did he choose to visit our city in such troubled times?"[36]

Ka, who suffers from writer's block, has managed to unlock his mind and compose a poem called "Snow," which describes a mystical experience. Ipek (his love) suggests that he go to see Sheikh Saadettin and confess that he associates religion with a backwardness that he does not want himself or Turkey to fall into. But instead, he feels a sense of comfort with the sheikh and begins to accept his new poems as gifts from God. Many events in *Snow* illustrate the tensions between the Islamic fundamentalists and the more liberal people of Kars. The plot darkens throughout the novel, and the reader encounters violent scenes as people from the village create internal tensions that lead to killing and death. Pamuk's novel, much like Mahfouz's writings, represents the conflicts within Islam, which are filled with local contradictions that arise when traditional attitudes are faced with those of modern Islam. It also presents a view of Muslims who are faithful to God and are fearful of extreme secularists and fanatics. Pamuk suggests that there is the slightest possibility that a balance can be maintained between both the religious and the secular. For example, in *Snow*, Ka has a conversation with Necip, a young religious student, who eventually dies when the growing tensions between secularists and Islamists explode during a televised event at the National Theater. Before Necip dies, Ka has a conversation with him in which he testifies not only to a belief in God that sustains many of the locals, but also to the fear that arises from this tension and the idea that only Westerners can question God. Necip tells Ka about a dream he has had, in which he fears his own disbelief in God, and that if it is true he will die. He further illuminates his fear by confessing:

> I looked it up in the Encyclopedia once, and it said that word *atheist* comes from the Greek *athos*. But *athos* doesn't refer to people who don't believe in God; it refers to the lonely ones, people whom the Gods have abandoned. This proves that people can't ever really be atheists, because even if we wanted it, God would never abandon us here. To become atheist, then, you must first become a Westerner.[37]

Necip's confession leads one to believe that the tension between East and West in Turkey is dependent upon Western influences that somehow direct human beings toward atheism. However, the main characters in *Snow* oscillate between religion and secularity until Ka appears on the scene to explain that one can have a mystical union with God and still have an open worldview. In this novel, Pamuk makes the case that the actions of fanatics, both religious and secular, can be dangerous, and Turkey, which is at the crossroads between East and West, has had to deal with deeper complexities than most Muslim countries. Pamuk and Mahfouz continually point to the dangers of such a tension, and also to the inevitable questions that arise from such friction, as Pamuk reveals in *Istanbul:* "Part of me longed, like a radical Westernizer, for the city to become entirely European. I held some hope for myself. But another part of me yearned to belong to Istanbul I had grown to love, by instinct, by habit and by memory."[38] The oscillation in Pamuk's memoir and novel, *Snow,* demonstrates that the colonial presence and, in the case of Turkey, Ataturk, had a significant influence on the way in which religion and modern identity have been shaped.

Hamid expresses a different literary tone in his writings; he uses the personal and anonymous third person to execute a novel that discusses religion through identity issues and nationalism. *The Reluctant Fundamentalist,*[39] his latest work, excludes any mention of faith identity, and presents it in a different context based on American life and materialism. Hamid enters the discussion of identity as he recreates 9/11 and the impact of its aftermath upon his own Pakistani identity. Hamid, like Pamuk and Mahfouz, clearly interprets religion to be cultural, social, and, more importantly, about identity politics. His writings express a desire to transform Muslim identity into a plethora of misperceptions and complexities of East and West. He has a flair for cynicism, and one can never be quite certain whether his main character, Changez, is trustworthy or is the anonymous listener, as illustrated by the following passage: "Ah, our tea has arrived! Do not look so suspicious. I assure you, sir, nothing untoward will happen to you, not even a runny stomach. After all, it is not as if it has been *poisoned.*"[40]

Contrasting with Pamuk's and Mahfouz's styles, Hamid manages to tackle the same issues of modern Islam and identity. He does not profess his faith, nor does he fail to remind the reader that he is a Muslim, but this does not presume that he is religious. As Hamid notes,

You seem puzzled by this—and not for the first time. Perhaps you misconstrue the significance of my beard, which, I should in any case make clear; I had not yet kept when I arrived in New York. In truth, many Pakistanis drink; alcohol's illegality in our country has roughly the same effect as marijuana's in yours. Moreover, not all of our drinkers are western-educated urbanites such as myself; our newspapers regularly carry accounts of villagers dying or going blind after consuming poor quality moonshine. Indeed, in our poetry and folk songs *intoxication* occupies a recurring role as a facilitator of love and spiritual enlightenment. What is it not a sin? Yes, certainly it is—and so, for that matter, is coveting thy neighbor's wife. I see you smile; we understand one another, then.[41]

Hamid's novel is a postcolonial narrative that introduces many words in anglicized Urdu and English slang used by the Hindus and Muslims of the Indian subcontinent. As one enters Hamid's world, one is aware that the writer is deeply invested in the local culture, and that he intermixes it with the larger narrative on American influences that construct this colloquial mongrel, as well as its customs, rituals, and Islam. *The Reluctant Fundamentalist* can be read as an allegory to Pakistani-Muslim immigration to the United States. The main character can also be compared to Hamid and his experience as a Muslim living in post-9/11 America. Pakistan and the West seem joined—the binary of the cultures is saturated, and one is left with the feeling that Muslim is in fact a mix of many different components. As Mahfouz has shown, Egypt and its history cannot be separated. Hamid demonstrates that it is not a matter of separation, but instead a mixture and an intermingling of cultures.

Hamid takes on this identity, which is portrayed by his characters as an oscillation between Pakistani and American tradition. His presentation of Islam suggests that it serves as a moral compass, but he indicates that Islam alone is not moral; the people who follow it are what create Islam and their culture. As Smith argues between what he calls the "actual" and "real," he states that "the work of an artist is religious art not by virtue of attaining a given goal but by virtue of aiming at it."[42] Pamuk, Hamid, and Mahfouz have shown in their work on identity that they are in agreement with Smith—Islam should be differentiated from the actual and the ideal, from what is and what ought to be.

As Hamid explores the cultural milieu of Changez, he also illuminates the intimacy of Muslims with the West (America), expressed not only as admiration, but also as confusion on how to react to post-9/11 events. The Muslim oscillates between his identity in America as a Princeton graduate working at a successful firm and his love for an American woman. As Hamid notes:

> I had always thought of America as a nation that looked forward; for the first time I was struck by its determination to look back. Living in New York was suddenly like living in a film about Second World War; I, a foreigner, found myself staring out at a set that ought to be viewed not in Technicolor but in grainy white and black. What your countrymen longed for was unclear to me—a time of unquestioned dominance? Of safety? Of moral certainty? I did not know—but that they were scrambling to don the costumes of another era was apparent. I felt treacherous for wondering whether the era was fictitious, and

whether—if it could indeed be animated—it contained a part written for someone like me.[43]

In Mahfouz's novel *The Beggar*, the main character Omar is also divided and loses his family and ethical principles in order to find wholeness. His desire is to be spiritual, but it results in materialism and lust. Although Omar is on an existential quest, he also represents the duality of modern Muslims. As Smith asserts, "The fundamental crisis of Islam in the twentieth century stems from an awareness that something is awry between the religion which God has appointed and the historical development of the world which He controls."[44]

This crisis or tension develops in the works of all three authors and indicates that modern Muslims are struggling with identity in various ways; for example, by addressing indigenous and external influences, as demonstrated by Geertz, and by considering historical congruity, as suggested by Smith. Pamuk and Mahfouz describe the crisis in various ways based on their different Muslim cultures, which share not only the transformations that have taken place in postcolonial identities, but also, more importantly, the spiritual crisis.

As Mahfouz illustrates, Egyptian identity is not static, and it has a long history of many different influences. He asserts, "We must not try to deconstruct this national character and reduce it to its original components, because that would cause it to lose all its cohesion. It would be like reducing water to oxygen and hydrogen—gases drifting away and disappearing in the air."[45]

In the works of these literary writers, there is always the presence of a colonizer, an outsider, a stranger who has somehow not only created a crisis, but also caused confusion about what modern Muslim identities are today. In Mahfouz's work, Egyptian Islam undergoes significant changes from Nasser to Mubarak, to revolution, to secularism, and to the Muslim brotherhood. Hamid directly critiques the image of Islam and its postcolonial influences to exchange them with local Muslim narratives, whether through language, literature, intermarriages, or social conditions. Pamuk's version of Turkish Islam encourages questions of religion and the gaze of the colonial traveler in Turkey, which creates a modern dilemma for Turks, as Turkey is the only openly secular country in the Islamic world. These writers shed light on the struggle taking place over questions that lie deep within each Muslim culture, and encourage reflection on both religious and modern ideas. Mahfouz, Pamuk, and Hamid have been recognized in the West, as well as in their own cultures, as authorities on their cultures and religion.

They are responsible for the powerful emergence of modern Muslim literature on different continents of the Islamic world, which represents a new awakening for Islam and Muslim identities, and the significant struggle and disintegration of those who want to hold on to traditional cultural and Islamic values.

Notes

1. Edward Said, *Orientalism* (New York: Vintage Books, 1979).
2. Gayatri Spivak and Sarah Harasym, *The Postcolonial Critic: Interviews, Strategies, and Dialogue* (New York: Routledge, 1990).
3. Said, *Orientalism,* p. 45.
4. Orhan Pamuk, *Istanbul: Memories and City,* trans. Maureen Freely (New York: Alfred A. Knopf, 2006).
5. Mohsin Hamid, *The Reluctant Fundamentalist* (Orlando, FL: Harcourt Press, 2007).
6. Ibid., p. 124.
7. Clifford Geertz, *Islam Observed: Religious Development in Morocco & Indonesia* (Chicago, IL: University of Chicago Press, 1968).
8. Ibid., p. 71.
9. Ibid., p. 106.
10. Naguib Mahfouz, *Palace Walk,* trans. William Maynard Hutchins and Olive E. Kenny (New York: Doubleday, 1989); *Palace of Desire,* trans. William Maynard Hutchins and Olive E. Kenny (Cairo: University of Cairo Press, 1991); *Sugar Street,* trans. Willaim Maynard Hutchins and Olive E. Kenny (New York: Doubleday, 1992).
11. Geertz, *Islam Observed,* p. 21.
12. Naguib Mahfouz, *The Beggar,* trans. Denys Johnson-Davies (Cairo: University of Cairo, 1989).
13. Naguib Mahfouz, *The Journey of Ibn Fattouma,* trans. Denys Johnson-Davies (New York: Doubleday, 1992).
14. Pamuk, *Istanbul.*
15. Please see discussion in Pamuk's "Under Western Eyes."
16. Ibid., p. 226.
17. Naguib Mahfouz, *Midaq Alley* trans. Trevor Le Gassick (Cairo: University of Cairo, 1992).
18. Ibid., p.1 4.
19. Pamuk, *Istanbul,* p. 14.
20. Naguib Mahfouz, *Naguib Mahfouz at Sidi Gaber: Reflections of a Nobel Laureate, 1994–2001: From Conversations with Mohamed Salmawy* (Cairo: University of Cairo Press, 2001), p. 92.
21. Orhan Pamuk, *Snow,* trans. Maureen Freely (New York: Random House, 2004).
22. Ibid., p.27.

23. Ibid., p.95.
24. Mahfouz, *Midaq Alley*, pp. 337–338.
25. Pamuk, *Istanbul*, p. 180.
26. Ibid., p. 182.
27. Rasheed El-Enany, *Naguib Mahfouz: The Pursuit of Meaning* (London: Routledge, 1993).
28. Pamuk, *Snow*, pp. 185–186.
29. Mahfouz, *Palace Walk*, p. 71.
30. Pamuk, *Istanbul*, p. 87.
31. Pamuk, *Sugar Street*, p. 307.
32. Pamuk, *Istanbul*, p. 209.
33. Naguib Mahfouz, *Children of Gebalaawi* (London: Heinemann, 1981).
34. Pamuk, *Snow*, p. 55.
35. W. R. Baker, *Islam without Fear: Egypt and the New Islamists* (Cambridge, MA: Harvard University Press, 2003), p. 57.
36. Pamuk, *Snow*, p. 151.
37. Ibid., p. 142.
38. Pamuk, *Istanbul*, p. 322.
39. Hamid, *Reluctant Fundamentalist*.
40. Ibid., p. 11.
41. Ibid., pp. 53–54.
42. W. C. Smith, *On Understanding Islam: Selected Studies* (New York: Mouton Publishers, 1957), pp. 8–9.
43. Hamid, *Reluctant Fundamentalist*, p. 115.
44. Smith, *On Understanding*, p. 41.
45. El-Enany, *Naguib Mahfouz*, p. 10.

CHAPTER 2

Tensions in the Nation: Pamuk and Svevo

David M. Buyze

Life had receded from me, losing all the flavor and color I'd found in it until that day. The power and authenticity I'd once felt in things (though, sad to say, without fully realizing it) was now lost.[1]
—Orhan Pamuk, *The Museum of Innocence*

The draining tenor of this existential reflection by Kemal, the protagonist of *The Museum of Innocence*, confronts a perspective on the authenticity of self, a conundrum that faces the modern world.[2] How is a life to be lived? How can meaning be given to a life, or how can one obtain meaning? What is the relationship of the self to society? What is love? These are questions that have concerned humanity since the inception of contemplating what it means to be human. The novelists Orhan Pamuk and Italo Svevo set out in their respective novels, *The Museum of Innocence* and *Zeno's Conscience,* to pose some reflections to these questions of what it means to be human in society, where the central concern is how to imagine a life other than one that is not solely structured and measured through society. The problem of identity is at the core of these novels, and it can be seen in how both novelists create a continual sense of critique that dislodges and questions societal discourses of identity and how these have structured consciousness. In this regard, the comparative analyses of novels by Pamuk and Svevo in this chapter provide a modicum that allows for a renewed understanding of local/global and existential tensions between the individual and the society. In thinking of the ambitions of Pamuk and

Svevo in these novels, Jacqueline Rose describes the power of literature in this manner in *The Last Resistance*: "If fiction plays a key role in what follows it is also for another reason: its powers to unsettle, like psycho-analysis, all idealised, official, rhetorics, whether of nationhood, race, religion or state—its powers of resistance, as one might say."[3] Rose's perspective provides a point of resonance for the literature of Pamuk and Svevo that is reflected in how their novels unsettle the discourses of national orientation, societal dimensions, and life that is situated in regard to Turkey and Italy, vis-à-vis literary introspective disturbances that are indelibly reflected and relevant to human experience.

In consideration of Pamuk's *The Museum of Innocence* and Svevo's *Zeno's Conscience*, it becomes increasingly clear to the reader that these two writers are writing against the social contract that is further con-strictive through how one is imagined to behave and think in ways that limit the imagination and the possibilities of experience. These constrictions and limitations occur in ways that not only impact the freedom of the self but that reconfigure how others are seen through the narrow prisms of race, class, religion, and nation as well. In a very significant manner, these two novels can be considered alongside a pri-mary psychoanalytic work such as Sigmund Freud's *Civilization and Its Discontents*, since both of these novels attempt to speak to the lack in the world today that societies have perpetuated, which has left the indi-vidual adrift when one desires to transcend and find ways to sublimate the limitations of a lack of meaning that is inherent in mass means of identifying and living.[4] A refined focus is also necessary in recognizing that such assumed tensions of what continue as varied ways of seeing epistemological difference, through such naïve determinations of East/West and traditional/modern, have faded and diminished through the effects of globalization in that all of human experience is indeed satu-rated, one within the other as is seen in a definitive aim of how Pamuk circumscribes his literature. In this regard, psychoanalytic discourse and experience is also not limited by national boundaries or cultural distinction as is recognized by Svevo and Pamuk considering the role of psychoanalysis in their novels. This can be further understood as is very apparent in a novel such as Hanif Kureishi's *Something to Tell You*, where psychoanalytic language is a distinct part of Pakistani and British expe-rience, and is no longer relegated to solely belong to Western paradigms of contemplating human life.[5] Writers such as these are narrating to the world that the distinctions assumed to be at hand between the colo-nial self/other relation might just be vanishing in how they have been known, or perceived to be understood, and that well-wrought categories of difference and altarity are indeed very unstable and inhabited with people that push back at how the masses in society want to contain and limit the intimacy and varied registers of consciousness, in thinking about the Other in one's society and nation in the world.

In contemplation of these issues, the reading and interpretation of literature needs to be further decathected from national orientation and identification, and it is clear that Pamuk and Svevo provide strategies by which one can think through the societal rhetoric of nation, race, class, and religion in how humans have negatively portrayed these dimensions through interpretative expectations of how one should live and exist in society. Pamuk and Svevo critique this through the personal struggle of the individual in exploring psychological issues and tensions that saturate the literature of these two novels to a degree that seeks to transcend the individual's situation, class conflicts, and life's predicaments within society. These two novels acutely revolve around personal relationships, and this becomes the manner of forging a sense of disruption of how one is seen, or desires to *pass,* or is perceived as *passing* in society as another type of identity. In these works, the themes of contingency, desire, consciousness, and intimacy are continually exfoliated in a very personal manner, which is always brushing up against the Other and reconfiguring the dimensions of society. Rose puts it very evocatively in this way, "Even when we dream, we are not alone. Our most intimate psychic secrets are always embedded in the others—groups, masses, institutions and peoples—from which they take their cue, playing their part in the rise and fall of nations. Not to recognize this is, finally, the greatest, most dangerous, illusion of them all."[6] Rose states this in concluding her chapter entitled "Mass Psychology," which nods to Freud's *The Future of an Illusion*[7] and his critique of religion in society, and both Pamuk and Svevo comparatively develop a critique of religion/secularity and Muslim and Jewish identity particular to its societal dynamics in the contexts of Turkey and Italy.

A further issue that persists in these two novels is the conundrum of solitude and desire for an "other," that is always at lack and remains unfulfilled and unresolved within the frustrations that the main characters, Kemal and Zeno, have with society. For these writers, the issues of intimate personal relationships as portrayed in these novels parallel problematic societal dynamics that require firm contemplation and analysis for the study of human experience. David Grossman acutely ruminates on this tension of the individual and the group or society in his essay "Individual Language and Mass Language" in *Writing in the Dark*, where he speaks to the crux of this in the reading of literature as a means to think otherwise in the contemplation of consciousness, and how it has been impacted by social rhetoric and conformity to a certain way and ideal of living. Grossman writes:

> A good book—and there are not many, because literature too, of course, is subject to the seductions and obstacles of mass media—individualizes and extracts the single reader out of the masses. It gives him an opportunity to feel how spiritual contents, memories, and existential possibilities can float up and rise from within him, from unfamiliar places, and they are his alone. The fruits of his personality alone. The result of his most intimate refinements. And in the mass culture of daily life, in the overall pollution of our consciousness, it is so difficult for these soulful contents to emerge from the inner depths and be animated.[8]

In *Writing in the Dark*, Grossman also proceeds to distinguish between the private and public idiom, and how a focus needs to resonate on the intimacy of private language as a means to brush up against the shallowness and predictability of the public-societal idiom that Pamuk also dwells on in *The Museum of Innocence*.[9] It is out of this nexus of contemplating the perspectives of Rose, Grossman, and Freud that an intensive consideration of the novels by Pamuk and Svevo is necessary, for it is possible within their narratives and ruptures of language that there exists ways to reconfigure consciousness from the insight of one's most intimate sense of reflexivity on the vitality of existence itself. Alternative manners to pondering a life in the world need to be considered, and Svevo and Pamuk open new vistas of thinking in their reconsiderations of imagining the self and other in society.

Orhan Pamuk's *The Museum of Innocence*

> The power of things inheres in the memories they gather up inside them, and also in the vicissitudes of our imagination, and our memory—of this there is no doubt.[10]
>
> Orhan Pamuk—*The Museum of Innocence*

Kemal, the main character of Pamuk's *The Museum of Innocence*, which is set in 1970s' Istanbul, is a collector of memories in his amassing of a caché of material objects that are assigned significance because of how he values them as representative of his love for Füsun. The focus on materialism in this novel is also indicative of a change in societies on a global level through the distribution of capital and how this impacts one's desire for the material, and a sense of one's self-worth that becomes manifest on a group level in recreating societal expectations that Pamuk capitulates as the pursuit of being modern and secular. In 1970s' Istanbul, this was outrightly seen as mimicking a desire to be European by a shedding of provincial mindsets that appeared well wrought within the religious; yet the paramount issue is that a simple shift to the material does not change perspective. Being religious or Muslim in Turkey as represented in the novel is characterized as an incidental trait, which foreshadows my comparative reading to Svevo's *Zeno's Conscience*, wherein the protagonist desires to escape how society wants to imprint Jewish identity on his sense of self. Pamuk writes in regard to how religion and secularity were impressed upon family and class structures in Turkey, as Kemal narrates:

> Neither my mother nor my father was religious. I never saw either of them pray or keep a fast. Like so many married couples who had grown up during the early years of the Republic, they were not disrespectful of religion; they were just indifferent to it, and like so many of their friends and acquaintances they explained their lack of interest by their love for Ataturk and their faith in the secular republic.[11]

In this milieu of meaning that shifts between religion and secularity in Turkey, *The Museum of Innocence* is also a novel that is deeply saturated in desire and loss amid the constraints of society, wherein Pamuk desires to make a shift away from a primary political focus, as he writes through Kemal, "Like most people in Istanbul, I had no interest in politics."[12] Pamuk rather situates a focus on existentialism and a search for meaning in the contemporary world in putting forward a more poignant understanding of subjectivity. This search for meaning is not some simple hero's journey, nor is it optimistic, but it enables one to consider that a "real life" is not simply one that is enabled or substantiated through society, but it is one that is of course still contingent on the others in one's life.[13]

As a corollary example, one of Pamuk's other works, which was very popular in Turkey, *The New Life*,[14] presents a very similar perspective in that a new life offered as a choice between the religious and the secular (although those terms are never explicitly used) is never under consideration, in that life in all of its multiplicity was never a simple choice between these two realms of meaning in society. As conveyed in the novel, this is a search for meaning or purpose through the old and new, the religious and the secular, and the traditional and the modern, which are all rendered as bereft of substance, since, for the characters there is no sense of identification or fulfillment in these suggested meanings of life. The succinct problem of how one identifies with being religious/secular or traditional/modern is the polarizing effect that is often adopted in repressing the constant interplay and exchange between such spheres of understanding. In this situation, the individual might only highlight the dogmatic or rigid sense of what is manifested in his or her consciousness as to how the world should be strictly seen and experienced, which is then often utilized as a frame by which to place judgment on others that veer from that worldview.

The New Life begins with the main character Osman, whose life is remarkably changed by a book that he reads, and who goes on a journey to discover this significance, which is simultaneously paralleled with a search for his illusive love, Janan. Osman begins to see and experience that the world does not mimic the wonders that this book held for him, and that an ideal existence can never occur. Osman wavers on the ephemeral state of human happiness and love that is always infringed upon by society and the world in how one must live in these continual senses of being at lack, in that meaning cannot be immediately provided by a text, a societal understanding, or a way of living that is adopted by the masses.

A quest for meaning is one that is often fraught with solitude and frustration in the inability to find the manner in which to sublimate one's desires in creating fleeting degrees of self-fulfillment. Such a story is that of Kemal and Füsun in *The Museum of Innocence*, a striking and discomforting love story, a narrative that resonates on the human predicaments of desire, despair, and loss. In this novel, Pamuk dramatically changes the tone of his writing in comparison to *Snow*,[15] although similarities can certainly be drawn of Kemal to Ka and the portrayal of their relationships to women, which are most often stuck in the vicissitudes of their imaginations.[16] Materiality and memory is a paramount theme in *The Museum of Innocence* that speaks to the fascination of society with the material and draws a distinct difference to the sorted love affair of Ka and İpek in *Snow*, which remained at a distance through political and religious ideologies, in suggesting that Pamuk is simultaneously exploring in *Snow* and *The Museum of Innocence* the respective distinct differences of perspective in provincial and urban life, which is indeed spoken to very directly in *The Museum of Innocence* as insular class tensions that persist in such dichotomies as traditional /modern, religious/secular, and evaluations on material objects that continue to perplex Turkish society and global experience. In the novel, these dichotomies are presented as dire ephemeral perspectives that shatter any sense of real and sustained engagement with life as there remains this underlying societal tension of what it now means to be an "ideal" or "pure" Turk, which, of course, brings to bear highly problematic ideas of identity. In a conversation between Kemal and his best friend Zaim, Zaim speaks of how the people living in the provinces embody a pure sense of being Turkish, which Kemal fails to understand.[17] It is in Kemal's failure to understand that this novel is majestic in exploring societal vacuousness, and it is also in Kemal's journey that he is ostracized from society, an occurrence that was precipitated by his affair with Füsun, the end of his engagement to Sibel, and the loss of his friendships. Yet, it appears that his relationships with others only allow the fissures of the membranes that hold society together to be illuminated more profoundly in evoking the dearth of meaning at hand in class, religion, secularity, and the political, since he becomes very disdainful of society, or indeed it appears that it is indicative that he always harbored such feelings. This is illustrated in the conversation with his brother Osman, where Osman articulates, "'You've disgraced yourself in society, but at least don't embarrass yourself at the firm,' he said mercilessly. (This despite the fact that he hated the word 'society' as much as I did)."[18] Kemal's pronouncement on their sibling hatred of societal vernacular also speaks to a condition of familial artifice that rather inflicted a pull with a desire to be as "modern" as possible within Western sensibilities, and that seemingly undercuts what it means to be Turkish. Indeed, as in any country, there is no longer a *type* that embodies a national sense of identity, and although the world may be seen in such a narrow prism this can no longer hold weight through the effects of globalization, and the positive confounding of what nationality holds in what, for example, Pamuk essentially describes as fractured communities from the provinces of Turkey and other peoples that include Italians, Levantines, and Greeks and that contrast the dominant urban Muslim Turkish neighborhoods.[19]

In this understanding, cultural difference appears as an urban illusion that is veiled within the nation through class, which holds a pretense of meaning for Turkish society, that Pamuk characterizes through Kemal as class difference struck with an ambience of insularity and utter fragility.[20] This is clearly further evident in a conversation when Sibel states to Kemal:

In Europe the rich are refined enough to act as if they're not wealthy. That is how civilized people behave. If you ask me, being cultured and civilized is not about everyone being free and equal; it's about everyone being refined enough to act as if they were. Then no one has to feel guilty.[21]

This degree of feeling cultured or civilized is most certainly situated as reliant on class or social status that is brought to a certain societal outlook, and that can be reflected on in today's world through the countless stories that reveal a fall from social stature through moral ambiguity and the ensuing crimes, which unravel the fragility of social fabric and class stature.

These types of cultural and social facades are further articulated by Pamuk as a degree of pretending to adhere to "tradition," as he writes through Kemal: "It was a great joy to study the myriad social refinements of which anthropologists seem to have so little understanding, and most especially these rituals that allowed families to act 'as if' they were respecting tradition, even as they broke with it."[22] In this manner, it remains rather confounding in the world today to think of tradition that remains stable or rigid, because this is, of course, always impacted by not only such acts as immigration/exile, but, more importantly, through human reinvention, imagining anew, and recreating what is held as significant in carrying out cultural processes that are always active, dynamic, and ever changing. The vernacular of ritual and tradition holds an archaic breath of human orientation, as can be noticed in the novel through Pamuk's critique of the traditional being equated to purity/virginity.[23] This type of consideration of being traditional is precariously marked, since it resides on the physical. The onus of one's subjectivity is given too much weight in the traditional, and Pamuk also stresses throughout this novel that greater meaning cannot be found in being considered modern, since this appears only as a temporary exercise of mind that lifts one out of the ordinary and the rumble of the structurations of everyday life. Being considered as strictly traditional or modern is no longer a place in this world that a human can inhabit, for they remain as ideal states of being that are always out of one's reach, and distinctly so because they are outward societal markers that deem an ideal of how one should live and exist. Either stance on living veers into an ideological perspective that defers epistemological reflection as it purports that the individual exists within one manner of how human experience has been imagined, which often hinges upon a shared communal act or investment in materiality that somehow always sets up some sort of forced interaction or a contrived defining of one's identity.

Pamuk strives to peel away these societal conditions in revealing the essence of being human as the residues of existence that persist in the ordinariness and the repetition of daily life. What further becomes revealed to the individual is the precarious sense of love and human relationships, the rapid passage of time that marks life, and the recurrent emptiness that often ravages attempts at meaning and the temporary satisfaction that sublimation provides in human desire and creativity. This is definitively apparent through Kemal when he reflects, "It was during those days that I first began to feel fissures opening in my soul, wounds of the sort that plunge some men into a deep, dark, lifelong loneliness for which there is no cure."[24] Kemal has become conscious of reflexively thinking otherwise about his subjectivity, and this is indicative of how he always feels out of place in society, yet this opens up the capacity in him to not only be self-critical but also able to develop a critical perspective about society, the nation of Turkey, and the meaning of existence for others. It would certainly appear that Kemal is no longer able to accept the version of reality as presented to him by society, and he intensely struggles against this. In a conversation with Zaim, where they are speaking of Sibel and his affair with Füsun, Zaim suggests to Kemal: "Take it on the chin and then it will be much easier for you to return to your real life, and before you know it, all this will be forgotten."[25] Kemal reflects on this, "I decided that Zaim was choosing his words— expressions like 'your real life'—just to inflame me."[26] Kemal decides that he does not need what amounts to a "real life," since he perceives this as only a fabricated existence in the manner of living one's life only to fulfill how it should be led as directed by societal norms and expectations. He chooses to live his life as a collector of material objects that represent his love for Füsun—he makes a choice to live between fantasy and reality, until he is able to achieve his fantasy of being with Füsun, which does come to fruition in the novel, although she is killed in a car crash shortly after their reunion, and Kemal chooses to live the rest of his life as a curator of her memory. It can also be suggested that Pamuk is reflecting on new manners to interpret and negotiate memory and fantasy/reality, as can be contemplated when Salman Rushdie writes, "If literature is in part the business of finding new angles at which to enter reality, then once again our distance, our long geographical perspective, may provide us with such angles."[27] Rushdie's idea involves finding ways to distance one's self from the habitual manners by which one falls into a singular understanding of what reality is, and perhaps as well, life is always a negotiation between fantasy and reality, between interpreting one's relationship to the world that is always, as Rose states, implicit in "our most intimate psychic secrets [which] are always embedded in the others—groups, masses, institutions and peoples—from which they take their cue, playing their part in the rise and fall of nations."[28] In *The Museum of Innocence*, it is distinctly clear that the character of Kemal is well aware of his involvement and investment with others and how he impacts their lives, how his life is impacted by others, and in turn how this pales against, and reconfigures, the state of the Turkish society and the nation.

Kemal recognizes the urgency of this in his own lifetime in an utterly existential moment when he reflects, "I noticed our canary in its cage. I thought about the past, and my life, the flow of time, the passing years."[29] This is even pressed to a further degree when he realizes the limits and rapidity of life, and, indeed, comes to a recognition about investment in the material world, as he contemplates at the deathbed of Füsun's father, Tank Bey: "But in the room there was no charge issuing from the objects that surrounded him in life; there was only the fog of death and the void."[30] This may appear as a grim note on which to end an analysis of *The Museum of Innocence*, yet as this is stated near the end of the novel, there is a purpose at hand here. A recognition of the brevity of life, and a realization of how to come up against the categorizations of society through a critical lens, will allow one to see through the stifled resonances of how such aspects as religion/secularity, traditional/modern, and the rhetoric of politics, class, and nationalism have constructed a life, an ideal of a life that was never meant to be lived in any sense as it was built on a societal fabric that left the self lacking, and excluded others. In *The Museum of Innocence*, Pamuk writes about a very different way of imagining leading a life that might well impact how reality is contemplated and configured in societies across the globe, if only one is willing to consider how things could be otherwise.

Italo Svevo's *Zeno's Conscience*

A word in the night is like a shaft of sunshine. It illuminates a stretch of reality and, confronted by it, the constructions of the imagination fade.[31]

Italo Svevo—*Zeno's Conscience*

Svevo's novel *Zeno's Conscience* is a narrative that portrays the interiority of consciousness and life in the contemporary world in overcoming negative discourses on identity and how they have impacted interpretations of subjectivity and consciousness. Svevo pressures what it means to be Jewish and secondarily how this was and is impacted by Italian national consciousness through the categories of race and religion in a critique of modernity. In parallel to Pamuk's *The Museum of Innocence*, it can be suggested that the categories of race, religion, nation/nationality, culture, and identity, are, as Svevo suggests, "constructions of the imagination," and that the articulation of new language and discourses must be imagined and learnt in the refiguring of consciousness and reality.

With Ettore Schmitz writing under the name of Italo Svevo, the literary and cultural critic is seemingly provided with an obvious strategy of how to approach the conundrum of his "identity" and his birthplace of Trieste, Italy, where languages, cultures, and nationalities mixed and coexisted. Many literary critics have rested on reading Trieste and the biographical material on Schmitz/Svevo as a way to read and interpret Svevo's literature and the novel *Zeno's Conscience*; however, I think that this demonstrates a certain blindness of reading and interpretation. Critics have also suggested that Svevo's literature has little to do with the Jewish experience, and this also suggests an inability to read or understand what Jewish means in the context of Svevo's project and what he is trying to approach as a problem of consciousness, which is also important to contemplate alongside Giorgio Bassani's *The Garden of the Finzi-Continis*.

Zeno's Conscience, published in 1923, prefigures the date of the racial laws in Italy and, of course, the *Shoah;* yet post-1880s' Italy already bore the yearnings toward a national identity and language that suggested ways of perceiving and distinguishing peoples that were seen and imagined as not fitting into the ideas and discourses of nationalism. In Elisabeth Schächter's *Origin and Identity: Essays on Svevo and Trieste*, she explains how, as of 1880, Svevo had experienced what we now term "racism," but that type of rhetoric, and imagining of difference, did not yet exist in how we think of the idea today.[32] Svevo's novel permits highly nuanced and introspective degrees of thinking through religion and consciousness that generate a deconstruction of the suspect categories of race and identity, and how they are enveloped in the sense and determination of religion. The interpretation of Svevo's portrayal of his orientation to Jewishness needs to be acutely interpreted as to what is at stake here for consciousness in today's world. The literary critics Schächter, P. N. Furbank, and Giuliana Minghelli have worked some important critical terrain in their reading of Svevo in regard to the connection between Otto Weininger and Svevo.[33] Weininger is referred to in *Zeno's Conscience*, but it has to be understood that Svevo is never direct, and perhaps a way to understand this is that Svevo's task as a writer is to make the unconscious speak as a means to rewrite an orientation to Jewishness itself. Jews were typified and stereotyped as having a collective negative "character" (inclusive to how they were seen racially and religiously) in Weininger's text *Sex and Character*, published in 1903, in which he set the oppositions of Aryan and Jew into the ultimate banality of nation-state discourse, which was carried forth under national socialism in Germany.[34]

The problem with the aforementioned literary critics in how they read and associate Weininger and Svevo is that, aside from some stray remarks in Furbank's *Italo Svevo: The Man and the Writer*, they tend to read Svevo's novels as reinforcing Weininger's discourse of seeing and representing the Jews as weak, inferior, incapable, and lacking in character to themselves and within the nation. This viewpoint is rather summarized by Giuliana Minghelli's *In the Shadow of the Mammoth: Italo Svevo and the Emergence of Modernism*, when she articulates, "The problem of the Svevian character is the absence of character."[35] Rather than situating this as a problem, it is necessary to articulate this as the exact force of Svevo's writing that is particular to *Zeno's Conscience* and in also recalling Robert Musil and how he critiqued modern subjectivity and national identity in *The Man without Qualities*.[36] Svevo strives and succeeds to rewrite and reinscribe a very different understanding of Jewish consciousness against Weininger's depictions of the Jewish character. It is very important to bear in mind that while in contemporary society the discourse of character is not utilized to demarcate collective senses of belonging, it can be firmly stated that in today's rhetoric, discourses on identity have subsumed character as the standard marker of difference. In this regard, Edward W. Said has stated in his article "Nationalism, Human Rights, and Interpretation": "The decline of national character studies portends the rise of the discourses of national identity."[37] Svevo's novel strives to move the reader and the human condition well beyond discourses of national identity and the ultimately hazardous limitations of how people fit into and do not fit into social structures of racial, national, and religious determinations.

Zeno's Conscience was published nearly 40 years prior to Bassani's *The Garden of the Finzi-Continis*, and Svevo's vision strikes as that which provides the reader and interpreter with a critical foreshadowing of the problems inherent in Italian and European society and human consciousness itself. The characters in Bassani's novel are reluctantly conscious of being seen as racially or religiously different as these pressures of identification, of being seen as Jewish in a negative societal sense, are

strictly imposed on them from the outside through society in the imagining of difference. Difference in the Jewish community is also implied
through class between the two principal families in the novel. Bassani
writes in this regard:

> That we were Jews, nevertheless, and inscribed in the ledgers of the same
> Jewish community, still counted fairly little in our case. For what on
> earth did the word "Jew" mean, basically? What meaning could there
> be, for us, in terms like "community" or "Hebrew university," for they
> were totally distinct from the existence of that further intimacy—secret,
> its value calculable only by those who shared it—derived from the fact
> that our two families, not through choice, but thanks to a tradition older
> than any possible memory, belonged to the same religious rite, or rather
> to the same "school"?[38]

It is apparent that Bassani writes against class distinctions of Judaism
that also fall into a rabbit hole of distinguishing the problematic dynamics of determining who is more authentically Jewish. In this regard, any
designs toward an idea of community falter greatly, and so the problems
are both simultaneously communal and national, and exclusion functions internally through the Jewish community and nationally through
the racial laws in Italy that saw Jews as not fitting into the idea of
the nation. This strikes with an ominous sense of clarity when Bassani
writes, "despite the deep rift made in citizenry by the racial laws,"[39]
and as he continues to articulate, "Even in a city as small as Ferrara,
you can manage, if you like, to disappear for years and years, one from
another, living side by side like the dead."[40] Through the fascist racial
laws that were established in Italy in 1938, Jews were stripped of Italian
citizenship, and even in this horrific milieu, the separations internal to
the Jewish community according to class created an abysmal degree of
societal isolation.

The kind of sentiments that Bassani speaks to are also illustrated
in *Zeno's Conscience* in a more general manner when Svevo writes, "I
believe we all have, in our conscience as in our body, some tender, concealed spots that we do not like to be reminded of. We don't even know
what they are, but we know they're there."[41] It could be suggested, from
this citation, that society, or, more specifically, the impulses and drives
to a national identity want to reveal and define the "concealed spots"
as to how they might mark or contaminate the quest for purity of language, culture, race, and religion. Indeed, the dangers in any quest for
purity need only be reflected to the Shoah and the rise of dictatorship

regimes where others disappeared or were exterminated or killed in such a quest.

H. Stuart Hughes important book *Prisoners of Hope: The Silver Age of Italian Jews 1924–1974* offers many insightful manners of thinking about Svevo, Bassani, and other writers, but unfortunately his lens of investigation is through the idea of identity, where he offers his central question at the beginning of his text. He states in reference to the Jewish presence in contemporary Italian culture and Jewish heritage, "What is left of identity when both language and religion are gone?"[42] Hughes pronouncement suggests a naïve understanding of language and religion in relation to understanding Judaism, since being Jewish is not dependent on being religious or speaking one certain language. Hughes reads Svevo incorrectly, and here is the precise problem in that there always remains a societal inclination to push toward forms of identity that revolve around group meaning or psychology, in diminishing how the individual envisions one's self in society, and indeed struggles against the well-worn ways of how one is supposed to live and identify according to societal or even national standards. Moreover, rather than trying to rescue the idea of identity, new sensibilities in language need to be created in order to reimagine reality in how others are seen according to the inherent constrictions at hand in, for example, the dynamics of race and religion, which is exactly a place where Pamuk and Svevo are writing. In this manner, Hughes refers to a remark by Svevo as cryptic, but I see this as speaking to Svevo's vision in a simple and clear manner, as Svevo exclaims, "It isn't race which makes a Jew, it's life!"[43] It is clear that Svevo is writing against how Jews were seen through the prism of race in Italy. It is also crucial to bear in mind, as Hughes does, that this utterance does not occur in one of Svevo's novels, but is rather found in one of his letters, since the pronouncement of such a statement would rather diminish the aim and intent of his novels. Indeed, if one were to gloss *Zeno's Conscience* for explicit references to Judaism, one would come up rather empty-handed, since the use of the word "religion" does not offer great insight to the reader as to what is essentially at stake in this novel. Perhaps, it is of importance to highlight one instance when Svevo mentions in *Zeno's Conscience* that, "religion is merely ordinary phenomenon."[44] The ordinariness of religion for Svevo capitulates an understanding that leaves the imprints of cultural, familial, and personal residues without the political, nationalist, and ideological overtones that intoxicate how religion is most often considered in today's world. *Zeno's Conscience* is a radical way of understanding an orientation to Jewishness, and beyond this, a text that permits a way to see beyond the religious and racial determinations of society that ultimately hamper and limit the use of language and how humans communicate and, likewise, see each other. It can be best suggested through Said's *Freud and the Non-European* that Svevo's approach to an orientation of Jewishness has to remain and be thought of as unresolved, in referring to how Said speaks of an unresolved sense of identity.[45] Svevo or Said are not looking for a resolution, as this would only lapse into a rigid sense of identity, and secondarily this would cause one to locate Svevo's perspective as to where it stands in his approach to Judaism as seen from religious/secular and societal/national definitions.

Svevo provides a powerful vehicle of subversion through this novel in how religious identity is imagined, which unfetters it from its social construction as a belief system or ideology in bearing witness to a very fractured Jewish sense of identity as ordinary lived experience that is not at the forefront of consciousness. Before the heightened senses of religion and race that mark difference in today's world, there was no necessity to "pass," as people were already well within the society at hand, in stressing that there yet is something very wrong with language and formations of consciousness today in how people are included and excluded. Svevo was acutely aware of the changes in society that were occurring in Italy and Europe, through how others were seen in the entwinement of being seen racially and then associated with a particular religion—which still remains a problem today for Jews and Muslims in the contemporary world.

On what begins as an existential note, the tropes of illness and disease that run throughout *Zeno's Conscience* are suggestive of the precarious contingency of life and broader social concerns about the human condition. J. M. Coetzee puts it as such, "The sickness of which Zeno does and does not want to be cured is in the end no less than the mal du siècle of Europe itself, a civilisational crisis to which both Freudian theory and Zeno's conscience are responses."[46] Svevo's response also explicates the ostracization that occurs in language, which resides primarily on the level of nationalist discourse where there are direct references to purity, race, and blood in the continual foreshadowing of dire change occurring in society, and how he sees himself as not being able to fit in and being pushed to the periphery of the social condition. An encroachment on consciousness occurs for Zeno through which he does not want to be forced to simulate the societal Jewish identity of a religious/racial expectation, which for him is indicative of sickness in the nation and the world. Svevo writes through the character of Zeno, "I don't have to force myself to have faith, or to pretend I have it."[47] There is also a secondary level of interpretation in Zeno's response, which is illustrated through his personal relationships with women, where he is indeed trying to reinscribe and elevate the status of women in society, again in writing against Weininger's simultaneous negative "characterizing" of Jews and women. Svevo's novel also bears the Freudian imprints of his thinking about the death of his father and his relationship to his psychoanalyst. There is no resolution for Zeno in either of these existential circumstances that simultaneously signify the dire sense of loss in life and an ongoing sense of therapy in learning how to live anew; yet in both realms this also concerns how to remember, think, and imagine differently about the self and others.

Zeno's Conscience provides a manner to think alternatively about human intimacy and social relationships through discursive fractures that strip the religious and the racial of objectivity, formality, and sociality, in creating a break or shift from senses of belonging and affiliation that challenge ways of seeing otherness and difference in the world as religion and race. Svevo's postcolonial gaze also firmly resonates to Bassani's *The Garden of the Finzi-Continis*, wherein the ordinariness of everyday life, to put it very simply, did never concern all of the severe and vast problems at hand in the categorizing of human experience through the lens of Jewish identity and the racialization of Jewish consciousness under Italian fascism. Correspondingly, in *Zeno's Conscience*, Svevo provides highly imaginative exfoliations of reality and consciousness in an unresolved orientation to human experience that reconsiders what it might mean to be Jewish in Italy and provides reflection in thinking on the significance of any religion, race, or nation in the world.

Conclusion

Svevo and Pamuk stress upon understandings of identity in how it has been perceived through religion and nationality that provide an impetus to reconsider how an individual thinks of belonging, and how society compels one to affiliate. Society is seen as very problematic in the consideration of perspectives on consciousness as it is, respectively, contemplated and interpreted through the characters of Kemal and Zeno in *The Museum of Innocence* and *Zeno's Conscience*. These novels by Pamuk and Svevo prefigure and remain amid momentous and catastrophic events in human history, in providing reassessments of what it means to be human in differing societies across the world today, which is struck within shifting national paradigms that call into question long-held ideas and ideals of what it means to dwell in a country and, more locally, a society that one inhabits across the world. People in every society need to think through the sedimentations of the varied aspects of identity and how it has been represented and signified through such dimensions as religion/secularity and traditional/modern, which remain in the thick of further dynamics of affiliation and exclusion that have been analyzed in this chapter. As has been seen through these novels, this can no longer remain in some sort of quasi-societal-national frame of responsibility, where the political powers and societal frameworks always seem to falter. The onus is on the individual to think against (as David Grossman suggests in *Writing in the Dark: Essays on Literature and Politics*) the public and political idioms, and it is the carving and imagining of innovations in private and intimate language and discursive exchange that can truly hold a place to lift humanity through the burdened and meaningless remains of language that render political and societal discourse with no verve.[48] The exchanges of private and intimate discourses have the capacity to brush up against and reconfigure the dominant public and political mass rhetoric. In this manner, this is a call for living in the power and presence of a life that can bear witness to a responsibility of lifting one's self above the masses, and where Pamuk and Svevo inspire is in their thinking of the limitless possibilities of the imagination for the individual in life and in society. In this, there exists a verve for the individual to insist on a place in the horizon for humanity that shatters the precepts of societies that have for so long needed to be undone in imagining a world that could be otherwise. A world where difference would no longer appear as the uncanny, foreign, or the alien, but rather a place in which each human being could really begin to imagine how to resonate in the perspective of the other. In this kind of thinking, there are spaces between to be diminished for the individual in society in relation to the Other, with a lessening of global tensions, and what may hopefully mark a shift to different considerations on life within the nation.

Notes

1. Orhan Pamuk, *The Museum of Innocence*, trans. Maureen Freely (New York: Alfred A. Knopf, 2009), p. 168.
2. In the latest "Orchestral Manoeuvres in the Dark" release entitled *History of Modern* (2010), there is a definitive moment in the track, "History of Modern Part II," when Andy McCluskey sings, "The last mistake, you ever make, thinking modern's new forever." This is important to contemplate

42 • David M. Buyze

in regard to cultural production and how periods of time and identity are ascribed meaning.

3. Jacqueline Rose, *The Last Resistance* (New York: Verso, 2007), p. 12.
4. Sigmund Freud, *Civilization and Its Discontents*, trans. James Strachey (New York: W. W. Norton & Company, 1989).
5. Hanif Kureishi, *Something to Tell You* (New York: Scribner, 2008).
6. Rose, p. 88.
7. Sigmund Freud, *The Future of an Illusion*, trans. James Strachey (New York: W.W. Norton & Company, 1989).
8. David Grossman, *Writing in the Dark: Essays on Literature and Politics*, trans. Jessica Cohen (New York: Farrar, Straus and Giroux, 2008), p. 83.
9. Pamuk, *The Museum of Innocence*, p. 174.
10. See Ibid., p. 324.
11. Ibid., p. 37.
12. Ibid., p. 309.
13. See Ibid., p. 417.
14. Orhan Pamuk, *The New Life*, trans. Guneli Gun (New York: Farrar, Straus and Giroux, 1997).
15. Orhan Pamuk, *Snow*, trans. Maureen Freely (New York: Vintage, 2004).
16. See Pamuk's *The Museum of Innocence*, p. 324
17. Ibid., p. 411.
18. Ibid., p. 230.
19. See Ibid., p. 290.
20. See Ibid., p. 105, 361.
21. Ibid., p. 219.
22. Ibid., p. 394.
23. See Ibid., p. 221.
24. Ibid., pp. 52–53.
25. Ibid., p. 417.
26. Ibid., p. 417.
27. Salman Rushdie, "Imaginary Homelands," in *Imaginary Homelands: Essays and Criticism, 1981–1991* (London: Granta Books, 1991), p. 15.
28. Rose, p. 88.
29. Pamuk, *The Museum of Innocence*, p. 370.
30. Ibid., p. 448.
31. Italo Svevo, *Zeno's Conscience*, trans. William Weaver (New York: Vintage Books, 2003), p. 194.
32. Elizabeth Schächter, *Origin and Identity: Essays on Svevo and Trieste* (London: Maney Publishing, 2000), p. 56.
33. In addition to Elisabeth Schächter's *Origin and Identity: Essays on Svevo and Trieste*, see also P. N. Furbank's *Italo Svevo: The Man and the Writer* (Berkeley and Los Angeles: University of California Press, 1966), and Giuliana Minghelli's *In the Shadow of the Mammoth: Italo Svevo and the Emergence of Modernism* (Toronto: University of Toronto Press, 2002).

34. See Otto Weininger's *Sex and Character*, authorised translation from the sixth German edition (New York: G. P. Putnam's Sons, 1906).

35. Giuliana Minghelli, *In the Shadow of the Mammoth: Italo Svevo and the Emergence of Modernism*, (Toronto:University of Toronto Press, 2002), p. 53.

36. Robert Musil, *The Man without Qualities Vol. 1: A Sort of Introduction and Pseudo Reality Prevails* & *The Man without Qualities Vol. 2: Into the Millennium, from the Posthumous Papers* trans. Sophie Wilkins (New York: Vintage, 1996).

37. Edward W. Said, "Nationalism, Human Rights, and Interpretation," *Raritan* 12.3 (1993): 32.

38. Giorgio Bassani, *The Garden of the Finzi-Continis*, trans. William Weaver (New York: Alfred A. Knopf, 2005), p. 27.

39. Ibid., p. 245.

40. Ibid., p. 246.

41. Svevo, p. 86.

42. Stuart H. Hughes, *Prisoners of Hope: The Silver Age of the Italian Jews 1924-1974* (Cambridge: Harvard University Press, 1996), p. 2.

43. Ibid., p. 39.

44. Svevo, p. 40.

45. Edward W. Said, *Freud and the Non-European* (New York: Verso, 2004), p. 55.

46. J. M. Coetzee, *Inner Workings: Literary Essays 2000–2005* (New York: Viking, 2007), p. 12.

47. Svevo, p. 403.

48. See Grossman, *Writing in the Dark*.

PART II

Pamuk's Textual Diversity

CHAPTER 3

Mirroring Istanbul

Hande Gurses

Orhan Pamuk's *Istanbul: Memories of a City* is a text that is impossible to define using the already existing vocabulary regarding genre. Both thematically and formally it stands on slippery ground, which is constantly moving, challenging any definition that would confine it within fixed boundaries. With its variety of ingredients that includes autobiographical details from Pamuk's own childhood memories, photographs from the family album, newspaper articles, paintings, as well as writings on Istanbul by various artists, *Istanbul: Memories of a City* reflects the different levels, temporal and spatial, through which the narrator has experienced the city. The narrative itself emerges as a reflection of Istanbul with its conflicting and diverse social, cultural, and financial aspects. Its nonlinear structural and thematic composition offers the reader the chance to experience the city in the same way that Pamuk did. The first-person narration and Orhan the narrator stress the autobiographical aspect of the narrative while also raising questions regarding the genre of *Istanbul: Memories of a City*.

In this chapter, I will discuss how the narrative functions like a mirror and what are the images that are reflected in that mirror. The narrative appears as a mirror in different respects: it shows how Orhan and Istanbul are depicted in each other's image while also functioning like a mirror itself and reflecting the city as Pamuk had experienced it. I will explore the different aspects of the narrative that function like a mirror while also discussing the implications of the distorting function of this mirror and analyze how the different Orhans and Istanbuls reflected in the text result in a perpetual displacement in the creation of an Orhan who is constantly feeling out of place.[1] Despite having spent most of his adult life in the same city, Orhan can never feel at home, and it is this state of being out of place that provides him with the singular perspective that results in the creation of *Istanbul: Memories of a City.*

The text, published, in 2003, in Turkish and in English in a translation by Maureen Freely, in 2005, is Pamuk's ninth book. It is composed of 37 chapters, an epigraph, a dedication,[2] an index, and various photographs of both the city and Pamuk. The narrative depicts the first 22 years of the narrator's life in Istanbul, as well as portrays the city in its different aspects. It is written in the first-person singular, giving the narrative an autobiographical tone. To distinguish between the writer and the narrator, Orhan will henceforward refer to the narrator and Pamuk to the author. This distinction is even more important than in most texts since throughout the narrative Pamuk questions the possibility of a single and pure "I" by perpetually displacing a single, unified, and homogenous Orhan and Istanbul. The narrator draws attention to the multiplicity of elements that prevent the labeling of the narrative as "autobiography." He makes it explicit that he will not be offering a "true" and "accurate" account of his memories:

> But these are the words of a fifty-year-old writer who is trying to shape the chaotic thoughts of a long-ago adolescent into *an amusing story.*[3] (my emphasis)

While writing his experience of the city, the narrator's main concern is to create a pleasant story by bringing together different elements of that experience. As is the case in all of Pamuk's narratives, in *Istanbul: Memories of a City,* the memories are presented as elements brought together to create a story where they have a perpetually shifting position, acquiring new meanings with each connection established. In other words memories become meaningful in the story that they are part of rather than possessing an ultimate and essential "truth" in themselves. In order to illustrate his position regarding memories, Orhan gives the example of a specific tense that is used in Turkish to talk about events that we have heard from other people as opposed to our personal experiences. He explains that if he believed in the distinction between two kinds of memories—pure experience and the stories that we hear from other people—he would have used that tense in his narrative in order to make that distinction. To use that specific tense would imply that there is a clear-cut line that separates the imaginary from the real, whereas for Orhan there is no such distinction:

> In Turkish we have a special tense that allows us to distinguish hearsay from what we've seen with our own eyes... Beautiful though it is, I find

the language of epic unconvincing, for I cannot accept that the myths we tell about our first lives prepare us for the brighter, more authentic second lives that are meant to begin when we awake. Because—for people like me, at least—that second life is none other than the book in your hand. So pay close attention, dear reader. Let me be straight with you, and in return let me ask for your compassion.[4]

The memories that the narrator includes in his narrative are not absolute "truths" with single and fixed meanings but rather are perpetually displaced, resulting in the creation of a space where meaning is disseminated. To illustrate the role of memories, the narrator states that neither his mother nor his brother remembered the fights, suggesting that he invented those anecdotes:

> Later, when reminded of those brawls, my mother and my brother claimed no recollection of them, saying that, as usual, I'd invented them, just for the sake of something to write about, just to give myself a colourful and melodramatic past... So anyone reading these pages should bear in mind that *I am prone to exaggeration*.[5] (my emphasis)

Like the Orhan of *My Name is Red*[6] who would tell lies to create a pleasant story, the Orhan of *Istanbul: Memories of a City* makes it explicit that he has a tendency toward the fictional. The narrator's confessions regarding the nature of his memories do not aim to offer the reader a "correct" account but rather underline how the distinction between truth and fiction is irrelevant within the textuality of the narrative. He thus draws attention to the composition of his narrative; by bringing different elements together, he doesn't aim to create an accurate "autobiography" but instead a "story" that allows reinvention with each reading.

The use of images throughout the narrative has a particularly crucial role. By bringing together photographs of Istanbul and photographs from his own family album, Pamuk creates a narrative where the images gain new meanings. These images are, for him, like memories. Once brought together, the individual images reflect the city as Orhan had experienced it. Rather than including postcard images of the city that show the recognizable landmarks, Pamuk prefers to use images of the backstreets of the city, dominated by darkness and poverty. For example, the images included in the fifth chapter entitled "Black and White" show an Istanbul that is not recognizable even for the locals. Using those images that reflect the sadness, the lack of light, and the ruins, Pamuk recreates the city, as he has perceived it. The images of Orhan are carefully chosen and illustrate how the city has shaped Orhan at different stages in his life. While depicting the pleasant trips that they made to the Bosphorus with his mother and brother, the picture of Orhan that is included reflects an Orhan (a boy instead of Orhan) who is happily smiling into the camera.[7] On the other hand, during his adolescent years, when preoccupied with different issues in his life, Orhan is seen in a rather melancholic mood, not looking at the camera, gazing at the city from the balcony of his house.[8]

Perpetual Reflections

Istanbul is depicted in the narrative as having a decentered, fragmented, elusive, and heterogeneous structure, very much like the narrative itself. Throughout the narrative, at different stages of Orhan's life, there is a different aspect of Istanbul that becomes apparent, which is also in parallel with the mood that Orhan is in at that specific moment. Those individual moments are brought together and compose the narrative as a fragmented structure. Rather than having a linear organization, the narrative appears through fragments, which prevents the establishment of a fixed center. *Istanbul: Memories of a City* is about the constant reinvention of both Istanbul and Orhan in each other's image:

> But here we have come full circle, for anything we say about the city's essence, says more about our own lives and our own states of mind. *The city has no other centre than ourselves.*[9] (my emphasis)

The above passage can be interpreted as a key that unfolds the complexity of the narrative in the sense that it illustrates the futility of any attempt to define the center of the narrative, and of the Istanbul that is created with this narrative. Similarly, the Orhan that the narrative creates is constantly moving. Just like Istanbul, Orhan too emerges as fragmented, changing, and shifting, preventing a firm and predetermined definition from being concluded. The impossibility to define a single and pure identity for Orhan is made explicit as early as the first chapter of the narrative entitled "Another Orhan." By underlining the presence of the possibility of another Orhan, who had an alternative life to his, the narrator highlights the fact that his narrative will not be a linear journey depicting the development of Orhan but will be fragmented and multifaceted, illustrating the different Orhans that emerge in parallel to the city that is constantly changing. The narrative opens as follows:

> From a very young age, I suspected there was *more to my world than I could see: somewhere in the streets of Istanbul, in a house resembling ours,*

there lived another Orhan so much like me that he could pass for my twin, even my double.[10] (my emphasis)

By introducing the idea of another Orhan at the beginning of his narrative, the narrator implies that the journey ahead will be a journey in search for the other Orhan. Throughout the narrative, we see the narrator in the streets of Istanbul trying to reconcile the various Orhans. However, gradually this desire leaves its place to acceptance in the sense that rather than looking for an absolute and originary definition of Orhan, the narrator prefers to explore the possibilities offered by the coexistence of the different Orhans who provide him with different experiences of the city.

The narrator explains that this imaginary "other" Orhan enabled him to travel wherever he wished without moving from his own house. As a person who has never left his own city, these possibilities offered by the "other" Orhan constitute a rich source for the imagination of the narrator. He states that the "other" Orhan and his connection to the city are the very sources that made him who he is, in the sense that the possibilities offered by the "other" Orhan provided the narrator with the fresh gaze that kept his connection to the city alive, while also contributing to the feeling of being "out of place":

> I've never left Istanbul—never left the houses, streets and neighbourhoods of my childhood... *I know this persistence owes something to my imaginary friend, and to the solace I took from the bond between us...* Conrad, Nabokov, Naipaul—these are writers known for having managed to migrate between languages, cultures, countries, continents, even civilizations. Their imaginations were fed by the exile, a nourishment drawn not through roots but through rootlessness; *mine, however, requires that I stay in the same city, on the same street, in the same house, gazing at the same view. Istanbul's fate is my fate: I am attached to this city because it has made me who I am .... This book is about fate.*[11] (my emphasis)

The city and Orhan are thus portrayed as interdependent. Orhan as he is reflected in Istanbul's mirror emerges as fragmented, perpetually changing, and refusing a restrictive, predetermined definition. In the same way, the city of Istanbul, as it is recreated in the mirror that Orhan holds, cannot be accommodated within a binary opposition between the East and the West, or the new and the old. The image of Istanbul that we see in the narrative is a fragmented and decentered one that invites individual experience. It is a city filled with the presence of ruins that blur the boundary between the new and the old. Both temporally and spatially the city of Istanbul embodies both sides of the binary opposition hence making it impossible to draw a clear-cut line. In Orhan's experience, the modern and Western Nişantaşı neighborhood, where he has lived all his life, and the old, poor neighborhoods, where he takes long walks, contribute to his experience of the city without separating one from the other, allowing him to discover the different Orhans alongside the different Istanbuls.

Before discussing the various elements that make the city a mirror for the narrator, I will discuss an actual mirror within the narrative:

> When boredom loomed, I would cheer myself up *with a game very similar to the one I would later play in my novels.* I would push the bottles and brushes towards the centre of the dressing table, along with the locked silver box with the floral decorations that I had never once seen my mother open, and, bringing my own head forward so that I could see it in the central panel of the mirror triptych, I would push the two wings of the mirror inwards and outwards until the two side mirrors were reflecting each other and *I could see thousands of Orhans* shimmering in the deep, cold, glass-coloured infinity.[12] (*my emphasis*)

This game that the narrator calls the "disappearing game" is not merely a game but it also invites reading as a reflection of what he is doing with *Istanbul: Memories of a City*. It shows the impossibility of a pure and single definition of identity for Orhan and portrays the perpetual displacement of the various Orhans.

The changes that take place in the Pamuk family and the narrator's emotions are also reflected in the city. The narrative starts with Orhan's childhood when the Pamuk family was still enjoying their wealthy and happy days. During those times, the narrator depicts the Nişantaşı district of the city, which with its modern buildings, boutiques, and cafes becomes a reflection of the family's social status. Gradually, however, the financial aggravations and the fights between his parents bring with them a change of houses, a constant move that takes the narrative and Orhan into different parts of the city, echoing the thematic displacement of the identities of both the city and Orhan. Approaching the end, although still living with his family in Nişantaşı, Orhan starts discovering the poor and old districts of the city, as his dominant feelings are unhappiness and confusion. Those neighborhoods of the city become the reflection of the melancholy that Orhan has been experiencing. The narrative hence combines the feelings of Orhan with the different views and neighborhoods of the city. While creating his narrative remembering, the narrator thinks of those landscapes with the emotions that he had looked at them in the first place. He doesn't merely see the city as a landscape, but sees his own feelings reflected back at him. He explains:

> I remember how troubled I was the first time I looked at this same view from the same angle, and notice how different the view looks now. It's not my memory that's false—the view looked troubled then because I myself was troubled, I poured my soul in the city's streets and there it still resides.[13]

The relation between Orhan and Istanbul is thus a two-way process in the sense that the narrator not only reflects his feelings onto the city's views, but also receives them back later on. Istanbul is marked with the memories of his feelings with which he has associated the city's views. In other words, the narrator, while remembering, is always writing the mediated version that is filtered by the memories he has of those views. Orhan's different distorted images that he sees reflected in the city are thus marked by the feelings he had at that moment, and once he remembers those images, he remembers them in relation with those feelings that contribute to the creation of "other" Orhans who experience the city in multiple ways.

Before looking at the specific instances where the feelings of Orhan have been marked by the views of the city—and vice versa—I should emphasize two motifs that characterize the narrative and the city for Orhan: *hüzün* and black-and-white. These two themes permeate both the city and the narrative. For Orhan, the city always appears full of hüzün. And the same is valid for the black-and-white. The monochrome image of the city is mainly communicated in the narrative with the various images. The photographs make the black-and-white a sensory as well as a conceptual presence for the reader. For the narrator, the city's black-and-white hue is like a shield protecting it from Western eyes. It fits the mood of the city, which is dominated by ruins and poverty. It is not only visual but also has poetic connotations reflecting the mood of the city's inhabitants. The narrator describes the places in Istanbul where one could see the atmosphere created by the black-and-white:

> There are places—in Tepebasi, Galata, Fatih and Zeyrek, a few of the villages along the Bosphorus, the back streets of Uskudar—where the black-and-white haze I've been trying to describe is still in evidence. On misty, smoky mornings, on rainy, windy nights, you can see it on the domes of mosques on which flocks of gulls make their homes; you can

see it, too, in the clouds of exhaust, in the wreathes of soot rising from stovepipes, in the rusting rubbish bins, the parks and gardens left empty and untended on winter days, and the crowds scurrying home through the mud and the snow on winter evenings; these are the sad joys of black-and-white Istanbul.[14]

This passage sheds light on the different scenes that the narrator has associated with the black-and-white image of the city. Black-and-white is not seen in its bright and clear aspect but is presented as a blurry tone that reflects the city's gloomy atmosphere. Rather than presenting the opposition between the two strong colors, the narrator offers a perspective of the general atmosphere created by the absence of colors. In other words the black-and-white doesn't appear in the narrative as the clear-cut distinction between two colors, as an opposition, but rather as a theme that describes the absence of colors in the city. The losses, the poverty, the ruins that emerge as the predominant presence in Istanbul, are thus reflected visually in the black-and-white vision that Orhan portrays. The lack of colors in the photographs and in the city while reflecting the way Orhan had perceived the city also adds to the temporality in the sense that, the memories as Orhan portrays them appear as having lost their lively colors.

The black-and-white also reflects the tones of gray that emerge in between the black-and-white as the blurriness of those shades is a visual reflection of Istanbul's cultural, social, and financial conditions as a city geographically and culturally situated between what is broadly referred to as the East and the West.[15] The city's inability to belong to either side of this implied binary opposition is also in line with the blurry tones of gray that mark it visually.

The blurring effect of the tones of gray, of the smoke that appears in the black-and-white city, also reflects the loneliness that marks Orhan's experience of the city. As the newly found Turkish Republic is trying to define itself, independent of the remnants of the Ottoman Empire, Istanbul no longer appears as a central, dominant source of power, but as a forgotten and isolated place. This peripheral state of being and the isolation also find expression in the smoke that creates the veiling effect:

When the smoke thickened into a cloud, especially when rising from all the funnels of all the ships moored around Galata Bridge, it was as if my world was being wrapped in a black veil.[16]

According to the narrator, the black-and-white is an emblem of the destruction that the city has been undergoing. For the narrator the black-and-white doesn't merely become apparent in a specific landscape, but it is a filter through which he has experienced the city. Throughout the narrative, the overwhelming presence and the veiling effect of the black-and-white appear in parallel to the concept of hüzün.

The narrator defines hüzün as the feeling of melancholy that is communal. Unlike melancholy, which is experienced personally, hüzün is shared, and, in Istanbul, all the inhabitants participate in the atmosphere created by it. Hüzün marks the whole narrative as well as the narrator's perception of the city. The narrator explains that, for him hüzün is not merely an attribute of the city, but rather it functions like a mirror that reflects our own feelings, such an inseparable part of the city that we see it as the reflection of our presence within the city:

> But what I am trying to describe now is not the melancholy of Istanbul, but the *hüzün* in which we see ourselves reflected, the *hüzün* we absorb with pride and share as a community.[17]

The inhabitants of Istanbul also see themselves reflected in the hüzün that the city generates. The narrator explains this effect by comparing it to the steam on the window:

> Offering no clarity; veiling reality instead, *hüzün* brings us comfort, softening the view like the condensation on a window when a tea kettle has been spouting steam on a winter's day. Steamed-up windows make me feel *hüzün*, and I still love getting up and walking over to those windows to trace words on them with my finger. As I trace out words and figures on the steamy window, the *hüzün* inside me dissipates, and I can relax after I have done all my writing and drawing, I can erase it all with the back of my hand and look outside. But the view itself can bring its own *hüzün*.[18]

Hüzün is very similar to the effect that the black-and-white has in the sense that they are both veiling, obliterating a clear view. The blurry space that emerges in between the black and the white, with the dominance of the shades of gray and smoke, is similar to the effect that hüzün has. They both function like a cover, a protective shield between the city and the individual. Both hüzün and the black-and-white reflect the feeling of isolation that marks the city since the decline of the empire.

However it needs to be underlined that this hüzün is not a damaging feeling; instead, it enables artistic creation with the steamed-up window that invites writing and drawing. The obliterating aspect of the steam allows the narrator to create his own impression of Istanbul through the veil that hüzün provides. In other words, it could be argued that both hüzün and the black-and-white function like a distorting mirror by preventing a clear reflection. Instead, they reflect distorted images of the city, which, in return, allows the inhabitants of the city to see themselves reflected. For Orhan too, these two dominant themes create a space where he can see the various distorted images of himself.

Among the various places in Istanbul that offer a distinct reflection of Orhan, Bosphorus plays an important role; it marks Orhan's memories as a source of joy and optimism. In the sixth chapter entitled "Exploring the Bosphorus," the narrator describes his first visits there with his mother and brother. This first encounter with this part of the city is a positive memory for Orhan, who remembers it with happiness and optimism even at later stages in his life:

> The little family quarrels, the rivalry with my older brother that turned every game into a fight, the discontents of a "nuclear family" wandering around in a car, hoping for a brief escape from the prison of their apartment—all this came to poison my love for the Bosphorus, though I could not bring myself to stay behind at home. In later years, when I would see other noisy, unhappy, quarrelsome families in other cars on the Bosphorus road, out on the same Sunday excursions, what impressed me most was not the commonalities between my life and others' but the fact that for many Istanbul families, the Bosphorus was their only solace.[19]

Notwithstanding subsequent familial tensions, the Bosphorus at later stages in life reflects his positive feelings back to the narrator, and thus becomes a source of joy and happiness.

However, there are other parts of the city that reflect a gloomier Orhan, which becomes apparent when the narrative and Orhan gradually move to the backstreets of the city, dominated by ruins and poverty. During his adolescent years, Orhan is no longer the optimistic and happy child who was visiting the Bosphorus but instead is depicted as confused and unhappy. He escapes onto the streets of Istanbul where he sees his own mood and confusion reflected in the city:

> I'd see myself in the mirror on the opposite wall, and I'd think my reflection too real, too crude to bear. These moments were so excruciating I'd want to die, but I'd continue eating my sandwich with ravenous anguish, noting how much I resembled Goya's giant—the one who ate his son.[20] The reflection was a memento of my crimes and sins, confirmation that

I was a loathsome toad. It was not just because the reception rooms in the unlicensed brothels in the back streets of Beyoğlu had these huge framed mirrors hanging on their walls: I disgusted myself because everything around me—the naked bulb above my head, the grimy walls, the counter at which I was sitting, the cafeteria's sickly colours—spoke of such neglect, such ugliness. And I would know then that no happiness, love or success awaited me: I was doomed to live long, boring, utterly unremarkable life—a vast stretch of time that was dying before my eyes, even as I endured it.[21]

The reflection that he sees in the mirror is not a pleasant one, reflecting an Orhan he finds repulsive, suggesting a profoundly contradictory self, as the allusion to the brothel invites us to review the loneliness he experiences at that period. Other districts of Istanbul reflect his loss and sadness back to him:

It may be because I first saw so many neighbourhoods and back streets, so many hilltop views, during these walks I took after I lost my almond-scented love, that Istanbul seems such a melancholy place to me. When the loss was still new, I saw my mood reflected everywhere.[22]

Again, the narrator's perception of the city is marked by the way he had first seen it. These parts of the city are melancholic mainly because it was the dominant feeling in the narrator while he was contemplating them.

Throughout the narrative the narrator presents various attempts at reproducing the city. He tries to seize the meaning of the city by reading it, walking its streets, and painting it. But it could be suggested that it is only by "writing" that he can reflect the city as he has experienced it, because writing allows the narrator to illustrate the constant displacement that is at work in his Istanbul. With its textual and visual elements and fragmented structure, *Istanbul: Memories of a City* illustrates the impossibility of a fixed and singular meaning for the city, the unfamiliarity of its backstreets, smoky skies, and ruins, compounding the estrangement of the reading experience. In other words, the narrative itself thus becomes a distorting mirror that reflects the city as Orhan had experienced it.

The narrator's learning how to read invites a comparison with the city as a text waiting to be read. Until that point, his experience with the city has been mostly based on the walks with his mother and what he saw on the streets; with reading, a new way to experience the city becomes available. The words are not meaningful unities for Orhan at this stage but a compilation of letters with sounds:

> From the moment I learned how to read, the imaginary world inside my head was adorned with constellations of letters. They did not convey meaning or even tell a story: they just made sounds.[23]

When he learns how to read, the city becomes an open book for the narrator. However, far from becoming transparent or clearly meaningful, the ability to read makes the world *more* rather than less needful of interpretation. Every detail belonging to his daily life henceforth becomes a significant element in his perception of the city. By reading the letters on an ashtray, Orhan makes those words part of his perception of the city, and eventually part of his narrative. Reading becomes so automatic that Orhan doesn't even need to think about it. That is to say, letters, immediately translated "into syllables and sounds," draw attention to their own materiality, and manifest their existence as *signifier* rather than as vehicle of a predetermined signified:

> The decree on some of the cement pavements around the Governor's Mansion in Nişantaşı, three minutes away from our house, was one of them. When I was walking with my mother and my brother from Nişantaşı towards Taksim or Beyoğlu, we'd play a sort of hopscotch on the empty pavement squares between the letters and read them in the order we saw them: ESAELP GNITTIPS ON.[24]

This opacity of language also brings us back to the concept of the mirror, in that the letters "ESAELP GNITTIPS ON" spell "No spitting please" backward. For the narrator, holding a mirror to his city doesn't imply a mimetic reproduction that aims to capture the singular "meaning" of the city. The mirror that he holds is a distorting one, which, instead of affirming the identity of the city with its recognizable and hence readable landscapes, reflects its ruined structures that appear as illegible.

Reading the city for the narrator becomes an important part of his relation with it. As he grows older the reading machine in his head continues to work. During his high school years, when he is feeling lonely among the crowds and unhappy with who he is, Orhan reads the city as if he is reading himself:

> All these give me to know that the rest of the city is as confused and unhappy as I am, that I need to return to a dark corner, to my little room before the noises and signs pull me under.

AKBANKMORNINGDONERSHOPFABRICGUARANTEE
DRINKITHEREDAILYSOAPSIDEALTIMEFORJEWELS
NURIBAYARLAWYERPAYINSTALMENTS[25]
So in the end I'll escape the terrorising crowds, the endless chaos, and the noonday sun that brings every ugly thing in the city into relief, but if I'm already tired and depressed, the reading machine inside my head will remember every sign from every street and repeat them run together like a Turkish lament.[26]

The very street signs of the city become a text, one, however, that translates his turmoil *into* language. The juxtaposition of unrelated fragments echoes, as we have seen, in the fragmentary structure of *Istanbul: Memories of a City*. Letters rather than offering a linear order that invites an ultimate meaning, appear as randomly brought together, hence echoing the nonlinear structure of both the city and the narrative.

Conclusion

As I have so far tried to portray, the city as Orhan has experienced it, is far from being a linear and fixed unity but rather appears as fragmented, constantly changing, shifting, and hence preventing a firm and absolute definition. In its different neighborhoods, in the predominant tones of gray, the city not only obstructs an ultimate rendering but also prevents its inhabitants from experiencing the security of such an absolute definition. Orhan as well as other inhabitants of the city witness the constant displacement by seeing themselves reflected in the permanent move that the city is subject to. Both Orhan and Istanbul, as he had experienced it, rather than appearing as beholders of a single and ultimate definition, appear as constantly shifting, hence always remaining "out of place." *Istanbul: Memories of a City,* by bringing different elements—visual, textual, literary, historical, and personal—echoes the structure of Istanbul as Orhan had experienced it, thus offering the reader yet another distorting mirror. In the distorting mirror of the narrative, both Orhan and Istanbul are presented as displaced identities that explore the possibilities offered by the perpetual reinvention. The reader, rather than following a predetermined route that would lead to a fixed point of arrival, is free to reinvent both Orhan and the city following his or her own individual itinerary in this fragmented structure.

Notes

1. E. Said, *Out of Place* (London, Granta Books, 1999) is also an autobiographical book where he depicts his experience of being away from home.

It is important to note that Said's feeling of "out of place" reflects his permanent state of being a "foreigner" as he lives away from home. Whereas I argue that in Pamuk's *Istanbul: Memories of a City*, this feeling is present despite the fact that Orhan has spent most of his adult life in the same city.

2. *Istanbul: Memories of a City* is dedicated to Pamuk's father Gündüz Pamuk who died in 2002.

3. Orhan Pamuk, *Istanbul: Memories of a City* (London: Faber and Faber, 2006), p. 290.

4. Ibid., p. 8.

5. Ibid., p. 265.

6. Shekure, one of the protagonists of *My Name is Red*, closes the narrative by indicating that her son Orhan is the "storyteller" and that he has a license to lie in order to obtain a pleasant story: "For the sake of a delightful and convincing story, there isn't a lie Orhan wouldn't deign to tell" (O. Pamuk, *My Name is Red* [London: Faber and Faber, 2001], p. 503).

7. Pamuk, *Istanbul: Memories of a City*, p. 45.

8. Ibid., p. 185.

9. Ibid., p. 316.

10. Ibid., p. 3.

11. Ibid., p. 5.

12. Ibid., p. 69.

13. Ibid., p. 313. The Turkish original of this passage is slightly different as it draws attention to the bringing together of the vistas of the city with the personal feelings. I suggest the following translation: "To look at the landscape of the city is to combine those vistas with the feelings that Istanbul offers while walking along the streets, cruising by the boat. However these are not the only ways to view the landscapes of the city; to view the city also means connecting your mood with the views that the city offers to you. Associating your feelings with the scenes of the city with talent and honesty also means combining those images that are marked in your memory with the deepest and frankest emotions such as pain, sorrow, melancholy and sometimes with happiness, joy of life and optimism." O. Pamuk, *Istanbul: Hatıralar ve Şehir* (Istanbul: Yapı Kredi Yayınları, 2003), p. 322.

14. Pamuk, *Istanbul: Memories of a City*, p. 35.

15. This geographical reference includes cultural, political, aesthetic, and historical distinctions, which have been discussed by various authors from different perspectives in a global context. In this chapter, the East/West dichotomy refers to the national cultural atmosphere that has emerged with the foundation of the Turkish Republic in 1923. Having lost its status as the capital of the empire, Istanbul becomes the space of encounter where the old/Eastern/traditional ways of living meet with the new/Western/modern forms that are introduced.

16. Pamuk, *Istanbul: Memories of a City*, p. 254.

17. Ibid., p. 84.

18. Ibid., p. 79.

19. Ibid., p. 53.
20. The giant in question is *Chronos*, time. It could be suggested that the passing of time for Orhan implies the decline and fall of the Ottoman Empire leading to the gloomy and poor Istanbul that he is experiencing.
21. Pamuk, *Istanbul: Memories of a City*, p. 278.
22. Ibid., p. 313.
23. Ibid., p. 117.
24. Ibid., p. 118.
25. Akbank, morning, doner, shop, fabric, guarantee, drink, it, there, daily, soaps, ideal, time, for, jewels, nuri, bayar, lawyer, pay, installments.
26. Pamuk, *Istanbul: Memories of a City*, p. 287.

CHAPTER 4

Problematizing East-West Essentialisms: Discourse, Authorhood, and Identity Crisis in Orhan Pamuk's *Beyaz Kale* [*The White Castle*]

Michael Pittman

"To understand what is unique about other cultures, other peoples, these things we can glean only from the careful, patient reading of great novels," he said. "It is by reading novels that we come to understand the complex world in which we live."[1]

—Orhan Pamuk

"Of what importance is it who a man is?" the Hoja would ask and reply: "The important thing is what we have done and will do!"[2]

The discourse around a so-called clash of civilizations between the West and the Islamic world continues to promote intense debate. In many ways, Turkey is and has been both geographically and textually at the center of this debate. This chapter will trace some of the nuanced expressions of this dilemma in Nobel Laureate Orhan Pamuk's third novel *Beyaz Kale* (1985) (*The White Castle*) through the lens of Michel Foucault's discussions of the author from his 1970 essay, "What Is an Author?" The aim of the discussion will be to highlight the complexities of the notion of author, and the power relations that are invoked within Pamuk's novel, as a microcosm of East-West relations, both past and present. The problems of authorhood, and an essentialized East and West, are conspicuously foregrounded in and around the formal text of *The White Castle* through the creation of a variety of marks signifying authorship and through the ambiguous identity of the author of a "discovered" story about a waylaid Italian scholar and a Turkish Hoja in seventeenth-century Istanbul. Throughout the novel, the identity of the narrator/author is put into question in a series of omissions, substitutions, and deferrals that mirror Foucault's concerns about the role of the novel and notions of objectivity in texts and discourse—the text not only resists grand narratives about the authors, but also resists or undoes the solidification of a series of historically dichotomized identities, including Europe and the East, or the West and Turkey, or the West and the Muslim world, etc.

The White Castle begins with the capture of a young, educated Italian man from Venice who is captured by the Turks and taken to Istanbul. The Italian is eventually given as a slave to a man known simply as "Hoja"—and we never learn the real names of these two central figures. Being well educated, the Italian is given a certain amount of respect and freedom by the Hoja. Though the Hoja is sure of the superiority of the Ottomans over Europeans, he is extremely interested in the Italian's knowledge of science and the power it represents. Throughout the story, the two men have extended conversations in which they question each other and reflect upon their own identity. Towards the end of the story, the two men design, at the behest of the sultan, a mammoth weapon and accompany it to battle the Poles in the attempted siege of the powerful and symbolic White Castle. The story concludes with the reflections of the now-retired Italian who lives in the bucolic environment of Gebze, some distance from Istanbul.

The White Castle: Shifting Narration/Identities

From the very beginning of Pamuk's groundbreaking novel, the preface plays a role in the obfuscation of authorial identity by introducing Faruk Darvinoğlu, whose name is signed in the conclusion of the preface as the discoverer and translator of the text to follow. In the preface, Darvinoğlu claims to have made in-depth, but inconclusive, research into the manuscript's origins and the identity of the author. Pamuk, even in this preface, tries to deconstruct the notion of a fixed author/narrator through Darvinoğlu's suggestion that the author of the found manuscript read travel books by Evliya Chelebi, a famous seventeenth-century Ottoman travel writer, as well as others, and remarks that the author "clearly enjoyed reading and fantasizing." However, the narrator remarks, nothing could be concluded unequivocally as to the identity of the author. Darvinoğlu describes his attempt to research the identity of the author in graveyards and archives (giving a certain touch of realism in mentioning specific locales in Istanbul, such as the famous Üsküdar graveyard), but concludes that only certain details are historically inaccurate and others are possibly true—though he gives no indication to the reading audience which may be true or false. After reading the story, he remarks that he enjoyed retelling it and discussing, "its symbolic value, its fundamental relevance to our contemporary realities, how through this tale (he) had come to understand our own time, etc."[3] The language in this comment suggests another layer to the significance of the text and alerts the attentive reader to the possible implications of the text as a whole.

Next begins the novel proper—the supposed "found" text opens with the narration of an Italian scholar and sojourner whose ship is overtaken by the Turks: "We were sailing from Venice to Naples when the Turkish fleet appeared." The Italian scholar is taken into captivity and later sold to a man identified simply as "the Hoja." The story takes us through the ups and downs of these two men "interested in science and knowledge" as they live together for the next 20 or so years. They grow together in their attempts to please the series of viziers and sultans for whom they work. Throughout their time together, they also struggle to define themselves as separate individuals, and they do so in a variety of ways. Through writing their own life stories, telling each other their dreams and memories, they come to know each other well. After many years of living and growing together, they are enlisted to create a "monster weapon" for the sultan, which they then accompany to the battle lines of Venice and an otherwise mysterious "White Castle." Finally, after a failed assault on the White Castle, they agree to exchange identities. The narrator then tells us that the Turkish Hoja returns to Italy in the place of the slave, and that the Italian slave takes the place of the Hoja.

However, it is at this juncture that what we have already understood about the writer of the novel is undermined again—all along we have been led to believe that the narrator of the events is the Italian scholar writing his memoirs. As the story closes, however, another turn is taken, and the narrator reveals that he is not actually the Italian slave but rather the Hoja, and that it is he who has written the entire story. Again, we are thrust into further indecision and ambiguity—the identities of the Hoja and the Italian scholar have slipped from certainty. We cannot at this point be sure that there ever was even an Italian slave, and we may even question if the Hoja is who he has claimed to be.

In the final chapter, we find an account of a visit by an Italian traveler who has apparently read a story about the now-famous Hoja in

Italy. The Hoja gives the man his story to read, and after perusing the story the Italian remarks that the Hoja must have no "real" ties to Italy as his descriptions of Italy seem inaccurate. The Hoja's description of the landscape of Italy in the story is revealed to be the view from the window at his home in Gebze (East of Istanbul). The images in the book have been revealed to be a reimagined representation of the view of his own world. The implication is now that the author has fabricated the whole story—but even this allows us to draw no conclusions, for at this point one can doubt the identity of the Italian visitor, who is providing this knowledge, simply as another character in the story. Even this cursory summary of the narrative scheme shows the slippage that occurs in the text. Questions about identity, reality, fiction versus nonfiction, and even writing as a way to determine the significance of these concepts are all foregrounded in *The White Castle*. These shifts of author/narrator openly and even radically question the naturalness of our assumptions in reading a text.

Foucault and the Disappearing Author/Authority

Since Foucault's 1970 now well-known essay on the author, the question of the author, and authorhood has been brought radically into question. Foucault begins his essay on the author with a quote from Samuel Beckett in support of his task: "'What does it matter who is speaking,' someone said, 'what does it matter who is speaking?'"[4] Through his historicization of the notion of the author, Foucault reveals the complex ways in which we value and place upon the identity of a particular individual the authorship of a text. As he remarks, it is the "privileged moment of individualization in the history of ideas, knowledge, literature, philosophy, and the sciences."[5] Foucault uses this strategy to liberate us from the notion of the author and the work resulting from this privilege of individualization that seems to us as indivisible, indestructible, natural, and, therefore, irreducible. In doing so, he creates a space in which we may question the "how" of writing: How is writing used? How does it function in relation to other texts? How does the subject appear in discourse? In reiterating the idea that today's "writing has freed itself from the dimensions of expression," he emphasizes the notion that there is no inside to a text, and that meaning does not lie hidden within a text nor does its author express anything from a secret interior.[6] There is no transcendent signified that we can decipher in order to find the "true" meaning of a text. Thus, as with the nature of the text, author, and identity, we find a mirror of this questioning in Pamuk's novel. Just as the figurative and literal mirrors in Pamuk's novel show us the different possible ways of reading into the novel, this breakdown and slippage also reveals connections to the discourse on East-West boundaries, and the problems of the "Other" in narratives that attempt to control, to impose, to essentialize, and to dictate the uneven presentation and representation of narratives and identity within the discourse of East-West identity of our time. What remains is that there is no author, no authority—though, for Foucault, this is ultimately a positive situation.

For Foucault, the author is not a necessity, though we are driven, if unconsciously, to seek one out. In *The White Castle*, this dilemma is consciously foregrounded by the creation of a variety of marks signifying authorhood within the text. Through the process of reading, the identity of the author/narrator is problematized. Of course, the initial author involved is Orhan Pamuk, and it is quite "natural" for a reader to assume that he is the "real" author of the work since his name is identified on the cover with a handsome photo and a few approving reviews. But once we leave the setting of the external clues (the cover of the book and title page) that connect his identity to the text in hand, we are conspicuously thrown into some confusion as to who exactly the author/narrator is. The narrator of Pamuk's novel is at moments *the subject* of the text, at others, the author of the text, and at other times an author is conspicuously absent. The author is at best an elusive entity—there are no conclusive determining factors in the novel that connect to a singularly identified personage. Pamuk's work plays with the idea of the author through the shifting identity of the narrator of the story or stories. If we take the work as a whole, including Pamuk himself, and the purported author of the introduction, the identification of the author is made all the more complex and indeterminable. Thus, there may be at least four entities at different moments in the text that tell us that they are or could be an author: first is Orhan Pamuk himself; another is Faruk Darvinoğlu, who is referred to at the beginning of the text, the one who introduces the text/manuscript to the reader. Alternatively, it may be one of the other two main characters that claim to have authored the text at different times: the Italian slave, or the Hoja. Pamuk writes against the usual grain of reading and discovery of an autonomous author or subject with a specific identity that bears certain unique or essential qualities. As Foucault remarks, the author-function "is not a pure and simple reconstruction made secondhand from a text given as passive material."[7] That is, several subjects or even different classes of individuals are referred to by the position given in the author-function of *The White Castle*. The disorder and the indeterminacy can be disconcerting for it also implies the unattainability of subjecthood both within the text and outside of it.

Reading and Desire

The White Castle draws the willing reader into the narrative and challenges the often unconscious desires around authorhood and identity, particularly as they have been constructed in the novel of the West. Through a close reading of *The White Castle* we may find, sometimes, in the interstices of story, the effects of the shifts of identity and the manifestations of an unconscious desire to assert and maintain control over the narrative in our own reading process. The narrative stretches the reader's attention, while inviting the reader to question his or her desire for this control. Yet, in reading the last chapter, as the story shifts from the point of view of the Italian slave as author to the Ottoman slaveowner, one may lose ground in this effort—that is, if one has not been already undermined in this process at an earlier stage. Even with the suggestions made in the preface that the author may or may not have been who he said he was, that he enjoyed reading and fantasizing, and that he could have borrowed the stories, one may proceed to read the text with the same assumptions and expectations about the naturalness of the position and identity of the author. This in itself reveals the strength of our unconscious desires to have a "unified" reading experience. In the story, it works almost on the level of a mystery—once we are alerted to the inconclusiveness of authorship. First, the Hoja narrating as author suggests that the name of the author is buried, "if not deeply," within the text. Second, there is a kind of invitation to seek the page through a rereading of the story, just as the Italian visitor had done, which would decipher the secret of the story. One may be driven to reread and search for the name and the source for the Italian's smile. This desire, only partially unconscious, seems to be driven by a wish to have control over the text, to know the identity of the author, and to have particular identifications with the time and place. But they are never quite fulfilled—even when one goes back and rereads the pages and discovers that the name of the Hoja is Ahmet, as he is named after his paternal grandfather. Nor when one finds the passage near the beginning of the book that purports to describe Italy, but which is revealed, at the end of the book, to be a description of the view from the Hoja's window at his home in Gebze. Knowledge of the names or places or even times in the story never fulfills the desire for control. Rather, they simply replicate a kind of endless deferral wherein we can never be completely sure of the text or the objective validity of our own reading of it.

In the course of their time together, Hoja Ahmet and the Italian slave write in order to discover what is innermost the truth of "what one really is." The act of writing enables and enacts personal intro-spection and a thorough purging of memories, past experiences, and faults. In these exercises, they simultaneously reflect the complexities of influence, collaboration, distance, and destruction embodied in the discourse of East and West. The all-night face-to-face writing exercises between the Italian and the Hoja serve as a reflection in the self-same search for identity. The Hoja and the Italian slave face each other while writing as if facing a mirror—their writing sessions easily likened to a session of psychoanalysis or a confession. The Hoja and the slave believe that the truth of their identity is found in the cathartic purging of the memory through the admittance of former wrongdoings. They have long conversations and arguments over the significance of their past and the tales that they write and exchange with each other. Over time, dreams that they have and tell each other, information from books they have read, and memories of their past lives become indistinguishable from one another. All of the stories they tell one another become a kind of distorting mirror for the selves that they see and think they understand. Mirrors of beliefs and ideas have become mirrors of self-conception or the lack thereof. These mirrors thereby provide a skewed reflection that produces a kind of schizophrenia in perception and there-fore self-conception. As a result, over these long years, the Hoja and the Italian slave come to represent, for each other, an Other. In the story, the Other is sometimes exactly like oneself, at different times the Other is simply "one of those fools." The process of playing out these activities such as writing, dreaming, conversation, and comparison as a means of attaining knowledge of Self and Other results in a decentering and a conflation of identities. Further, this conflation and confusion of iden-tity seems to declare the irresolvability of such issues as Self and Other, source and influence, presence and absence, reason over emotion.

The Novelization of the Hoja and the Slave's Will to Know

Pamuk's work overturns Western notions of authorhood and identity particularly by challenging or co-opting a Western reconstruction and representation of history and literature, simultaneously revealing the power/knowledge struggle. One of the most important ways this is achieved is through the means, modes, and figurations of a historically

Western genre, the novel, set in the guise of a historical document. The secretary of the Swedish Academy, Horace Engdahl, in a report about the rewarding of the Nobel Prize for literature in 2006 to Pamuk, remarks, "He has stolen the novel, one can say, from us westerners and has transformed it to something different from what we have ever seen before."[8] Pamuk's transformation of the novel in *The White Castle* dramatizes the struggle of East and West and situates the center of this struggle in Istanbul, at the traditionally historic crossroads of the East and West. At the level of the main narrative, the relationship between the Hoja and the Italian scholar reflect the attempt to understand what often seems incomprehensible about the Other, to have knowledge and power over the Other. The doppelganger motif in the story serves to show that there is a wish on the part of the Hoja to see himself like the knowledgeable Italian slave, to become just like him, to exchange lives with him. The two are described as brothers in the story both by themselves and by others around them. Are they actually alike in appearance and demeanor or is it the other's "imagination" or "lack of food"? Upon seeing the Hoja for the first time, the Italian scholar thinks that he looks just like him but when he reconsiders he writes: "I realized that it had been a year since I last looked in a mirror."[9] Throughout the story there is a continual comparison by the Italian scholar with the Hoja and by the Hoja with the scholar and "the others." The Hoja is portrayed as being obsessed nearly to the point of paranoia with comparing and distinguishing himself from the others. The Other as long as he thinks he is or can be like him is worth loving, to be longed for and to be emulated. The Other, who he can never be like or with whom he finds fault, is the fool. The slave becomes a point of fixation for the Hoja upon which he projects alternately the desire to be like him as a model of power and knowledge, and conversely as the Other against which he can define himself as different and unique. The Other is a constant presence and threat, yet he strives to be like him and define himself against him. Throughout the story the Hoja mentions "those fools" whom he feels contempt for, who are imperfect in all the ways that he is not. He frames them in simplified versions of the reality in order to explain them away. He is always condemning the vizier, the sultan, the Italians, and the slave as one of *them*. He writes of these various others in a paper he characteristically entitles, "Fools I Have Known Well."

The Irresolvable Other

The issue of Otherness is foregrounded by the Hoja as the narrator when he speaks of the Italian scholar as "Him" with a capital "H."

This "Him" represents and becomes the Other, albeit an Occidental one, and the power that the West holds, as well as an assumption of a direct connection with the source of truth. The novel suggests that the assumptions made during the seventeenth century about the power and knowledge that the West possesses and the desirability of their possession by the then Ottoman Empire, then as now, affect the exchange between the East and the West. *The White Castle* that appears at the end of the story becomes a symbol of the West and the origin of "Him." Such unfulfillable aspirations as to be like the West, then as now, are reflected in the description of the "White Castle" that the sultan's forces attempt to overtake:

> I didn't know why I thought that one could see such a beautiful and unattainable thing only in a dream. In that dream you would run along a road twisting through a dark forest, straining to reach the bright day of that hilltop, that ivory edifice; as if there were a grand ball going on which you wanted to join in, a chance for happiness you did not want to miss, but although you expected to reach the end of the road at any moment, it would never end.[10]

The Hoja is the intelligent Turk who is interested in and inspired by the knowledge of the West, but who is never able to completely fulfill the promise of knowledge and concomitant control because the goal of fulfillment, like the white castle, is a fiction.

The production of fictions is central to questions about the skewed discourse of Orientalist texts. Pamuk introduces passages in the conversation between the Italian visitor and Hoja that caricaturize and idealize the assumptions made by the West about Turks. A popular Western opinion of the Turks is characterized by the statement of what "He" had written about them and is injected into the dialogue by the Italian visitor:

> He was not a true friend of the Turks . . . He'd written unflattering things about them. He'd written that we were now in decline, described our minds as if they were dirty cupboards filled with old junk. He'd said we could not be reformed, that if we were to survive our only alternative was to submit immediately, and after this we would not be able to do anything for centuries but imitate those to whom we had surrendered. "But he wanted to save us," I put in.[11]

It is "He" who wishes to help the declining Ottomans who do not seem to be able to help themselves, and whose time is past, and who need reform and guidance from the West. This statement can be seen as an approximately accurate opinion that the West held regarding Ottoman Turkey, "the sick man of Europe," in the seventeenth and later centuries that motivated them to influence the country economically through the allowance made by its weakening political and military position.

Conversely, a more positive opinion about Hoja expressed by "Him" also reflects another type of Western stereotype of Turks in their relationships with their neighbors and the West. It is framed in a seemingly positive, but stereotypical and naive way:

> I had been ashamed after mercilessly beating up one of my childhood friends from the neighborhood and wept with regret, I was intelligent, I had in six months understood all the astronomy He taught me, I loved my sister very much, I was fond of my religion, I performed my prayers regularly, I adored cherry preserves, I had a particular interest in quilting, my stepfather's profession, like all Turks I loved people, etc., etc.[12]

Both of these characterizations of the Hoja reflect a stereotype of Turks from an ultimately artificial point of view, though one that is still prevalent in current discourse about the generosity of Easterners. In the story these identifications amplify and illustrate the way that discourses have portrayed and portray the relations between East and West by attempting to simplify the identity of one by the other into a neat, understandable, and controllable form.

In the concluding passages we finally encounter the white castle, which embodies all of the contradictions of the discourse in a symbolic manner. The whiteness of the castle becomes a symbol of unrealistic and false purity, an ideal of concepts or terms such as capitalism, democracy, and power, which is never attainable and therefore remains an utter and irreconcilable difference. The purity of the castle, like the supremacy of the discourse of reason of the West, is a fiction, and continues to be propagated in texts, both fiction and nonfiction. Yet, *The White Castle*, as the discourse of immutable reason and transcendence that the West is founded upon, still represents an ideal, though ultimately unattainable. It is this death, too, that Foucault calls our attention to. Along with the death of the author goes subjecthood and transcendence, and the removal of transcendence evaporates a privileged position of reason and rational discourse over presumably irrational positions associated with the East, or more particularly in current discourse, the "Islamic World." The privileged foundation of this logic has given rise to many of the master narratives justifying political and social domination of our age. The problem of irreconcilability remains. No matter how much we might turn over the binary oppositions that these narratives are founded upon, we are still subjected to them while they prevail and function as the basis of social, economic, and political ideologies. The complexities of the situation are invoked within the novel as a microcosm of the macrocosmic picture of East-West relations. The layering of the text and the complications that are invited concerning the identity of author reflect the complexities faced in discerning and declaring identity for oneself and for one's culture as over and against another culture. It is the representation of such identities in and through Orientalist discourse that has played and continues to play a large role in relations between the Middle East and the West. The position of criticism toward this book shifts as the identity of the author shifts. It is this shifting ground that Pamuk plays with and the equivocal status of the author that implicates the variety of possible authors, their connotative identities, and us, as readers. Yet, in this implication, it is we who are opened to yet other possibilities, other avenues of elaboration, and investigation—to understand our complex world and finding ways of working together. So, by way of concluding—and to mirror Pamuk's comment about the potential of the novel to help us "come to understand the complex world we live in," with which I began—I offer a quote from Edward Said reflecting in *"Orientalism* 25 Years Later," shortly after the US invasion of Iraq:

> *Rather than [focus on] the manufactured clash of civilizations, we need to concentrate on the slow working together of cultures that overlap, borrow from each other, and live together in far more interesting ways than any abridged or inauthentic mode of understanding can allow.*(my emphasis)[13]

Notes

1. Interview with Orhan Pamuk, "Pamuk Talks Power," Daily Stanford Daily Stanford, October 23, http://www.stanforddaily.com/2007/10/23/pamuk-talks-novels-power (September 28, 2010).
2. Orhan Pamuk, The White Castle (London: Faber and Faber, 1990), p. 149.
3. Ibid., p. 11.
4. Michel Foucault. "What Is an Author?" in Modern Criticism and Theory: A Reader, 3rd ed., ed. David Lodge (White Plains, NY: Pearson/Longman Publishing, 2008), p. 281.
5. Ibid., p. 281.

6. Ibid., p. 282.
7. Ibid., p. 288.
8. Ian Traynor. 2006. "Nobel Prize for Hero of Liberal Turkey Stokes Fears of Nationalist Backlash," The Guardian, October 13, http://www.guardian .co.uk/world/2006/oct/13/books.turkey (March 12, 2009).
9. Pamuk, The White Castle, p. 22.
10. Ibid., p. 143.
11. Ibid., p. 154.
12. Ibid., p. 158.
13. Edward Said. 2003. "Orientalism 25 Years Later: Worldly Humanism v. the Empire Builders." Accessed March 10, 2009. http://www.counterpunch.org /said08052003.html (March 13, 2009).

CHAPTER 5

Framing *My Name Is Red*: Reading a Masterpiece

Esra Almas

A great painter does not content himself by affecting us with his masterpieces; ultimately he succeeds in changing the landscape of our minds.
—*My Name Is Red*, p. 195

With the 2006 Nobel Prize in Literature, Turkish novelist Orhan Pamuk who, in the words of the Swedish Academy, "has discovered new symbols for the clash and interlacing of cultures," has been internationally acknowledged as a master-writer.[1] Subsequent to the award, *My Name Is Red* (1998, 2001), Pamuk's most acclaimed work and winner of the IMPAC Dublin Literary Award in 2003, has been framed as a masterpiece by the accolades of both the writer and the text.[2]

The notion of masterpiece is not an external fact about, nor simply a value associated with *My Name is Red*, but literally a constitutive aspect of the work itself. Set in the Istanbul of the 1590s, the novel tells a story of murder and love that revolves around an unfinished masterpiece. The sultan secretly commissions an illuminated book that will be sent to the Venetian Doge in the Islamic millennium. Meant to depict his dominion over both worlds and to testify to the Ottoman supremacy in the East as well as in the West, the sultan requests the miniatures be painted in the European manner. This leads to an unprecedented commotion among the miniaturists, who are ambiguous about Western methods of painting, and among the Islamic zealots, who regard painting as heresy. Recounted through 21 distinct voices, ranging from corpses to Satan, interwoven with romance, Islamic legends, and Koranic parables, as well as with discussions on style, time, and perspective, *My Name Is Red* is a treatise on art, a historical novel that reflects sixteenth-century Istanbul, and a representation of the now-forgotten art of miniature painting.

In this chapter, I argue that framing Pamuk's most acclaimed novel as a masterpiece helps situate both writer and book within the dynamics of contemporary culture. A problematic term in literary studies, the use of masterpiece in literature dates back to the nineteenth-century break from the Greco-Roman classics, and hence to an increasingly globalized understanding of literature.[3] Today, however, the term evokes the idea of "master" narratives, pieces, and authors, all categories that have been heavily critiqued in postmodern literary and cultural studies. I explore a series of frames that work to constitute the novel as a "masterpiece," indeed to "assign" it the status of masterpiece in contemporary discourse, from its launch and reception, to the related figure of "master-writer." Moreover, the notion of the masterpiece works, in turn, to frame ideas concerning murder, anachrony, multiplicity, Islam, and finally, writing miniatures. Deploying a kaleidoscopic perspective that resembles the book's form, I identify the varied frames that have worked to give the novel its "masterpiece status" and more specifically, to show how *multiplicity,* itself one of the frames I delineate, is not only intrinsic to situating this work as a masterpiece, but also reflects on an understanding of both the concept and the work. I propose, finally, that a critical deployment of these varied frames shows how *My Name is Red* frames, troubles, and ultimately reconfigures our cultural meanings of masterpiece.

Frame 1: Publicity

My Name Is Red was published in Turkey in 1998 and was immediately the center of media attention; its record sales (150,000 copies in a year) and extensive advertisement campaigns were unprecedented for a work of literature. Indeed, Pamuk was accused of "inundating" the media with publicity, thereby robbing his readers of the pleasure of reading it in solitude. Moreover, the novel was considered a difficult read, with exaggerated sales figures (Yılmaz 50–51).[4] The English translation of the novel, by Erdağ Göknar, came out in 2001 and sold 160,000 copies. The novel was featured on the cover of *The New York Times Book Review.* The cumulative effects of publicity and critical attention worked swiftly to establish the novel as a masterpiece in the West, and it was nominated for the IMPAC award.

The Turkish and English editions of *My Name Is Red* further illustrate some interesting differences in the novel's framing. The 1999 Turkish paperback edition cites no praise on the front cover. The long summary on the back cover opens with a comment by Pamuk, calling it his most cheerful novel. Ironically, however, the novel is referred to as "a requiem for the forgotten beauties of the ancient art of painting."[5] The two commentaries at the bottom display rather broad perspectives. The first one from *Frankfurter Allgemeine* reads as praise of Turkishness: "The young Turkish novelist shows Europe how to write a novel." The second commentary, from *The New Statesman*, concerns Pamuk's works in general: it suggests reading him as a must. There is also a short biographical note on Pamuk, mainly about the international recognition of his work. This Turkish edition of the novel is framed as a *master's* piece. The 2003 paperback edition of *My Name Is Red* in English, on the other hand, emphasizes its artistic value. The cover reviews focus on the novel, and not the writer. The front cover includes praises from *The Guardian, The New Yorker*, and *The Observer,* and the IMPAC, whereas the back cover commends the author as a possible Nobel Prize winner (Freely), and the book for reflecting the tensions between East and West ("Winner"). John Updike's review compares Pamuk with Proust and Mann, while a review by Kelly puts him in company with Umberto Eco. The framing of *My Name Is Red* in the Turkish and English publications, in short, highlights the discrepancy between the Turkish and the Western media, and between its national and international reception.

Frame 2: The Master-Writer

Pamuk's writer persona incorporates that of a master-writer, one relating simultaneously to both "Eastern" and "Western" traditions of storytelling:

> I learn and pick-up things from other authors. I've learned from Thomas Mann [...], Italo Calvino [...], Umberto Eco, [and from] Marguerite Yourcenar. [...] What inspired me most for *My Name Is Red* were the Islamic miniatures [...] drawn to illustrate the best scenes of stories that once upon a time everyone knew by heart and today, because of westernization, very few remember.[6]

Here, Pamuk emerges as a writer with an understanding of "tradition" in the sense invoked by T. S. Eliot in "The Tradition and the Individual Talent" (1919), his seminal essay on poetry as a meeting ground of tradition and the creative powers of the poet.[7] Tradition, from Eliot's perspective, "involves a perception, *not only of the pastness of the past, but of its presence*" (n.p.; emphasis mine). Tradition, including both past and present, suggests a present of multiple temporalities, crowded with echoes of the past. It culminates in "historical sense," one which "compels a man to write not merely with his own generation in his bones, but with a feeling that the whole of the literature of Europe from Homer and within it the whole of the literature of his own country has a simultaneous existence and composes a simultaneous order." For Eliot, historical sense leads the writer to a rather Eurocentric understanding of individualism, as a reflection of local literature. Pamuk's sources of inspiration reveal a similar perspective, and his authorship of *My Name Is Red* is also about being framed by past master-writers and masterpieces.[8] Yet, Pamuk's statement dislocates Eliot's definition, as the tradition it reflects draws not only from Europe, but also from the Islamic East. The tradition in the novel, in other words, is a twofold one, where not only past and present, but East and West converge. In perhaps a curious reenactment of the Eurocentric character of individualism, Pamuk cites specific names from the Western novelistic tradition, while he refers anonymously to the Islamic tradition of miniatures. Nonetheless, in the case of *My Name Is Red*, the master-writer's perspective of his piece encourages alternative vantage points to view both the novel *and* its status as masterpiece.

Frame 3: IMPAC Citation

Among the mostly favorable international reviews of *My Name Is Red*, the judges' citation for the IMPAC has become the most memorable one. The citation, primarily repeating the themes generally associated with Pamuk's works, merits reflection for a number of reasons regarding the form, content, and politics of the novel:

> A work of intense beauty, Orhan Pamuk's *My Name Is Red* opens a window into the reign of Ottoman Sultan Murat III, inviting us to experience the tension between East and West from a breathlessly urgent perspective.[9]

The window metaphor here evokes the thematic and aesthetic concerns of a novel that is, above all, about perspective. The window has featured in discussions of painting since Leon Battista Alberti's treatise on perspective, *De Pictura* (1991: 55).[10] The window analogy in the IMPAC

Citation relates the novel's masterpiece status to how it functions; the novel is a "window into the reign of Murat III." This, of course, leads one to question the ontological and epistemological implications of the metaphor. The window trope assumes that a work of art is transparent. The reader, therefore, is posited in a privileged situation to see through both. *My Name Is Red* is not simply an outlet into the past; it is a frame, a subjective re-presentation of a historical period. The window metaphor, focusing on the truth-value of the novel, is therefore problematic as it forecloses a reading motivated by the aesthetic concerns that frame the novel.

The citation emphasizes the perspective of the window not as a subjective point of view, but as a vantage point from which to view the past and the present. From the "breathlessly urgent perspective" that the window furnishes to the reign of Murat III, what the readers may view is "the tension between East and West" in its quasi-atemporality. The masterpiece status of *My Name Is Red* is therefore linked to its framing of East-West conflicts. Similarly, its political significance is often linked to present-day conflicts between Islam and West, especially after September 2001. Indeed, the American launch of the novel coincided with the events of 9/11, and the novel was considered a source of insight into current conflicts.

Within this presentational context, then, *My Name Is Red* appears as a retrospective story, which is more about the present and the future than about the past. Yet literature is a medium of storytelling in which form is equally important as content. As a "voice" in the novel reminds us, "it's not the content, but the form of thought that counts" (*MNR* 353–354). In this novel, which is narrated through multiple voices, perspective is neither transparent nor does it offer direct access to its object. On the contrary, the use of multiple perspectives draws attention to perspective itself, encouraging us to look "at" it rather than "through" it. The novel invites its readers to adopt an unsteady vantage point that requires constant reconfiguration and readjustment.

Frame 4: Framing a Murder with Masterpieces

Set in Istanbul during the winter of 1591, at a time when the Ottoman Empire was beginning to wane, *My Name Is Red* recounts the nine days following the murder of Elegant, a master miniaturist. Along with three other miniaturists, Elegant has secretly been commissioned by Enishte, whom the Ottoman sultan has asked to compile a "masterpiece," an illuminated book that will be sent to the Venetian Doge in the Islamic millennium. To depict the sultan's dominion over both worlds and to testify to Ottoman supremacy in the East as well as the West, the sultan has asked for miniatures painted in the European manner. The book itself is thus intended to be an encounter between the two ways of seeing. This encounter, however, is one marked with conflict and strife. Within the iconoclastic tradition of Islam, painting is a controversial topic. Realistic painting is considered the painter's claim to be as creative as God and hence a means of competing with Allah, the master-creator, which is the greatest of sins. Within this framework, painting in Western style, including the use of human perspective, connotes arrogance before God, as it prioritizes a human point of view over the godly one.[11] The only admissible painting style within this worldview is the art of miniature painting, a search for divine vision, "the act of seeking out Allah's memories and seeing the world as He sees the world" (*MNR* 96).[12] Miniatures primarily serve as a means of complementing the story and a repose for the eye; they "are the story's blossomings in colour" (*MNR* 30).

The miniatures in the secret book also include a portrait of the sultan, a practice regarded as doubly transgressive as it not only elevates a human point of view, but further idolizes it by putting a lifelike image at the center of a painting. The sultan's miniatures pose a threat to all who are even peripherally involved. For Enishte, whose own encounter with Venetian portraiture is also the reason why the sultan commissioned him, the secret book is to be a pinnacle of both the Ottoman miniature and his career. Yet, he believes it is also a threat to his life. The miniaturists who contribute to the book, on the other hand, feel they are betraying their art and their "master," Master Osman, who has taught them illumination. The religious bigots under Erzurumi Effendi, who relates the present weakening of the state to the abandonment of "true" Islam, seek to destroy the book, its promoters, and eventually the art of miniature. Ultimately, the miniatures in the secret book are a threat to the very art itself, both by the antagonism they generate and by advocating values diametrically opposed to the very precepts of the art itself, which is to erase all traces of the illuminator's style in order to achieve a representation of the world as God would see it. The killing of Elegant, apparently for all of the above reasons, unleashes a series of events prompted by these fears.

Miniatures in the secret book, as well as the art of miniature, also frame the love story. Black, Enishte's nephew, returns to Istanbul from a 12-year exile to help Enishte complete the secret book. Black's misfortune has also been brought about by way of portraiture: enamoured with

Shekure, Enishte's daughter, Black declares his love through a scene from *Khusrev and Shirin* (*MNR* 46–47), a popular Persian epic love story, and a cherished subject for miniaturists, following Bihzad, the Persian master miniaturist.[13] The love affair between Black and Shekure is a contemporary take on the romance, yet it takes quite a different course. In the romance, Shirin, an Armenian princess, falls in love with Khusrev, the crown prince of Persia, upon seeing his picture. For Black, however, a miniature portrait offers insufficient means of generating love. In his miniature, the nondescript faces of the two lovers are replaced with his own and with Shekure's. Revealing his identity and his feelings in a miniature, Black violates both the very precept of anonymity in miniature and of familial bonds. He is subsequently banished not only from Enishte's household, but also from Istanbul. Ironically, 12 years later, portraiture becomes a means to obtain Shekure's hand. Now a widow, Shekure has returned to her father's house with her two sons, Orhan and Shevket, to avoid Hasan, her brother-in-law and pursuer. So when Black steals a furtive glance of Shekure and is reminded of the romance, his love for her is rekindled. "When I recognized (a) similarity, oh how I burned with a love such as they describe in those books we so cherish and adore" (42). Black, yearning to revive the romance, recognizes the depth of his feelings only when his experiences remind him of a scene from the story. Life then imitates art, and the utmost aspiration is to imitate a masterpiece.

Black's investigations concerning the murder resemble a treatise on art and serve as an introduction to Islamic aesthetics: he has tête-à-tête conversations with Butterfly, Olive, and Stork, the three artists who help with Enishte's book, on issues that define a miniaturist: style, time, and illumination. This treatise on art entails a worldview in which Europe, to borrow Dipesh Chakrabarty's title, is "provincialized" (1999).[14] The discussions between Black and the miniaturists refer to parables and stories from the mosaic that constitutes the Islamic world: Turkish, Turkmen, Mongol, Arab, Indian, Chinese, and Persian thought, philosophy, and art. In each conversation, characters recount stories from Islamic lore, legends, even fables, to illustrate their point. Through these dialogues, we are introduced to a different way of seeing, to a world of masterpieces where meaning precedes form, word precedes image, and where style is considered a flaw.

Traditional stories and meditations on art become crucial in solving the mystery and literally framing the murderer. By decree of the sultan, Black has recourse to masterpieces and to the master miniaturist, Master Osman; they spend two nights at the Imperial Treasury studying the masterpieces in order to identify the style in the miniatures found on Elegant's corpse. Master Osman identifies the murderer as Olive, but also blinds himself, with the same needle Bihzad had, to attain the ultimate darkness, "God's pureness," and to protect one's honor, which is here equated with vision, from unwanted influences (*MNR* 396). Black, enamored of Shekure rather than of miniatures, captures Olive, who is about to flee to India to devote himself, under the Shah of India, to the purity of his art. Olive's yearning for purity of vision finds an ironic answer as Black blinds him with Bihzad's needle.

The novel concludes with a bleak denouement: Black is "crippled" after his struggle with Olive. Olive manages to escape, but is killed by Hasan, Shekure's brother-in-law. Black and Shekure's marriage is overshadowed by Black's failure to kill Olive, as well as his inability to complete Enishte's deadly book. The remains of the book are confiscated and placed in the Imperial Treasury; the art of miniature evanesces as the Ottoman Empire comes increasingly under the influence of religious extremism. In a bittersweet conclusion, telling her un-paintable story to Orhan, Shekure finds her sole consolation in writing, the space where all conflicts and identities blend within Orhan's "delightful and convincing stories" (*MNR* 503).

Frame 5: Anachrony

Reminiscent of the IMPAC citation, the novel's status as masterpiece has also been related to its depiction of the predicaments surrounding present-day Turkish identity. A historical novel, *My Name Is Red* is set in sixteenth-century Istanbul. The conflicts it portrays, however, relate more to the present than to the past. Concerns over Westernization as a loss of Turkish identity and individuality characterize the novel, but not the period it portrays. Whereas portraiture is repeatedly represented in the novel as a great affront to Islam and to Ottoman society, in that period it was already a branch in its own right.[15] Master Osman, the traditionalist painter in the novel, for whom portraiture is a "disgraceful affront to his dignity" (*MNR* 408), was actually the leading portraitist of the period, famous for his portraits of the sultans. Osman was also renowned as an innovator and promoter of realism (And 2002).

Another master miniaturist of the period was Velican (Olive in the novel), who was renowned for his charcoal illustrations of animals, with most of his surviving works containing his signature (Meredith-Owens 20; And 53).[16] In the novel, however, Olive is a painter whose passion for Western painting leads him to utter disillusionment and ultimately to rejection of Western methods, including signature. Stealing the sultan's unfinished miniature from Enishte after killing him, Olive tries to make a self-portrait in the space assigned for the sultan. The result is a realization of his inadequacy related not to his individual talent, but to a lack of tradition: painting in the European style requires "a proficiency [...] that will take years to attain" (*MNR* 487). In contrast to Enishte, who suggests, in a tone reminiscent of Eliot and of reviews of *My Name Is Red*, that masterpieces arise out of unprecedented encounters between two styles (195), Olive emphasizes that encounters without mastery and knowledge risk resulting in mere imitation. In the same vein, Olive responds to Black's scorn of his desire to "practice genuine artistry," with a warning against *all* attempts at Westernization:

> For the rest of your lives you'll do nothing but emulate the Franks for the sake of an individual style. [...] But precisely because you emulate the Franks you'll never attain individual style. (*MNR* 489)

The paradox in Olive's words points to the complexities of the novel and its discussions of aesthetics. Art is inescapably linked to imitation. However, imitation for its own sake and with no attempt to move beyond it can only result in a loss of authenticity. Olive's argument is a dialogue with the present; his words resonate with recent criticism of pro-Western self-modeling that has characterized the policies of Republican Turkey.

As the story of a struggle between pro-Westerners and traditionalists, the past in the novel is one that echoes the present, the space "where the subconscious of our contemporary neurosis is captivated by an anachronistically established 'East-West' confrontation" (Çiçekoğlu 3).[17] The novel blurs the lines not only between the past and the present, but also between author and character, fact and fiction. Pamuk's author persona is present within the novel, inserting details of his childhood into the narrative: the mother and her two sons are nominally and anecdotally the same as their real life counterparts ("Conversation"). In the same vein, Shekure, the final voice in the novel, announces the writer of her story as Orhan, and his preoccupation with the symmetry rather than the truthfulness of his story. Pamuk writes, "For the sake of a delightful and convincing story, there isn't a lie Orhan wouldn't deign to tell" (*MNR* 503). Shekure's announcement is both a warning against "literal" readings of the novel and an emphasis on its aesthetics. Form and not content, aesthetics and not truthfulness, provide the key to construing the perspective that the novel offers.

Frame 6: Multiplicity and Literary Style

With its interrogation of the conflicts between "two ways of seeing," the novel works to demonstrate how perspective determines perception.[18] Set over nine days, the story is recounted through 21 distinct voices, ranging from corpses, to the color red, and to Satan. This multiplicity of voices enhances the sense of plural meanings and possibilities, a tactic that has important thematic connotations for the novel. This is a narrative strategy that puts the reader on stage, transforming the practice of reading from that of passive reception to active production. Reading in this sense becomes a *play*, linking literary, musical, and recreational practices. Pamuk himself voices his concerns for polyphony when writing the novel, yet with the intention to "entertain his readers with kites and yo-yos" (1999).[19] In the same vein, the storyteller, the voice of the inanimate objects, refers to the East-West dichotomy as a means of achieving more amusement: "I only want to amuse myself frontside and backside, to be Eastern and Western both" (*MNR* 431). The reader then, is encouraged to *play* (in and with) the text as both a musical and entertaining activity.

Multiple viewpoints appeal to postmodern aesthetics, but they also perform as the mirrors in a kaleidoscope, which reflect changing patterns with each rotation of the tube. In the 59 chapters that make up the novel, no two consecutive ones are in the same voice. Re-presenting the same events through rotating perspectives, writing is indeed kaleidoscopic: almost every episode starts with retelling the events in the previous one, but from a different vantage point. In chapter 28, for example, the murderer visits Enishte, and the chapter ends with his confession. Chapter 29 starts at the same point again, but is rendered through Enishte's point of view. The point of view is reversed to present the perspective of the seen. As such, despite the repetitions and overlaps of events in subsequent episodes, since each is recounted from a different vantage point, the overall picture differs with each voice. The reading process is then about constantly reviewing and questioning the text. Even within the same "voice" we detect alternative ones, ideas vying for recognition, as in the murderer's split subjecthood that we read as two distinct voices, and in the gap between what the narrators share with the reader and what they articulate to the other characters in the novel. Unitary and objective meaning, as well as identity, is challenged, as there is no fixed ground, nor an authoritative voice on which to base a definitive reading.

Frame 7: Islam

My Name Is Red includes numerous discussions of the Koran and the Islamic canon that form the basis of the interdict against portraiture, refracted through its kaleidoscope. For example, Satan, voiced by the storyteller in Chapter 47, refuses to be associated with portraiture. Boasting that he "never bowed down before man," at the cost of banishment from heaven, this Miltonian Satan is now resentful that painting, portraiture, and perspective are attributed to the only angel that refused to acknowledge man's superiority (*MNR* 352). Satan attributes human vanity to God's ways, thus transforming the understanding of right and wrong, virtue and sin. Is this a paradox, or a critique of Islamic precepts? From Satan's perspective, the proscription of painting seems contrary to Islam as a religion where human beings are considered superior to angels. Satan's final words provide another twist: "It's not the content, but the form of thought that counts. It's not what a miniaturist paints, but his style" (*MNR* 353–354). The kaleidoscope moves once more to shift the pattern: the highly charged argument about religion turns into a question of aesthetics.

Satan's inquisitiveness stands diametrically opposed to Islamic fundamentalism, as portrayed through Erzurumi Effendi's adherents. As shifting perspectives and fleeting identities are considered heresy, an affront to "true" Islam, the Erzurumis seek ways to destroy the multiplicity of meanings that they associate with the art of miniature. Throughout the novel, the Erzurumis symbolize the threat that Islamic fundamentalism poses to any encounter between East and West. Indeed, religious bigotry is the underlying reason for the murders: Olive kills Elegant because he fears Elegant will report the heretical miniatures to Erzurumi Hodja. The Erzurumis kill the storyteller, who gives voice to the drawings of the miniaturists in coffeehouses to entertain his audience through responding to the course of events and thereby criticizing fundamentalism. The ensuing mayhem ultimately leads to the waning of the art of miniature.

In its representation of Islam, the novel engages with the destructiveness of religious fundamentalism. In one of its final images, Sultan Ahmed dreams that he sees the Prophet denouncing the heretical creations of the "infidel" and demolishing the monumental clockwork organ, itself a masterpiece and a gift from Queen Elizabeth I (MacLean 4).[20] Sultan Ahmed eerily evokes another enemy of clocks and time, the Imam in Rushdie's *The Satanic Verses* (1988), who destroys all the clocks in his city (214).[21]

Perhaps the most striking reference to the Koran is an anachronistic one. In this novel about Islamic precepts, the Koran is the divine masterpiece, the book that characters refer to when in need of self-justification. In the final dialogue between Olive and Black, however, a quote from Kipling's "The Ballad of East and West" (1895)[22] seems to make more sense than the Koran when discussing East-West relations:

> "*To God belongs the East and the West,*" I said in Arabic, like the late Enishte.
> "But East is east and West is west," said Black. (*MNR* 488)

To include the Koran as ultimate masterpiece in the context of the characters' multiple discussions about masterpiece is to introduce the divine as a mere perspective. In contrast to Kipling, Black does believe in the meeting of East and West as a means of creating a new space. The novel allows that encounters between the two are wrought with distress and destruction, but it does not adhere to a strict East-West opposition.

Frame 8: Writing Miniatures

Based on the opposition between word and image, the novel in fact brings them together in ekphrasis, verbal representation of visual art. In that sense, the aesthetics of the novel is reminiscent of word-image dualism, which also defines the novel and ekphrasis as a genre. Yet, in *My Name Is Red*, opposites converge within the aesthetics of the novel. An even more surprising encounter between opposites is the one between the art of the miniature and the postmodern stylistics of the novel, insofar as both are concerned with the meeting of reader and text. The characters in *My Name Is Red* are conscious of the reader watching them; they address the reader and talk about the gap between their thoughts and their words, as well as between their words and deeds. The murderer challenges the reader to discover his identity through his style (chapter 2), while Shekure threatens not to tell her story unless the reader takes her word on her beauty (chapter 9). When Shekure voices her interest in the reader, she not only reminds the reader of the fictionality of the work, but steps outside her frame in an attempt to include the reader within the story:

> Don't be surprised that I'm talking to you. [...] Just like those beautiful women with one eye on the life within the book and one eye on the life outside, I, too, long to speak with you. (*MNR* 51)

Direct address to the reader is not simply a means of connoting post-modern stylistics; it is a deliberate attempt by Pamuk to "write" a miniature, to engage with the art treated in the novel.

Pamuk also voices the aesthetic concern of the novel as "blending the more distilled and poetic style derived from works in the style of Persian miniatures with the speed, power, and character-driven realism of the novel as we understand it today" (2007: 265).[23] This act of blurring the boundaries between in and out, fact and fiction, character and reader, is also a tool that questions our preconceived notions about Islamic and Western aesthetics, specifically in relation to postmodernism and the art of miniature painting. By writing miniature and giving voice(s) to the mute art of Islamic painting, the novel liberates the art from its traditional role of confinement within the peripheries of books.

This story from multiple and shifting points of view acquires unusual reverse angles, in a style evocative of both postmodern aesthetics and the multidimensional character of miniatures. Art, in the Islamic context, is "a way of implying the impossibility of knowing reality as it is and of knowing the Absolute because the Absolute manifests itself in infinite ways" (Erzen 72).[24] As aesthetic spaces where reader and writer meet in a common quest for the unattainable, Islamic miniatures serve primarily to signify mutability and the multiple, illusory nature of knowledge and hence appear closer to postmodern or present-day "Western" sensibilities than portraiture or classical painting.

Conclusion

Beneath the unresolved conflicts between East and West, Islam and Europe, word and image, writing replaces image as the means to attain delight, to voice distanced tales, and ultimately to create masterpieces. After recounting the havoc that befell the art of miniature, Shekure speaks of the two paintings she has longed for: her portrait and a picture of bliss—a picture of nursing her children. The picture of bliss, para-phrasing an eponymous poem by the celebrated Turkish poet Nazım Hikmet Ran, renders the wish itself a masterpiece.[25] The novel, by its own admission, aims to become a masterpiece, by writing the un-paint-able and replacing the lost masterpiece.

The notion of masterpiece in the novel, then, is one that links not only tradition and the individual, but also past and present, East and West, miniature and portraiture, and finally, postmodern aesthetics and Islam. The novel sets out to be a masterpiece in the sense that Enishte defines it: "A great painter does not content himself by affect-ing us with his masterpieces; ultimately, he succeeds in changing the landscape of our minds" (*MNR* 195). Through an unusual framing of its subject matter and the multiple viewpoints it offers, *My Name Is Red* demonstrates that the landscapes of our minds are also framed by the vantage points from which we define them.

Notes

1. "The Nobel Prize in Literature 2006." Nobelprize.org. Web. May 2008. http://nobelprize.org/nobel_prizes/literature/laureates/2006.
2. The International IMPAC Literary Award is the world's most lucrative literary prize of 100,000 Euros.
3. For the historical context of the term "masterpiece," see David Damrosch, *What Is World Literature?* (Princeton, NJ: Princeton University Press, 2003).
4. Melike Yılmaz, "A Translational Journey: Orhan Pamuk in English." MA thesis Boğazici University, 2004.
5. This quote and the following ones are from the 1998 Turkish edition of the novel by İletişim.
6. "A Conversation with Orhan Pamuk." Randomhouse.com. *The Borzoi Reader Online*. Web. May 2008. http://www.randomhouse.com/knopf /authors/pamuk/qna.html.
7. T. S. Eliot, "Tradition and the Individual Talent." *The Sacred Wood: Essays on Poetry and Criticism*. 1920. Bartleby.com, 1996. Web. May 2008. http:// www.bartleby.com/200/sw4.html.
8. Like Pamuk's other novels, *My Name Is Red* is in dialogue with both the concept of "masterpiece," and with "masterpieces" themselves. Note the thematic recurrence, in Pamuk's work, of the desire to write a masterpiece. *The White Castle* (1985) is a manuscript discovered by a historian, one of the voices of an earlier novel, *Silent House* (1983), which features a grandfather who devoted his life to writing an encyclopedia that would cure the East of its backwardness. In *The Black Book* (1990), the protagonist becomes a master-columnist; *The New Life* (1994) is centered around a book that changes the lives of its readers; and *Snow* itself is triggered by Pamuk the author/character's search for his friend's masterpieces in Kars.
9. "Winner 2003." Impacdublinaward.ie. Dublin City Public Library, 2007. Web. May 2008. http://www.impacdublinaward.ie/2003/Winner.htm.
10. Leon Battista Alberti, *On Painting*. 1540, trans. Cecil Grayson. 1972, ed. Martin Kemp (London: Penguin, 1991).
11. See page 193 for a discussion on the status of painters in Islam. The accusation, as Enishte points out, is not from the Koran, but from a Hadith, a saying attributed to the Prophet.
12. Page numbers refer to Erdağ Göknar's translation, published by London: Faber-Farrar, 2001.

13. The romance of *Khusrev and Shirin*, a classic text of Persian literature, was written by Genceli Nizami in the twelfth century and became a popular subject for miniaturists, notably Bihzad.
14. Dipesh Chakrabarty, *Provinicializing Europe: Postcolonial Thought and Historical Difference*. (Princeton, NJ: Princeton University Press, 1999).
15. Portraiture goes back to 1460s, when Mehmed II invited painters from Italy to the Porte.
16. G.M. Meredith-Owens, *Turkish Miniatures* (Oxford: Oxford University Press, 1969). Metin And.. *Türk Tasvir Sanatları* [*Turkish Descriptive Arts*] (İstanbul: İş Bankası Yayınları, 2002).
17. Feride Çiçekoglu, "A Pedagogy of Two Ways of Seeing: A Confrontation of 'Word and Image' in *My Name Is Red.*" *Journal of Aesthetic Education* 37.3 (Fall 2003): n.p. Print.
18. This expression alludes to Çicekoğlu's work on the novel.
19. Orhan Pamuk, *Öteki Renkler* [*Other Colors*] (İstanbul: İletişim, 1999). For a discussion of the novel's playfulness, see Yıldız Ecevit, *Türk Romanında Postmodernist Açılımlar* [*Postmodernism in Turkish Novel*]. (İstanbul: İletişim, 1996).
20. The "clockwork musical organ" was a gift for the then-new Sultan, Mehmed III, sent February 1599. The "clock" "was destroyed by Mehmed's son, Ahmed I, who considered keeping it a heresy." Gerald MacLean, *The Rise of Oriental Travel: English Visitors to the Ottoman Empire, 1580–1720* (London: Palgrave, 2005). See also Nazan Aksoy, *Rönesans İngiltere'sinde Türkler* [*The Turks in Renaissance England*]. (İstanbul: İstanbul Bilgi University Press, 1990).
21. Salman Rushdie, *Satanic Verses*. 1988. (London: Vintage-Random, 2006).
22. Black's words quote part of the first line of the poem: "Oh East is East, and West is West, and never the twain shall meet." Rudyard Kipling. "The Ballad of East and West." *A Victorian Anthology, 1837–1895*, ed. Edmund Clarence Stedman. 1895. Bartleby.com, 2003. Web. May 2008. http://www.bartleby.com/246/1129.html.
23. Orhan Pamuk, *Other Colours* (London: Faber-Farrar, 2007).
24. Jale Nejdet Erzen, "Islamic Aesthetics: An Alternative Way to Knowledge." *Journal of Aesthetics and Art Criticism* 65.1 (Winter 1997): 69–75.
25. "Can you paint happiness, Abidin? Not in a conventional, easy way, though. Not the picture of a mother feeding her rosy cheeked infant," Ran, Nazım Hikmet, "Saman Sarısı" ["Straw Coloured"], 1963 (İstanbul: Yapı Kredi Yayınları, 2007) (my translation).

CHAPTER 6

On the Road or between the Pages: Seeking Life's Answers

Fran Hassencahl

"I no longer knew what kind of person I was. I was someone who had prodigally squandered and lost the core of his soul on the road, trying to make Janan fall in love with him, to locate that realm, and to dispatch his rival. I did not ask him about this, O Angel, I asked him who you are."

"I have never encountered the angel the book talks about," he said to me. "It might be that you behold the angel at the moment of death, in the window of some bus."

—*The New Life*

Sal Paradise, Jack Kerouac's alter ego, in his autobiographical novel, *On the Road,* wakes up in a cheap hotel room near the railway station in Des Moines, Iowa, and discovers as he looks at the cracks in the ceiling and hears footsteps in the room above him that for the first time he did not know who he was. He writes, "I wasn't scared: I was just somebody else, some stranger...I was halfway across America, at the dividing line between the East of my youth and the West of my future." His answer to his identity question is to "stop moaning." He picks up his bag, says goodbye to the hotel clerk, and goes to find some apple pie and ice cream for lunch.[1] While he travels, Sal periodically thinks about returning to college and wonders whether his children viewing family snapshots will think that "their parents had lived smooth, well ordered, stabilized-within-the-photo lives...never dreaming the raggedy madness and riot of our lives."[2]

The main character, Osman, in Orhan Pamuk's novel *The New Life,* which Pamuk admits is also somewhat autobiographical, experiences a similar awakening.[3] Osman, like Sal, leaves his university studies and takes a harrowing three-month-long bus trip across Turkey with Janan, a fellow student, to find Mehmet, her boyfriend. Osman clings to the fantasy that Janan is his intended, and he can persuade her to fall in love with him. All three read a remaindered book, by Uncle Rifki, a retired railroad inspector, who wrote children's comics and articles for *Rail* magazine. Osman becomes mesmerized by this book, which "revealed, so it seemed to me, the meaning of my existence."[4]

One day during another bus trip searching for Mehmet, Osman and Janan sit together in a different seat from their usual one. As they view from a new angle the television screen hanging from the center of the front windshield, Osman recalls, "we felt we were about to discover the secret of the concealed and incalculable geometry called life; and just as we were eagerly figuring out the deep meaning behind the tree shadows, the dim image of the man with the gun, the video-red apples, and the mechanical sounds on the screen, we would realize that, goodness, we had already seen this movie!"[5] Readers later discover that Mehmet left the university and his family to embrace a monk-like existence copying that remaindered book, which delivers no answers, but like the bus videos and Rifki's comics for children, offers comfort through familiarity.

We can argue that *The New Life* belongs to the literary genre of "the road novel." Generally, we consider that the road novel describes the American experience, but as Brian Ireland points out, "The trail is not limited solely to Americans."[6] The road trip could be the search for the American or the Turkish dream. Usually the main characters in road novels are young males who question their goals, the morals, and everyday lives of their parents, and focus on exploring their sexuality. Both Sal and Osman believe that orgasm is a way of achieving beatitude, but Osman has to be satisfied with one kiss from his beloved Janan, whose name means "soul mate" in Turkish, whereas Sal beds many women without forming any long-term attachments.

Usually the characters who travel either a literal or a metaphorical road in a road novel end up disappointed, because they find no answers to the big questions of life. Sal seeks his future in the West, but after his arrival in California, he finds that the road ends at the ocean and "there was nowhere to go but back."[7] At the moment of the final bus crash, Osman regrets his choice of the front seat and knows that he is not going to make that planned return to his wife and daughter in Istanbul.

Both *The New Life* and *On the Road* are written against the backdrop of social and political change, which provide fertile ground for conspiracy thinking. Road-novel characters also live in an existential moment and wonder what is the point to their lives. Both of these issues are addressed here.

Osman and Sal Confront Social and Political Change

Jack Kerouac writes about a postwar American soon to be immersed in the Cold War and under the threat of the atomic bomb. Old Bull Lee after a day of gambling with Sal laments that scientists rather than investigating future catastrophes, "are only interested in seeing if they can blow up the world."[8] *The New Life* is set against the backdrop of the changes that opened Turkey up to new ideas and transformed economic life during the 1960s and 1970s. Feroz Ahmad characterizes Turkish political life in the sixties as "dramatically different from what it had been in earlier decades." He explains that constitutional changes provided the opening for "ideological discourse." Marxist literature became available "even in the small towns," and students began to challenge the politicians in Ankara and question whether the United States was the loyal friend that it claimed to be.[9] The Cyprus question intensified under rising Turkish nationalism. Workers frustrated by high unemployment and rising expectations began to press for labor unions and the right to conduct strikes. The response of the Right was swift with assassinations and intimidations. The generals intervened in 1960, 1971, and in 1980 to establish martial law and severely curtailed the freedom of the press and unions.

Choosing New Identities and Asserting One's Individuality

Ireland observes that the theme of transformation of identity or rebirth occurs frequently in road novels, and that many of the character see the road as a way of escaping "constricting cultural conformity" and emphasizing their individuality and freedom of choice.[10] *The New Life* is set in Turkey, which values collectivity and conformity. Individual needs for happiness are met by the social and economic security that comes from following the rules of the culture and obeying family prescriptions. Orhan Pamuk writes in *Other Colors* about his experiences with the push and pull of collectivism and individuality. His father and grandfather studied engineering at Istanbul Technical University, and the family expected young Orhan to allow familial and class boundaries to guide his career choice. Only his father sympathized with his son's rebellion, because he had wanted to become a poet, but was not strong enough to release himself from the family mold.[11]

The escape from cultural conformity brings loneliness. Pamuk explains to an interviewer from *The Paris Review* that although he was raised to value the community, his decision to become a writer removed him "from the pleasant company of that community" and brought loneliness. He tells the reviewer and reiterates in *Istanbul: Memories and the City* that this loneliness was beneficial, because it "made my imagination work."[12] In his Norton Lectures at Harvard in the fall of 2009, Pamuk argues for the necessity of imagination. "Wondering about which parts are based on real-life experience and which parts are imagined is but one of the pleasures we find in reading a novel."[13] Pamuk adds that authors "are also entirely alone, just as we were when we wrote the opening sentence of our very first novel." [14] For Pamuk, both reading and writing a novel are solitary experiences.

Osman in *The New Life* also embraces loneliness and cautions the reader that he committed an unforgivable crime. He is not thinking of the time when in an almost empty movie theater he deliberately shot Mehmet, his rival for the love of Janan, but rather that he has violated cultural conventions. He, like Pamuk, "had desired to set myself apart from others, some one special who had a goal that was entirely different."[15] Osman abandoned his university studies and regular grooming for a life of bus travel, where his only clean clothes came from the small shops in towns when layovers for the next bus occurred. The opening lines of *The New Life* are: "I read a book one day and my whole life was changed." The reader, Osman, a university student studying civil engineering, describes an experience not unlike that of St. Paul on the road to Damascus. Osman explains the impact of this book as "such a powerful influence that the light surging from the pages illumined my face; its incandescence dazzled my intellect but also endowed it with brilliant lucidity. This was the kind of light within which I could recast myself. I could lose my way in this light; I already sensed in the light the shadows of an existence I had yet to know and to embrace."[16] He does regret leaving his old life and recalls the guilt that he felt, because he read a book that "estranged" him from his mother's world.[17]

The characters in *The New Life* and *On the Road* struggle with everyday existence, but they also attempt to understand and control the future courses of their lives. Caught in an existential moment and excluded from a cultural, collective identity, they begin to wonder who they are. Often the establishment of an identity depends upon a threat of or an experienced exclusion. Zygmunt Bauman observes, "'Identity' is a simultaneous struggle against dissolution and fragmentation; an intention to devour and at the same time a stout refusal to be eaten."[18] Polarization occurs, which Bauman characterizes as a situation where identity becomes a two-edged sword. On the one side are the individuals who resent conformity and wish to strike out in new directions. On the other side is the group or the collective who see such behavior as deviant and in need of correction or punishment.[19] Under such circumstances, each side of that sword may feel rejected or isolated. They begin to see others as "Other" and develop fears about how the "Other" plans to treat them. George Lakoff points out in *Moral Politics* that these cultural metaphors often dictate our thinking and behavior.[20] This search for an explanation for their powerless situation often gives rise to conspiracy thinking. People need to make sense of their world. Richard Hofstadter argues in *The Paranoid Style in American Politics* that an entire society or culture can feel powerless and at the mercy of forces such as postwar technological and social changes that they cannot comprehend or understand.[21] Osman in *The New Life* encounters a peddler who tells him that Turkey has suffered a great defeat, "The West has swallowed us up, trampled upon us in passing. They have invaded us down to our soup, our candy, our underpants; they have finished us off. But someday, someday perhaps a thousand years from now, we will avenge ourselves; we will bring an end to this conspiracy by taking them out of our soup, our chewing gum, our souls."[22] The peddler's belief in subtle foreign forces that threaten or will change his life is a common aspect of conspiracy thinking.

Dr. Fine, the father of one of the students who left home in search of the new life promised in Uncle Rifki's book, represents those who feel excluded and believe their world is changing because of uncontrolled external forces. These reactions can be attributed to the model of East meets West or tradition meets modernity or postmodernity and globalization.

For Fine, a businessperson in central Anatolia, these changes threaten traditional family relationships and business practices. Fine descends into a paranoid rant against the West, "The Great Conspiracy." The

West cleverly through techniques of advertising and distribution draws consumers away from the true path of traditional cool yogurt drinks and sour cherry juices into a situation where their minds are muddled by drinking Coca Cola. New ideas entice youth to rebel against their parents.

Choice and adolescent rebellion are not part of Dr. Fine's world. Dr. Fine studied law, because his father wanted him to, and he, most likely, married and learned to love the woman chosen for him by his mother. When Dr. Fine's only son Mehmet, a dutiful and brilliant son, heir to the family farm and business, and a student of medicine in Istanbul, sends him a letter indicating that he no longer wants contact with his father, his response is disappointment and anger at such rebellion. Even though the generations may no longer live in the same household, the family functions as a collective, and deference to the patriarch still dominates Turkish culture. Fine attributes his son's behavior to the reading of a book and arranges for the death of the author, Uncle Rifki, whom he sees as responsible for luring away his son.

Blaming these events on the West, an evil outside force, is the best explanation for events and changes that Fine cannot comprehend. Fine views the forces that took his son from him as similar to the forces that threaten his general hardware store, a "mom and pop" business. "Unconcerned that only old men and flies dropped by the store, he continued stocking only those products which had traditionally been available to his forefathers."[23] His business, like his lost son's room, is a museum. He cannot bear to part with his son's comic books and still-muddy soccer shoes. He considered stocking modern products in his store but found that he could not tolerate the dissonance that these lackluster items created when placed next to his existing stock. He compares it to the putting of a cage of chattering finches next to a cage of nightingales that become distressed by the presence of these ordinary birds. Fine, like Kemal in Pamuk's *The Museum of Innocence* who collects objects used by his lost love Füsun, believes in the memory of objects, "the presence of a magical necessary and poetic sense of time that was transmitted to us from objects when we come into contact using or touching some simple thing like a spoon or a pair of scissors."[24] For Dr. Fine these new products from the West lack a referent, a connection to the past, and threaten the identity of Turkey by erasing its collective cultural memory.

The Bankruptcy of the Narrative

The students in *The New Life* optimistically place their trust in the power of the narrative, in the stories that the book tells. Much to their disappointment, the stories possess no magic; they are just words on the page. Ian Almond refers to the Hoja and his Venetian prisoner's sadness in Pamuk's *The White Castle* when they discover that there are no grand narratives, no hidden secrets, or supernatural voices speaking.[25] Almond posits that Pamuk's characters share Derrida's deconstructionist analysis of Western metaphysics as the search and yearning for the "primordial meaning of the sign."[26] As posited by Lyotard in 1984 in *Condition postmoderne*, we experience the bankruptcy of the metanarrative in the postmodern period.

Osman finds no God-ordained meaning, but a complex system of hierarchies and dualities of meaning written by ordinary men. At age 35, Osman muses over his disappointment about not finding when he was 22 the new life promised in Rifki's book. Mehmet warned Osman that the new life they sought existed only in the text and that "it was futile to search for what he had discovered in the text outside of the text, in actual life." He tells Osman that there is no "Original Cause" and "that we are all copies."[27] Mehmet finds peace and a life purpose through the routines of copying and selling the book that started the three on their quest. Like Krapp in Beckett's play *Krapp's Last Tape*, he senses that his moment of happiness has come and gone, and all that remains is to replay the tapes of distant memories.

After reading the books from Uncle Rifki's bookshelf and many others borrowed from libraries, Osman discovers that Rifki did not say anything new, but drew upon his library to write his book. When Rifki wrote the illustrated stories for children in the railway magazines, he took characters and plots from American comic books such as *Tom Mix* and *The Lone Ranger*. Uncle Rifki's writings are a cultural construction, or as Barthes describes it, a "tissue of quotations."[28] There is no new message, only the reproduction of already-produced words and images. Unlike the angels, who spoke to Mohammad, there are no more angels speaking. All that remain for Osman are photocopies of angels from great European paintings, sent to him by a correspondent in Germany, which have become playthings for his daughter to place on the bookshelves and windowsills.

Each reader is responsible for deconstructing the meaning of Rifki's text. Pamuk purposely plays with the reader by only revealing a few fragments that its author Uncle Rifki borrowed from both Eastern and Western writers. Pamuk says that he intends, "that the reader would learn nothing of the book the hero had read, only of what happened to the hero after he finished reading it." Consequently, this is a mystery story where the reader deduces from these clues back to what might be the content matter of the book.[29] The act of reading and believing its message creates a community of seekers and connects individuals who otherwise would not have had a reason to interact or any topics to discuss.

In this respect, the search for meaning becomes more important than the meaning drawn from the text. Sal and his companions hitchhike and travel by bus and sometimes drive stolen cars and see the country as an "oyster for us to open; and the pearl was there."[30] Osman and his fellow students also seek to escape from old routines and the familiar possessions binding them to an "old world." They travel without plans or a specific destination. Their search, which requires traveling by bus across Turkey, provides a distraction, an opportunity to focus upon the moment. From experience, I can say that riding the buses in Turkey is sometimes a heart-pounding adventure. Once you board the bus and find your seat number, your future is no longer in your hands, which brings a sense of freedom. Time is suspended. Pamuk describes it, "Whenever the driver slams on the brakes or the bus whips around in the wind, we open our eyes instantly to stare into the dark road, trying to figure out if the zero hour is upon us. No, not yet!"[31] Each trip promises the ultimate answer to life, but becomes just another search, just another bus trip. Ultimately, the students discover that they have watched thousands of kissing scenes and hundreds of action films on the TV sets suspended in the front windshields of the buses. The action films feature car chases, crashes, and lots of blood and gore that dominate the world of male movie attendance in the Middle East. The towns, whose names Osman knows from Uncle Rifki's tutelage about train stations, all possess similar crowded bus terminals where people carry "plastic bags, cardboard suitcases, and gunnysacks." Similar to their experiences viewing bus videos, our travelers find comfort from a sense of déjà vu.

Given the state of some Turkish highways and the lack of regulations for the drivers' training and sleep time, some bus trips in rural Turkey do suggest that passengers should have their lives in order. Our students become fascinated with the romantic idea of death. From their youthful perspective, death is not finality, but is a crossing over into a plane of existence better than their current life with platters of meat and potatoes and the predictable green salad prepared by their mothers who as desexualized beings fall asleep every night in front of the TV. The students hope to travel from the present created world to the world of the Creator. Like many seekers, they seek a guide, the angel, or the shaykh, who will guide them on their journey into the presence of God. For Osman this angel appears in female form, whereas in Islam, angels are genderless. Similar to the beliefs in Judaism and in Christianity, the Angel of Death, Izra'il, will appear to be beautiful to those who have lived a good life. For those who lived a bad life this angel resembles a frightening demon or beast. The angel who appears at the last moments of Osman's life is a bright light and does not intervene in events or show any compassion. This angel is not a guide and does not absolve Osman for shooting Mehmet, his competitor for the love of Janan. It only observes from a distance and does not resemble any of the European and Ottoman artists' depictions of angels as beautiful beings.

Pamuk may be alluding here in his road-trip novel to the Sufi tradition and the veils that distract the believer and block the Light of the Divine Presence. These veils keep the believer from leaving the West of existence and entering the East of the rising sun and the shining light of God.[32] Pamuk states that he is interested in Sufism as literature and finds that reading their writings lifts his spirits. He is too much of a rationalist to engage in the discipline of Sufism. Pamuk says, "I live like a man committed to Cartesian Rationalism to the nth degree."[33] Pamuk, however, works to develop credible and interesting characters and finds the everyday experiences as well as the ideas and spiritual quests of other people to be worthy of observation.

Our characters in *The New Life* believe that union with God occurs not in life but rather through the experience of physical death. They do not seek the second Sufi option of the annihilation of self, of the ego.[34] The three students form their expectations about death and life through their individual interactions with a text that promises a new life, a better plane of existence, rather than from participation in the collective experience of the mosque. Osman muses, "If life was indeed like what I read in the book, if such a world was possible, then it was impossible to understand why people needed to go to prayer."[35] None of the characters observe prayer times, study the Qur'an, or attend services on Friday.

Sal, like Kerouac, is a fallen-away Catholic. Sal prays that God will help the grape- and cotton-picking migrants in California, but knows, "Nobody was paying attention to me up there. I should have known better."[36] For him, angels do not guide or protect. They exist as attractive statues placed in various niches in cathedrals. Paradise is something lost after leaving the womb; it cannot be regained. Consequently, Sal and his fellow travelers focus on the present and fill their days and nights by forming relationships, listening to jazz, and consuming alcohol and mind-altering drugs.

Settling for Rather Than Finding Life's Meaning

Unable to find the promise of the new life, to bring back the magic that will propel him beyond the veils of the East and the West, Osman settles back into that pathetic old environment, finishes his degree, and marries a woman who lives on his street. He takes a nine-to-five job at City Hall and characterizes himself as broken and old. He feels powerless to change the course of his life. He clings to his memories of the shared bus seats and hotel rooms and regrets his loss of Janan. He veneers his search for inner peace through drinking *raki*, sharing the sofa with his daughter's blue teddy bear, and losing himself "in a fog" before the "images that didn't seem too terribly vulgar" on the television screen.[37]

At the close of Sal's road trip, he too, has settled back into a more ordinary existence and goes on a double date to the Duke Ellington concert at the Metropolitan Opera in New York City. Sal has rejected cultural conventions, but he has not reached a greater plane of knowing. He speculates as he sits on a broken river pier looking at the New Jersey sky and watching the coming darkness of the night, "Nobody knows what's going to happen to anybody besides the forlorn rags of growing old."[38]

The Social Construction of Reality

Neither Osman nor Dr. Fine can come to grips with the disconnect between what they want the world to be like and what they experience the world to be. Osman remembers his disappointment that the worlds and adventures in Rifki's comics ended, and that the "magical realm was just a place made up by Uncle Rifki."[39] When Osman discovers that there is no ultimate meaning, he feels sad, but also feels free. He concludes, "Now that I had no more hope and desire to attain the meaning and the unified reality of the world, the book, and my life, I found myself among the fancy free appearances that neither signified nor implied anything."[40] He no longer has to search; he can embrace the ordinary life of being a husband and a father who liked to watch soccer on TV and take his daughter to the train station to watch the trains and to buy candy. Ironically, when he begins to come to terms with his search for a heavenly future and accept an earthly present, he is transported through the windshield of a crashed bus into that future, the new life that he once sought.

Neither Osman nor Sal follows the classic model of the hero or what traditional myths ascribe to be the archetype of heroic action. They venture beyond the ordinary experiences of life and encounter a variety of demons, but they do not return enriched or more powerful or able to share what they have learned with others. Unable to overcome these threats, they wait for the emergence of someone who can banish or eradicate the evil and restore the community back to a harmonious paradise.[41] They cannot transform society, banish the demons of growing older, and find their guiding angel or an affirming belief in a creator, who is more than what Sal characterizes as a "Pooh Bear." Osman eventually returns home to his mother where, "We breakfasted quietly as in the old days"[42] and finishes his university degree. His mother never asks him about his loss of Janan after Osman introduced her as his wife during a brief check-in phone call from a small-town bus station. Sal retreats to his aunt's house in New Jersey and laments the loss of his father figure and traveling companion Dean Moriarity.

Osman and Sal are not political or attracted to ideologies. Unlike Dr. Fine, they do not attempt to organize a resistance for or against the forces that influence their lives. Osman does not harbor hostilities toward the West and carries a nostalgic appreciation of the past and the future as experienced in his childhood reading of Uncle Rifki's stories. When Osman receives Dr. Fine's offer to become a replacement for Fine's presumed dead son, Mehmet, and take over his business in the small town of Güdül where ads proclaim that circumcisions are performed in "the good old way" without using lasers, he declines to return to a small-town past and returns to Istanbul.

Both young men conclude that meaning is made from their lived lives and their relationships with other people. At first Osman seeks information about the future, his purpose in life, and the big question as to whether he can bed and wed the beautiful Janan through reading a written text. Osman eventually settles into a career, marries, and becomes caught up in the human experience or what Rollo May describes as, "Eros is the drive toward union with what we belong to—union with our own possibilities, union with significant other persons...in relation to whom we discover our own self-fulfillment."[43] Osman and Sal find no guiding God, no heavenly message. Reality is a social construction built from the timbers of their life experiences and relationships.

Constructing Meaning from Blending Old and New Ideas

Uncle Rifki in *The New Life* attempts to bridge some of the identity issues that Fine perceived to be challenging Turkish identity by proposing that strength could be garnered by blending rather than polarizing the traits of the East and the West. Rifki wrote these stories to encourage Turks to move from their position as victims and to believe that they could be clever, strong, and brave, "A kid from a poor neighborhood in Istanbul can draw a gun as fast as Billy the Kid or be as honest as Tom Mix."[44] Peter from Boston and the Pertev from Istanbul celebrate universal virtues of the past by participating in the adventures of the American cowboys and the Indians, and, what was also uppermost in Rifki's mind, the building of a transcontinental railroad in Turkey like the one in America. It is unlikely that Peter and Pertev would have resorted to violence over the affections of Janan, who eventually marries another seeker and moves to Germany. They would have come to an understanding, a gentleman's agreement. Rifki's characters embrace modernity without abandoning the virtues of the past. The East and the West as characterized by Peter and Pertev are able to cooperate and to bring about a new world, perhaps the new secular world similar to that promised by Atatürk.

Unlike Lyotard and some postmoderns, Pamuk has not given up on the power of the narrative. He still sees the potential of a new life in the sense that the boundaries that demarcate "us" and the "other "can be modified through the experience of reading. The novel permits the readers nestled in their armchairs to join the author in the imagining of the other and the "pains and troubles" of another's life. For Pamuk, this is a liberating experience, "By putting ourselves in another's shoes, by using our imaginations to shed out identities, we are able to set ourselves free."[45] Unlike Dr. Fine, Pamuk does not fasten upon the fear of a great conspiracy. He, like Uncle Rifki, finds permeable boundaries between the East and the West. Pamuk's Osman wishes for a transcending story to explain and give direction to his life. He learns that the word cannot be trusted, because it has not given him the power to control or predict the future. Osman finds no truly great ideas. Pamuk, in an interview with Jörg Lau from *Die Zeit* in 2005, observes that Turks torture themselves with the difficulties of living with these big, abstract ideas, of surviving them, and finding happiness. He tells Lau that after his portrayal of politics and religion in *Snow*, he is finished with big ideas and ready to experience the beauty of life experiences rather than to mull them over and agonize about what they mean.[46] Osman, or his alter ego Orhan Pamuk, like the soccer players on the television screen, replays his life in slow motion and resolves to accept life experiences as they unfold.

Pamuk is a bridge from Turkey's Ottoman past to the modern Turkey that is still establishing its identity and debating the efforts to move to a democracy that can guarantee freedom of speech and press and give power to elected leaders rather than to military officers. Both camps, the secularists and the Islamists, have differing views about the modern state. Alev Çınar finds that the Islamists define Turkey as an "Ottoman-Islamic" state, and the nationalist heirs of Atatürk see Turkey as secular and West-oriented.[47] Both groups struggle to accept diversity of opinion and to trust the other not to use religion or the military as a means of control. Change is difficult and Turkey experienced Ataturk's mandated reforms that forced citizens to accept Western dress and alphabet. Dr. Fine's cuckoo clock may proclaim, "Happiness is being a Turk," but questions still remain as to what is the nature of Turkish identity and to what extent does that modify as Turkey experiences the push and pull of the East and the West.

Pamuk hopes for a third way, a synthesis of both cultures. He is not afraid to look back at the Ottoman history and to question the grand narratives of nationalism of the new republic. In so doing, Pamuk joins other writers, such as poet Nazim Hikmet (1902–1963), satirist Aziz Nesin (1915–1995), and novelists Yaşar Kemal 1923– and Ahmet H. Tanpınar (1901–1962) who not only created great literature, but also were unable to separate their craft from the question of what Turkey will be like in the future.

Notes

1. Jack Kerouac, *On the Road* (New York: Penguin Books, 1957), p. 15.
2. Kerouac, p. 253.
3. Orhan Pamuk, *Other Colors: Essays and a Story*, trans. Maureen Freely (New York: Alfred A. Knopf, 2007), p. 259.
4. Orhan Pamuk, *The New Life*, trans. Güneli Gün (New York: Farrar, Straus, and Giroux), p. 12.
5. Ibid., p. 112.
6. Brian Ireland, "American Highways: Recurring Images and Themes of the Road Genre," *Journal of American Culture* 26.4 (2003): 675.
7. Kerouac, p. 77.
8. Ibid., p. 153.
9. Feroz Ahmad, *Turkey: The Quest for Identity* (Oxford: Oneworld, 2003), p. 128.

10. Ireland, p. 476.
11. Pamuk, *Other Colors*, pp. 261–262.
12. Ibid., p. 377.
13. Orhan Pamuk, *The Naïve and the Sentimental Novelist* (Cambridge, MA: Harvard University Press, 2010), p. 36.
14. Ibid., p. 185.
15. Pamuk, *New Life*, p. 289.
16. Ibid., p. 3.
17. Ibid., p. 8.
18. Zygmunt Bauman, *Identity* (Cambridge, UK: Polity Press, 2004), p. 77.
19. Ibid., p. 76.
20. George Lakoff, *Moral Politics: How Liberals and Conservatives Think* (Chicago, IL: University of Chicago Press, 2002), p. 44.
21. Richard Hofstadter, *The Paranoid Style in American Politics and Other Essays* (Cambridge, MA: Harvard University Press, 1996), p. 290.
22. Pamuk, *New Life*, pp. 290–291.
23. Ibid., p. 128.
24. Ibid., p. 127.
25. Ian Almond, "Islam, Melancholy, and Sad, Concrete Minarets: The Futility of Narratives in Orhan Pamuk's *The Black Book*," *New Literary History* 34 (2003): 75.
26. Ibid., p. 81.
27. Pamuk, *New Life*, p. 227–228.
28. Roland Barthes, *The Rustle of Language*. trans. Richard Howard (Oxford, UK: Blackwell, 1984), p. 63.
29. Pamuk, *Other Colors*, p. 259.
30. Kerouac, p. 138.
31. Pamuk, *New Life*, pp. 54–55.
32. William C. Chittick, *Sufism: A Short Introduction* (Oxford, England: Oneworld, 2001), pp. 12–13.
33. Pamuk, *Other Colors*, p. 261.
34. Chittick, pp. 85–87.
35. Pamuk, *New Life*, p. 14.
36. Kerouac, p. 97.
37. Pamuk, *New Life*, p. 240.
38. Kerouac, p. 307.
39. Pamuk, *New Life*, p. 12.
40. Ibid., p. 289.
41. John Shelton Lawrence and Robert Jewett, *The Myth of the American Superhero* (Grand Rapids, MI: William B. Eerdmans, 2002), p. 6.
42. Pamuk, *New Life*, p. 234.
43. Rollo May, *Love and Will* (New York: W. W. Norton, 1969), p. 74.
44. Pamuk, *New Life*, p. 188.
45. Pamuk, *Other Colors*, p. 228.

46. Jörg Lau, "The Turkish Trauma," *Die Ziet*, April 18, 2005, under "signand-sight.com," http://www.signandsight.com/features/115.html (accessed August 18, 2008).

47. Alev Çınar, *Modernity. Islam, and Secularism in Turkey: Bodies, Places, and Time* (Minneapolis: University of Minnesota Press, 2005), p. 9.

PART III

Pamuk's Snow

CHAPTER 7

The Imagined Exile: Orhan Pamuk in His Novel *Snow*

Hülya Yılmaz

My aim here is not to relate how I came to write a novel called *Snow*. [...] The subject that I am coming to understand more clearly with each new day, [...] is, in my view, central to the art of the novel: the question of the "other," the "stranger," the "enemy" that resides inside each of our heads, or rather, the question of how to transform it. [...] So, yes, one could define the novel as an art that allows the skilled practitioner to turn his own stories into stories about someone else, but this is just one aspect of the great and mesmerizing art that has entranced so many readers and inspired us writers for going on four hundred years. It was the other aspect that drew me to the streets of Frankfurt and Kars: the chance to write of others' lives as if they were my own. It is by doing this sort of thorough novelistic research that novelists can begin to test the lines that mark off that "other" and in so doing alter the boundaries of our own identities. [...] I am speaking now of the novel as a way of thinking, understanding and imagining, and also as a way of imagining oneself as someone else.[1]

The concept with which Orhan Pamuk associates his novel *Snow* in his speech as the recipient of the 2006 Nobel Prize for Literature—the novelist's imagination as a chance to alter one's own identity by transforming the "other" into the self—constitutes this chapter's core concern. "[G]reat literature speaks not to our powers of judgment, but to our ability to put ourselves in someone else's place,"[2] the author states. "The world to which I wish to belong is, of course, the world of the imagination," he announces, adding, "it is the imagination of the novelist that gives the bounded world of everyday life its particularity, its magic and its soul."[3] *Snow* is a canvas on which Pamuk designs a soulful life of particularity and magic for his protagonist Ka—a word choice that conveys his creative idiosyncrasy from the onset as it evokes "kar," snow, in his native tongue as well as Kars, the Turkish city where he unfolds Ka's life in momentous transformations. Ka's born identity also attains distinctiveness, for Pamuk has him eliminate both his names, implicating him with a violation of the country's law on family names.[4]

The magical realm that Pamuk passionately stresses on nonfictional platforms, "to leave behind this boring, dreary, hope-shattering world we all know so well, and to escape into a second world that was deeper, richer and more diverse,"[5] materializes in *Snow*. Moreover, his oft-articulated need to imagine the "other" he ponders most on resolves in his creation of Ka and in a re-creation of himself. "Since my novel *Snow* was published," he states, "every time I've set foot in the streets of Frankfurt, I've felt the ghost of Ka, the hero with whom I have more than a little in common."[6] His much-sought self-representation and literary reinvention transpire through his hero but who is also the narrator. Molding Ka's struggles for self-discovery and identity transformations into Orhan—the posited author, blending then into both as the real author—he escapes into the second world of greater depth, richness, and diversity that he has been seeking all his life.

Pamuk relates that he continuously yearned a beginning, a middle, and an end, when life's different challenges had thrown him into various directions and determines that only novels can offer such relief.[7] His novelistic imagination, in fact, facilitates his protagonist this complete circle. Simultaneously, he embarks on his own wondrous journey into an imagined world where he alters the boundaries of his own identity. In *Snow*, his work that I examine as a fictional autobiography of exile in negotiation between Edward W. Said's theory on metaphorical exile and Mikhail M. Bakhtin's theory on the dialogic imagination in the novel, Pamuk draws a path of significance for not only his protagonist but also his narrator within the framework of existence and consciousness in exile. By merging into his posited author, whom he alters into his protagonist toward the novel's end, he persists in his claim for a distinct individuality for himself in the role of an exile, and thus succeeds in subsisting outside the context of his most feared status, namely, that of a Turkish writer in whom no one could be interested.[8]

His hero is a Turk, Pamuk proclaims.[9] Not merely a home-bound Turk, however, with this hero he emulates Nazim Hikmet, "arguably the most acclaimed modern Turkish poet, who died in Russian exile in

1963 at the age of 61" and whose poetry is "[p]erhaps the single most powerful source of inspiration for Turkish writers of Germany."[10] He covets what Azade Seyhan perceives in Nazim as a "poetic Trauerarbeit (work of mourning)."[11] One only needs to recall the pathos Pamuk assigns to his protagonist in witnessing a young student's tragic death during one of the novel's key narrations—the multichapter secularist play—and to his narrator, for having to endure the loss of his friend in an execution-style death.[12] Into his Nazimian *work of mourning*, Pamuk—a learned student of German literature at large[13]—then blends the novels of Turkish German writers in closest connection to Nazim, their ideal of literary excellence: Alev Tekinay, Emine Sevgi Özdamar, and Zafer Senocak.[14]

With his motif of the small book of poetry—which his narrator chases over multiple chapters on numerous travels of quest with painful anticipation[15] and also by altering his hero's born identity—Pamuk imitates Tekinay's protagonist in her dervish novel.[16] A vibrant product of theatrical thrill spanning over nine chapters—disguised as the intriguingly unfolding story of the revolutionary play of catastrophic outcome—then shows Pamuk enter a new venue toward self-representation and literary reinvention. He now imitates the distinct landmark of Özdamar's novels of a Turkish and Kurdish cast—a theatrical and performance-based approach, as Monika Shafi also examines.[17] A composite of Sevgi's writings[18] underlines her markedly individual method within which she situates quests for identity and self-discovery: her imaginary scenes display a stagelike atmosphere, not lacking a touch of parody of some intensity. These characteristics of Emine's work—unique within the Turkish German context of literature—resound in *Snow* not only in their staging intensity and complexity but also with their tragic-comical effect, as Pamuk takes *Snow* with its revelation of historically impactful yet unpredicted and dreamlike developments to a point of absurdity in the Brechtian sense, of whose work Sevgi is a devoted reflection.

An extensive part of *Snow*, then, emerges as a replica of Senocak's novel *Dangerous Relationships*.[19] Pamuk reproduces the Senocak archetype as a polyvocal history within the ideal of a German-Jewish-Turkish triangular affiliation, factoring in Greek-Armenian-Turkish angles. His paradigm, too, reveals a substructure, also made up of three components but in the form of Turkey's secularists, Islamists, and Kurds. Using Senocak's technique of stream of consciousness, Pamuk, too, portrays through flashback summaries the impact of deterritorialization on the Greek and Armenian communities. The country's Kurdish population, then, provides him with the overriding element of his biography of the Turkish nation.[20] Through his protagonist he recalls Turkish history—a memory compilation that spans over several chapters, traveling in the past toward the present, then to the past again, and thus, enters from one door of a uniquely laid-out museum of imagination, and leaves out from another.[21]

A chaotic and ambiguous process of transitioning between the compelling sources of his inspiration—as summarized—unravels the numerous transformations of Pamuk's identity that he develops within the framework of metaphorical displacement. Retransforming his protagonist into exilic consciousness, he capitalizes on the immense capacity of the novelistic art in facilitating infinite venues of discourse for his literary reinvention. The agonizing obsession for self-distinction he shares with his posited author takes him—as a condition of exilic existence—on to different levels of his evolving identity: he blends into his narrator as himself.[22] In this stage of his dual-identity formation,[23] desperately seeking self-representation and literary reinvention, Pamuk assumes an outsider status as the trope for his artistic composition and system of imagery.

The concept of the intellectual as outsider brings to memory Edward W. Said's theory of exile as power, a hypothesis vital to my argument.[24] Neither a diasporic nor an exilic author, Pamuk embraces metaphorical exile, lending his *Snow* universality, and himself, the status of a writer of worldliness—a desire his numerous public statements declare. As an intellectual exile—a permanent exile in Adorno's terms—he exhibits much ambiguity. After all, as an outsider by choice—as Adorno would argue—his intent is not to be subjected to easy and immediate understanding. In accordance, Pamuk emerges in a complex state of in-betweenness: he exists in a third space perceiving the self in transition. This unsettling state of being shifts between a romanticized exterior belonging to an aesthetic world of creativity, that is, the world of poetry, and loss, that is, every component of the real world. *Snow*, thus, assumes a turbulent quality that the posited author represents in the narrator role and also as the merging real author, that is, his *double-voiced narrator*— the aspect of the novelistic genre Bakhtin analyzes.[25] Said argues that this third-space existence does not have to result in self-detriment, but rather allows the writer chaotic ambiance from which to achieve worldly affiliations, and hence, a higher state of intellectual authority:

> [Exile] does not respond to the logic of the conventional but does rather become more audacious and ready to changes. Thus the worldly

affiliations of the exile, in other words, the disinterested attitude makes the text also independent of bondages like nation, religion or culture and the space of writing becomes a free speech of different overlapping criticisms. Exile in this sense becomes a powerful weapon in the hand of the intellectual.[26]

The intensity with which Pamuk transitions between his efforts to shape and reshape the "other" to contour his vision of distinguished identity does, indeed, lend his art chaotic ambiance. It is with this privileged resource that he escapes into that second world of his lifelong desire—the world of imagination, the invention of which has been his sole quest in life. What Said argues in *Joseph Conrad and the Fiction of Autobiography* with regard to Baudelaire's conceptualization of the dualism permanently inherent in the artist, namely, being possessed with the power of being simultaneously oneself and someone else,[27] suits Pamuk's core objective, as I claim with emphasis, to rid his problem of having to assert himself an individual of significance as a writer. In reference to George Lukacs' theory of the novel, Said states, "The novel, a literary form created out of the unreality of ambition and fantasy, is a form of 'transcendental homelessness.'"[28] Transcendental homelessness enables Pamuk to attain the position of the insider's outsidedness in the Saidian sense through which his quest for paths of significance, for self-definition, and identity re-creation resolves in *Snow*. The unreality, then, of ambition and fantasy—of which Lukacs speaks—disentangles in Pamuk's dialogic imagination, as embedded in his double-voiced narrator. The dialogic relationship between *Snow*'s real author, narrator, and imagined author finds its succinct articulation in the following elaboration by Bakhtin:

> The author manifests himself and his point of view not only in his effect on the narrator, on his speech and his language (which are to one or another extent objectified, objects of display) but also in his effect on the subject of the story—as a point of view that differs from the point of view of the narrator. Behind the narrator's story we read a second story, the author's story; he is the one who tells us how the narrator tells stories, and also tells us about the narrator himself.[29]

While the experiences of migration and travel of his protagonist unravel, the second story—Pamuk's story as the real author—also arises quite radically with his narrator's own travel accounts.[30] The merging of the speakers corresponds to the concept that Bakhtin deduces for the genre of the novel: the dialogic tension between the protagonist and the narrator and between their ideologies allows a change in authorial intentions. Bakhtin argues that this alteration of authorial intentions may appear as differences between the two speakers of the novel—the narrator and the author—although in some incidences an absolute blending of voices may occur.[31] Pamuk illustrates what Bakhtin identifies as "dialogized ambiguity"[32] and thus maintains the aura of chaotic ambiance for his fictional and semifictional speakers. In one of the most distinct scenes, however, all three speakers do, in fact, blend into one another: Orhan replies to Ka's question about his plans for his next project with the exact title of Pamuk's 2008 novel, *The Museum of Innocence*.[33] Within the context of this phenomenon, Said's analysis of Conrad's letters proves critical as it directly relates to my argument: in his discussion of the fiction of autobiography, Said examines the probable relation between Conrad's thoughts on himself and his short fiction. Said's contention, namely, the problematic of a personal dialectic, and the reflections of such matters on the literary as well as nonliterary work of a writer, stands in vital relevance to my reading of Pamuk in *Snow*. For, he articulates his problem of self-definition and self-regard in identical acute desperation, whereas I claim the same personal conflict between the man and the writer to be also at play with Pamuk. The following nonliterary account underlines anew the same problematic:

> I work seven days a week, from 9 in the morning till 8 at night. I have the titles of the next eight novels I want to write. I feel myself pitiable, degraded on a day that I don't write. [...] I was at the end of my tether when my first book was published. For eight years, I didn't make a penny. I worked so hard, didn't drink, didn't enjoy life.[34]

Pamuk's public words of torment over his work and his definition of the self resurface in *Snow* in the following inner speech of his double-voiced narrator, the "other" into whose identity Pamuk blends as himself:

> It was as if I'd discovered yet another weakness in myself; it was a painful reminder that while Ka had lived his life in the way that came naturally to him, as a true poet, I was a lesser being, a simple-hearted novelist who like a clerk sat down to work at the same time every day.[35]

"Pain and intense effort are the profound keynotes of Conrad's spiritual history, and his letters attest to this,"[36] is Said's assessment of Conrad. The same consideration holds true for Pamuk. His posited author as well as his protagonist torment themselves in *Snow*, for they constitute an unknown writer.[37] In his examination of Conrad's claims of individuality, Said determines this exilic writer's dilemma to be the result of his desperate need to have a role to play in order to leave an indelible mark of his existence. This predicament, Said observes, is the drive behind Conrad's intense and persistent efforts to "escape from the anonymity of common human destiny," as "the only way to confirm the reality of his individuality."[38] This "involved personal dialectic," thus, inspires him toward "the creation of another character for himself."[39] Like Conrad, Pamuk, too, strives arduously for an escape from falling victim to anonymity. The following public display of his dilemma reasserts my claim that Pamuk, too, suffered the excruciating need to compose literature of world significance. However, as he was painfully aware, being a mere Turkish writer was to be a problematic:

> When I was in my twenties and trying to find a publisher for my first novel, an eminent writer from the generation that came before me once asked me in jest why I'd given up painting. A painting did not need to be translated. No one would ever translate a Turkish novel into another language, and even if someone did, no one living in a foreign country would be interested enough to read it.[40]

Asserting in the same speech, "that the urge to sit down and to write has something to do with our identity—what others call our 'national identity,'"[41] Pamuk stresses his quest for a distinctive identity with worldly affiliation and supranational outlook for himself as a writer:

> [T]he novelist speaks with conviction about the poetry he sees in his personal life, or the shadows that darken it, but critics and readers read his books as expressions of a country's poetry, and a country's shadows. Even the novelist's most private imaginings and creative idiosyncrasies are taken as descriptions of an entire nation, even as representations of that nation. It wasn't just when my books were translated into German, but also when they were translated into other world languages: as they worked to find me readers, my friends and editors would say the same thing, not just in Germany, but all over the world: "Don't take this the wrong way, Mr. Pamuk, your book is beautiful, but unfortunately there is no interest in Turkish culture in our country." Like any young man who has been denied a position just because he was born in the wrong place, I found this depressing, but I knew they were right. I felt like some sort of demented intellectual, banging on for years about a subject no one was interested in.[42]

In this context, *Snow*'s double-voiced narrator regains attention with his demented state to the extent of devastation following the death of

his successful poet friend—for that loss signifies the eternal destruction of hope to find his own unique identity. While Ka finds salvation
in the creation of his own *Snow*,[43] Orhan stands yet again before his
all-consuming dilemma. The publicly pronounced agony Pamuk has
endured in his life, thus, finds its echo in Orhan's desperate chase after
Ka's *Snow* and his self-torment about his unsuccessful search for distinction. Taking his protagonist in his suffering into a state of in-betweenness and assigning him a strong yearning to be like his dead friend,
Pamuk revisits his own lifelong desire to become and be the "other"
whose lives he always longed to transform into his own. Accompanying
Orhan in numerous settings and situations on the path of his self-discovery, Pamuk situates him in an array of identity problems: on his
arrival at and presence in Kars and interactions with Ka's contacts, he
replicates Ka;[44] he aspires to covet Ka and confronts his jealousy over
him.[45] In fact, his imaginary duplication of his beloved friend assumes
a concrete form in his own physical being, as he begins to do everything
"just like Ka."[46] Anguish and disenchantment enrapture Orhan in an
all-consuming desperation of his personal dialectic:

> It was as if I'd discovered yet another weakness in myself; it was a painful
> reminder that while Ka had lived his life in the way that came naturally
> to him, as a true poet, I was a lesser being, a simple-hearted novelist who
> like a clerk sat down to work at the same time every day.[47]

Echoing one of Pamuk's nonfictional pronouncements, Orhan identifies in himself *the writer clerk*:

> What sorrow I felt to imagine my friend pointing out the building in the
> distance. Or was it something worse? Could it be that the writer clerk was
> secretly delighted at the fall of the sublime poet? The thought induced
> such self-loathing I forced myself to think about something else.[48]

In another public statement on his self-regard against the backlash
of his indistinctive identity as a writer, Pamuk recalls the feelings of
unease and discontent that the immensity and affluence of the world
publishing industry prompted in him about his actual status—small
and insignificant:

> Even as I walked from hall to hall, floor to floor, building to building,
> feasting my eyes on the colorful array of books from all over the world,
> and marveling at their variety as I leafed through their pages, I could

see how difficult it would be to make my voice heard, to leave a trace, to make sure other people could distinguish me from others.[49]

Pamuk's grueling efforts to assert an individuality and a writer's status of distinction resurface in one of Orhan's lowest moments, as he contemplates about the expectation of the residents of Kars to find a "a hero, some great man"[50] in him:

Alas, I was to disappoint them with my bad Istanbul habits, my absent-mindedness and lack of organization, my self-regard, my obsession with my project, and my haste; what's more, they let me know it.[51]

The strong interaction between the real author's novelistic fiction and his personal statements in public gains a sharp contour in *Snow*—as shown through an entanglement of various emotional adventures within the context of which the voices of the narrator and the posited author blend into the speech of the real author of both positions, and thus, into his dialectical life. On the distinctive condition and consciousness of an exile, Said claims the following:

Much of the exile's life is taken up with compensating for disorienting loss by creating a new world to rule. It is not surprising that so many exiles seem to be novelists, chess players, political activists, and intellectuals. Each of these occupations requires a minimal investment in objects and places a great premium on mobility and skill. The exile's new world, logically enough, is unnatural and its unreality resembles fiction.[52]

In the unnatural and unreal world of his creation, Pamuk operates with resourcefulness and a highly inventive mobility to compensate for his lack of a real exilic standing. His approach to his novel *Snow* is one of an exile by choice to lend power to his artistic work in which he creates a new world to rule—as I have emphasized before. With the invention of this new world, Pamuk reconciles his existential dilemma that his nonfictional communication persistently underlines as the crisis that has made him feel degraded throughout his writing career. In, with, and through *Snow*, Pamuk discards his repute as an insignificant writer from an insignificant country. Through his novelistic art, he empowers himself with a *perpetual self-invention*[53]—to borrow a term coined by Said. *Snow* unfolds as the product of multiple acts of transplantation as well as psychological metamorphosis—the exilic reality of which Bharati

Mukherjee speaks,[54] in which Pamuk adopts a metaphorical state of exile liberating himself from a conventional life and from his usual career on an ever-evolving process of self-discovery and self-invention.[55] The problematic he shares with writers of fiction, namely, the "complicated struggle to balance the problems of one's own selfhood against the demands of publishing and speaking out in the public sphere,"[56] finds its resolve in *Snow*. His state of metaphorical exile allows Pamuk to attain a higher state of authority in the example of not only Nazim but also Auerbach, Conrad, Adorno, Said, Rushdie, Naipaul, Djebar, and Honigmann—all writers, in enforced or voluntary exile. It is with this fictional status of an exile that Pamuk affords eccentric angles for his authorial vision, enlivens his vocation, and obtains privileges without having ever been in a state of exile.

The higher state of authority Pamuk attains throughout *Snow* is especially notable in his full consumption of the Turkish past—just as the 1999 Nobel Prize laureate German writer Günter Grass is preoccupied with the German past.[57] From the margins of his imaginary retreat—first, in the role of his protagonist and then through his narrator—Pamuk observes the multitude of complications on Turkey's political scene that Kars embodies: he ventures into a journey of what Bakhtin identifies in the novelist as an *"authoritative discourse*, and an *internally persuasive discourse."*[58] As the sole authoritative speaking person—or, "an *ideologue"*[59] in Bakhtin's terms—Pamuk sets out to re-present history through what Bakthin identifies as *"ideologemes."*[60] Transforming the self into the "voice of conscience,"[61] he, thus, participates in historical becoming and in social struggle—taking on the privilege that Bakhtin discusses as an integral element of the novelistic art.[62] Pamuk adjusts his work as a historical novel. With this alteration, he accomplishes a unique representational discourse in which a "modernizing, an erasing of temporal boundaries, the recognition of an eternal present in the past"[63] dominate.

My observation of Pamuk in the role of a historian revives Said's argument not only on Conrad's historian-like outlook on his life[64] but also on his "especially anxious interest in the history and dynamics of political existence."[65] A particularly critical relation of Said's study to this chapter lies in the articulation of "the artistic cosmology of narrative fiction and its dependence upon the recollecting subjective consciousness."[66] As Conrad is said to have practiced with this approach to truth in his short fiction, *Snow*—the novel that Pamuk emphatically singles out as his only political work[67]—unravels the author's tendency to historical truth in "the deliberate artistic manipulation that sought to bring the past into a causal relation with the present."[68] Pamuk takes possession of the "magical alteration of the objective reality"[69] that Said assigns as a dominating element to Conrad's fiction:

> Most of Conrad's short fiction [...] dramatizes the problematic relation between the past and the present, between then and now. It may be Conrad's own sense of the past conflicting with his sense of the present, or it may be a character's sense of the past disturbing his (the character's) sense of the present—the distinction is impossible to make.[70]

As if to imitate Conrad, Pamuk stages the historical accounts in *Snow* in such a manner "that the tales attempt to create an extended moment in which past and present are exposed" and "the relation between past and present is treated in profoundly dramatic terms."[71] On this aspect of Conrad's work, one that I claim to be the case for Pamuk's *Snow*, Said states the following:

> There is [...] the quality of attempted *intrusion*: the intrusion of the past into the present, and the intrusion of the present into the past. The real aim of the tale becomes that long, extended moment wherein past and present are brought together and allowed to interact. The past, requiring the illumination of slow reflection on former thoughtless impulses, is exposed to the present; the present, demanding that "desired unrest" without which it must remain mute and paralyzed, is exposed to the past.[72]

Throughout his historical accounts, Pamuk blankets himself with a distinct aura of detachment positioning himself as an outsider, all along representing the past and the present through what Said considers in Conrad to be "equivalent, in Sartre's terms, to the magical alteration of the objective reality."[73] His laborious struggles toward the construction of his fictional autobiography of exile involve "what Foucault once called 'a relentless erudition,' scouring alternative sources, exhuming buried documents, reviving forgotten (or abandoned) histories."[74] With his tireless resourcefulness, he discovers alternative sources, unearths buried documents, and resuscitates forgotten or abandoned histories. He fully benefits from the vast capacity that Seyhan details on autobiographical narratives of exile:

> Autobiographies of exile can variously and simultaneously assume the form of personal testimony and biography of parents, ancestors, or community. They can also be "the diary of a place (often a city); a polyvocal

history; a meditation on language, love, and metaphysics," and, in some cases, "an unauthorized biography of the nation."[75]

As if to exhaust the dimensions of narrations within exilic autobiographies of Seyhan's outline, Pamuk's autobiography of metaphorical exile—as demonstrated throughout the chapter—assumes the forms of personal testimony,[76] a biography of ancestors and community, the diary of Kars and also of Frankfurt, a polyvocal history, a meditation on love[77] and metaphysics, and an unauthorized biography of the nation. The *relentless erudition*[78] of Foucault's identification in a writer's struggles for the creation of his work "involves a sense of the dramatic and of the insurgent, making a great deal of one's rare opportunities to speak, catching the audience's attention, being better at wit and debate than one's opponents"[79]—a fact that has become evident in this chapter on the basis of Pamuk's nonfictional stance that I have cited in arguing for the pain and intense effort being—in the model of Conrad—the profound keynotes of Pamuk's spiritual history.

Having dedicated his painfully intense labor to writing and having persisted in his lifelong quest of creating for himself his own tale flavored with worldliness, Pamuk does, indeed, succeed in catching the attention of an audience worldwide—of which Foucault speaks in different contexts. Pamuk's efforts to self-reinvent find their complete execution in his novel of imagined exile, the work that enables him to accomplish the long-awaited *process of signification*[80]—to echo the Saidian concept. For, not unlike Conrad, "he, too, was a man of action urgently in need of a role to play so that he could locate himself solidly in existence."[81] With *Snow*, Pamuk succeeds in evading his most-dreaded fear: being condemned to anonymity. He achieves a self-representation that lends him the stories of a multifaceted "other" whose life of enrichment and intriguingly ambiguous associations he successfully covets, attaining a new identity for himself. It is in this fictional autobiography of exile that Pamuk's often-changing directions of his early years to identify a career for himself and to ease his intellectual unrest, his preoccupation with having to write for worldly significance, and his existential predicament, come to rest at last.

Notes

1. Orhan Pamuk, "In Kars and Frankfurt," trans. Maureen Freely. 2005 Commencement Speech

2. Ibid.
3. Ibid.
4. The Surname Law, promulgated on June 21, 1934, enabled Turkey's Muslim citizens surnames in the model of her Christian and Jewish citizens.
5. Pamuk, "In Kars and Frankfurt."
6. Ibid.
7. Ibid.
8. Orhan Pamuk, Frankfurt Fair 2008 Opening Speech. Pamuk's most notable remarks on Turkey as being his most disheartening ordeal occur in this speech.
9. Ibid.
10. Azade Seyhan, "Enduring Grief: Autobiography as 'Poetry of Witness' in the Work of Assia Djebar and Nazım Hikmet," *Comparative Literature Studies* 40.2 (2003): 159–172, 167.
11. Ibid., p. 163. See Nazım Hikmet, "It Is Snowing in the Dark," *Son Şiirleri. Şiirler 7*, Adam Yayınları, 1987, and "In Beyazıt Square," in: *Beyond the Walls* (London: Anvil Press Poetry, 2002), p. 218. See also Nazım Hikmet, *Poems* (New York: Persea Books, 2002). For comparison, see Pamuk's narrative mourning of Necip's death by a bullet in the forehead and its impact on Ka, and also Ka's execution-style death.
12. See Nazım Hikmet, *Human Landscapes from My Country* (New York: Persea Books, 2002). In Orhan Pamuk, *Snow*, trans. Maureen Freely (New York: Vintage International, 2005), see pp. 6 and 7.
13. *Buddenbrooks*, the first novel of the 1929 Nobel Prize laureate Thomas Mann, a German novelist and essayist, reveals itself as the source of Pamuk's inspiration for his first novel, *Cevdet Bey ve Oğulları*.
14. See Alev Tekinay's dervish novel, *The Crying Pomegranate* (Frankfurt, Germany: Suhrkamp Phantastische Bibliothek, German Edition, 1998); her short story "Jakob und Yakup" in: *Es brennt ein Feuer in mir* (Frankfurt, Germany: Brandes & Apsel, 1990); Emine Sevgi Özdamar's *Life Is a Caravanserai: Has Two Doors—I Came in One—I Went Out the Other* (London: Middlesex University Press, 2000); *Mother Tongue*. Toronto: Coach House Press, 1994); and *The Courtyard in the Mirror* (Köln, Germany: Kiepenheuer & Witsch, 2001); and Zafer Şenocak's *Dangerous Relationships* (München, Germany: Babel Verlag, 1998). With *Snow*, Pamuk replicates the exilic consciousness, humanism, and poetic symbolism of Nazım while he disentangles an ambivalent plot of multiple negotiations between Tekinay's treatment of Islamic mysticism, Özdamar's construction of ancestorial biographies through a Turkish and Kurdish cast, and Şenocak's unauthorized biography of the Turkish nation. I also assert that Pamuk's thorough knowledge of the "othering" of Erich Auerbach with a displacement—of all the places in Turkey—to his beloved İstanbul, and of his critical writings enabled through the periphery, a context of his continuous fascination as I have argued throughout, does seem to have helped him refine his construction of the ideal exilic writer and work.
15. *Snow*, p. 279, 280, and 232.

16. Tekinay's protagonist has an altered born identity—Ferdi T.—as does Ka; for both, self-fulfillment is tied to the composer of a small book of poetry, and elements of Sufism are blended prominently into *Snow* in the model of Tekinay's dervish novel. See Mevlana Celaleddin Rumi, *Divan-I Kebir*. Ankara, Turkey: İş Bankası Yayınları, 2008), and for one of the most comprehensive studies on Rumi's Sufi poetry and symbolic imagery that Tekinay makes frequent use of in her novel, see Annemarie Schimmel, *Mystical Dimensions of Islam*. Chapel Hill: University of North Carolina Press, 1975).
17. Monika Shafi focuses on *The Bridge of the Golden Horn*. See "Joint Ventures: Identity Politics and Travel in Novels by Emine Sevgi Özdamar and Zafer Şenocak," *Comparative Literature* 40.2 (2003): 193–214.
18. See *Life Is a Caravanserai: Has Two Doors—I Came in One—I Went out the Other; Mother Tongue, The Courtyard in the Mirror,* and *The Bridge of the Golden Horn*.
19. While Emine's mentioned novels and *Snow* share identical authorial and political concerns, a comparative look at Şenocak's 1998 novel had to suffice here.
20. *Snow*, pp. 12, 14, 21, 26, 28, 56, 224–227.
21. *Snow*, pp. 20–22, 34, 36, 302, 318, 397, 461.
22. Ibid., p. 245, 246.
23. Shafi, p. 197. For an extensive discussion of diasporic literature, see also Azade Seyhan, *Writing Outside the Nation* (Princeton, NJ, and Oxford: Princeton University Press, 2001), and Leslie Adelson, *The Turkish Turn in Contemporary German Literature* (Palgrave Macmillan, 2005).
24. Edward Said, *Representations of the Intellectual* (New York: Vintage Books, 1996). p. 59.
25. Mikhail Bakhtin, *The Dialogic Imagination* (Austin: University of Texas Press, 1981), p. 312.
26. Said, *Representations of the Intellectual*, p. 59.
27. Said, *Joseph Conrad and the Fiction of Autobiography* (New York: Columbia University Press, 2008).
28. Ibid.
29. Bakhtin, pp. 313–314.
30. A distinct if not extinct name, Sargut Sölçün, a Turkish German literature scholar in Germany, an assistant professor of German literature at Hacettepe University, Turkey, where I was a student during his tenure, is disguised as the novel's Tarkut Ölçün—an affirmation of what Pamuk claims in reference to aspects of himself in *Snow*.
31. Bakhtin, p. 315.
32. Bakhtin, p. 325.
33. *Snow*, p. 280.
34. "In Kars and Frankfurt."
35. *Snow*, p. 448.
36. Said, *Joseph Conrad and the Fiction of Autobiography*, p. 4.
37. Note their identification as a "so-called poet," their fear of becoming the other's

"posthumous shadow," the "many moments" of feeling like one another and "dreaming" of one's own "place in the universe," just as the other.

38. *Snow*, p. 38.
39. Said, *Joseph Conrad and the Fiction of Autobiography*, p. 39.
40. "In Kars and Frankfurt."
41. Ibid.
42. Ibid.
43. *Snow*, pp. 278–279.
44. Ibid., pp. 411–412.
45. Ibid., p. 412.
46. Ibid., pp. 446–447.
47. Ibid., p. 448.
48. Ibid., p. 455.
49. Ibid.
50. Ibid.
51. Ibid., p. 458.
52. Edward Said, *Reflections on Exile and Other Essays* (Cambridge, MA: Harvard University Press, 2000), p. 181.
53. Edward Said, *Letters of Transit* (New York Public Library, 1999), p. 111.
54. Ibid., p. 70.
55. Ibid., pp. 62–63.
56. Ibid., p. 23.
57. Shafi, p. 195.
58. Bakhtin, p. 342.
59. Ibid., p. 333.
60. Ibid., pp. 332–333.
61. Ibid., p. 349.
62. Ibid., p. 331.
63. Ibid., pp. 365–366.
64. Said, *Joseph Conrad and the Fiction of Autobiography*, p. 11.
65. Ibid., p. 15.
66. Ibid., p. 102.
67. "In Kars and Frankfurt."
68. Said, *Joseph Conrad and the Fiction of Autobiography*, p. 95.
69. Ibid., p. 105.
70. Ibid., p. 91.
71. Ibid., p. 99.
72. Ibid., p. 93.
73. Said, *Joseph Conrad and the Fiction of Autobiography*, pp. 104–105.
74. Said, *Representations of the Intellectual*, p. xviii.
75. Seyhan, "Enduring Grief: Autobiography as 'Poetry of Witness,'" pp. 161, 172.
76. The immediately evident surface elements of a personal testimony include their Istanbul origin; educational background; privileged upbringing; and unawareness of poverty (see pp. 19, 57, 280, 319, 320, 323).

77. See *Snow*, pp. 370, 371 where Orhan dwells over Ka's love for Ipek after Ka's death and fantasizes to be Ipek's love.
78. Said, *Representations of the Intellectual*, p. xviii.
79. Ibid.
80. Said, *Joseph Conrad and the Fiction of Autobiography*, p. 70.
81. Ibid., p. 12.

CHAPTER 8

Silence, Secularism, and Fundamentalism in *Snow*

Esra Mirze Santesso

In *Snow*, Ka, a struggling poet returning from a decade-long self-inflicted exile in Germany, is commissioned by a national news-paper to report on young, religious girls committing suicide in Kars, in Eastern Turkey. Once a cosmopolitan city with "thousand-year-old churches," "a large Armenian community," Persians, Greeks, Kurds, Georgians, and Circassians, Kars is now a poverty-stricken pro-vincial outpost suffering from "destitution, depression, and decay."[1] As Ka makes the journey on a bus in the thick of winter, it begins to snow, which he sees as "a promise, a sign pointing back to the happiness and purity he had once known as a child" (4); he is inspired to write a poem, titled "The Silence of Snow." The "inner peace" that the poet initially feels, however, is gradually replaced by an apprehension brought about by the escalating snowstorm; it becomes "tiring, irritating, terrorizing," creating "a fearful silence" among the passengers (5). As the bus con-tinues its journey, it literally distances Ka from the familiarity of the Western values of Istanbul. Upon arrival, he feels culturally displaced in "a ghost town" of idleness and extremism, where human rights are violated and privacy laws are meaningless. Most importantly, the jour-ney to the periphery of the nation forces Ka to enter into the ongoing political struggle between secularists and Islamists, and to rethink the usual rhetorical depiction of this struggle.[2]

The silence of snow—both the actual backdrop of Kars as well as the poem Ka continues to work on throughout the book—can be viewed as an extended metaphor for the silence, the lack of dialogue, between

Eastern and Western Turkey, as well as between the different factions of Kars, which act as a microcosm of the nation. On the surface, the author's engagement with various forms of political discourse rests on a traditional binary: secularism versus Islamism.[3] Pamuk initially follows this binary—a constant presence in the Turkish media—as he describes secularism as a liberal philosophy that rejects state-sponsored religion, and Islamism as a political movement dedicated to the revival of religion, and a fundamentalist interpretation of the sacred text. Yet, as the novel proceeds, Pamuk begins to conflate the two positions, pointing to the way both glorify a "golden age" and a long-term goal (Kemalism and its commitment to secular modernization and the Muslim brotherhood and its sharia law). Most importantly, he demonstrates that both positions are invested in silence: secularism "maintains complete silence regarding absolute or permanent values," while Islamism depends on the act of silencing nonbelievers, as well as other possible forms of reading and interpreting the Qur'an.[4] In *Snow*, Pamuk concentrates on how both discourses finally fail, how they cancel each other out and consequently generate moments of silence.

In his portrayal of the relationship between Islamists and secularists, Pamuk is diligent about not depicting either camp in a monolithic way; rather, characters reveal complex subject positions, subscribing to various, even contradictory, tenets. Consider, for example, the way the author separates pious believers who fear "fall[ing] under the spell of the West," at the expense of "forgetting [their] own stories" (81), from political Islamists, who seek power by feeding on the fears of religious groups (their slogan: "Give your vote to the Prosperity party, the party of God, we've fallen into this destitution because we've wandered off the path of God" [26]). He also avoids presenting the secularists as a unified group, differentiating between moderate secularists who are "prepared to live" with the Islamists "as long as [they] don't use intimidation or force to make Westernized women wear scarves" (151), and fanatics "who detect [...] a political motive every time [they see] a covered woman in the street" (22). This nuanced portrayal of characters allows the reader, especially the Western reader, to recognize that the political "binary" is something of an illusion, and that more radical members of each side seek to silence the dissonant voices within in order to simulate unanimity.

The most controversial aspect of the novel has been its treatment of fundamentalism. The idea of "fundamentalism" is particularly vexed in the Turkish context; though 97 percent of the population identify themselves as Muslim, there is a tendency in the secular media to label any public displays of faith as "fundamentalist." Furthermore, as some scholars have pointed out, fundamentalism—a concept deeply rooted in the Judeo-Christian tradition—can be a misleading term when it comes to describing certain aspects of current Islamic movements (even though, as Bobby S. Sayyid argues, "Islamic fundamentalism has [now] become a metaphor for fundamentalism in general)."[5] And, of course, there is no consensus even among believers about what fundamentalism actually means. Yet, while Islamic fundamentalism clearly cannot be regarded as a coherent and consistent *strategy* (fundamentalists in rural Turkey have little in common with fundamentalists in urban Malaysia) what does unify the *movement* at a very basic level is, first of all, a desire to promote "the principles of religion" (however loosely defined, but in any case, understood as divinely revealed and unchanging rules) over those values that are seen as offshoots of Western modernism.[6] This anti-Western sentiment is of central concern to Turkish authors and scholars, and is especially alarming for secularists who fear that the deprivatization of religion will eventually present a threat against individual freedom, endangering the democratic structure of a state surrounded by nondemocratic neighbors. Taking its cue from these ongoing debates, *Snow* presents a philosophical conundrum: what is at stake when a state committed to secular guarantees of individual rights decides it must limit the rights of Islamic fundamentalists who support the desecularization of civic life? Is it legitimate to silence one group so that another may speak freely? If so, are universal and democratic rights in permanent opposition to each other?

Pamuk's pluralistic discussion of these questions—in particular, his evenhanded treatment of Islamists—has been the object of criticism in Turkey. Pamuk has defended himself:

> Our secularists, who are always relying on the army and who are destroying Turkey's democracy, hated this book because here you have a deliberate attempt by a person who was never religious in his life to understand why someone ends up being what we or the Western world calls an Islamic fundamentalist. It is a challenge and duty of literature to understand the passions of anyone.[7]

Both sides, in other words, have been trying to silence the other; the author must let them speak. Pamuk does just this through the dialogic form of the novel. By representing a dissonant array of voices, he draws attention to the complexity of identity politics, and consequently articulates the dilemma of the modern, progressive Muslim nation attempting to impose secular values upon a religious population. This dilemma, as *Snow* suggests, generates a deeper philosophical question about whether the civil rights of particular groups may be sacrificed in order to uphold the rights of others.

Pamuk's investment in an honest representation of ideology allows him to make unexpected observations about fundamentalism; as the novel proceeds, he begins to redefine this term, expanding its significance beyond the religious context. He reintroduces "fundamentalism" as first and foremost a textual practice, finally formulating a broader characterization of fundamentalism as a political practice in which text is always privileged over speech. The irony is that, with this definition, Pamuk is also able to classify a group of extreme *secularists* as fundamentalist. *Snow* follows the way a group of secular radicals mirror their religious rivals: just as Islamic fundamentalists use the decrees of the Qur'an as infallible guiding principles, for example, secular fundamentalists rely on the constitution as doctrine—and both use their text as a way of discouraging speech and debate. Thus, Pamuk attempts to blur the lines between religious inflexibility and secular despotism, describing *both* positions as essentially fundamentalist, *both* dedicated to silencing the other. By paying particular attention to various forms of fundamentalism (textual, religious, and secular), Pamuk examines the predicament of subscribing to rigid doctrines that promise stability at the expense of plurality. It is my contention that this politically charged novel is Pamuk's response to the silences, taboos, and indictments that are the by-products of both religion and nationalism. What I analyze here is the author's complication of the fundamentalist/secularist binary by introducing the concept of silent space, and articulate what that silence means for Turkey's future.

Pamuk emblematizes the modern legacy of this struggle by developing two symbolic themes in his novel. The first revolves around the headscarf, which has political ramifications well beyond religious practice. Pamuk's treatment of the controversy allows the reader to observe a rather unusual alliance between fundamentalism and the rhetoric of universal rights. The second revolves around the idea of language itself, especially the idea that textually obsessed fundamentalists lose their ability to listen to spoken language. A key demonstration of the failure of oral communication arrives in the novel's great set piece: a military coup carried out by a struggling actor. Ultimately, by identifying silent space as a position associated with fundamentalism, Pamuk warns that silence is often a precursor to violence.

* * *

In the early years of the republic, by accepting laicism as the basis of democracy, the Kemalist government made a conscious effort to distance Turkey from its Islamic, imperialist past. It is important to note, however, that *laïcité*, "despite its ideology of the strict independence of religion and state, has a long tradition of the *gestion* ("management") of religion."[8] Many scholars have pointed out that the new state's increasing desire to *remove* religion, rather than manage it, ironically paved the way for its politicization: "The effect of this [separation]," as Sayyid argues, "was to reactivate Islam as a political discourse. [. . .] Once the caliphate had been replaced by the discourse of Kemalism it became possible to think about the need for an Islamic state."[9] In attempting to silence the believers, in other words, Kemalists gave them a new language to use. In the late 1990s—the time in which *Snow* is set—the tension between the two camps reached a peak when secularists' efforts to modernize Turkey, and gain full membership in the European Union, mobilized conservative Muslims nervous about state-sponsored Westernization.[10] The resulting political and ideological movement came to be known in Turkey as "Islamopolitics," a political movement dedicated to the Islamization of civic life.[11] Certain seemingly minor facets of everyday life became highly politicized: food and drink sales, holidays, even clothing.

Perhaps the most significant battleground between secularists and Islamists was the banning of the headscarf.[12] While the unveiling of women was a visible sign of secularization in the early years of the republic, the beginning of the 1980s saw a considerable number of women returning to the headscarf. This alarmed the secular regime, which feared "creeping Islamism," a growing promotion of sharia over the secular constitution. To prevent the veil from becoming a rallying symbol, the Higher Education Authority announced in 1982 its policy to remove female students with headscarves from university lecture halls. This pronouncement was supported by the Supreme Administrative Court, which asserted that

> beyond being a mere innocent practice, wearing the headscarf is in the process of becoming a symbol of a vision that is contrary to the freedoms of women and the fundamental principles of the republic.[13]

The court decision reflected the general secular view of Islamism as a "structural crisis," threatening the nation's democratic principles.[14] For the secular elite, it was acceptable, even necessary, for government to silence symbolic expressions of sentiments that might threaten the secular nation.

Within this political frame, *Snow* rethinks the headscarf controversy by depicting a group of girls who inadvertently become instruments of a political struggle. Once they put on scarves they are sought out by both sides—but rather than entering into the debate, the girls ultimately "kill [. . .] themselves abruptly, without ritual or warning, in the midst of their everyday routines" (13). The suicides of the girls generate a national uproar from both sides: Islamic fundamentalists blame the secularists for persecuting believers, while the secularists condemn religious practices that treat women as second-class citizens. The headscarf girls, trapped between clashing political positions (patriarchal traditions, secular ideology, and the manipulative politics of both sides), view suicide, the ultimate act of self-silencing, as the only way they can draw attention to their voicelessness. The Islamists are quick to speak for the victims, objectifying the girls as political rebels who have willingly sacrificed their lives for their religious convictions. By turning them into martyrs, they see a political opportunity to blame the secular state for its targeting of Islamic women. Pamuk, however, rightly notes that Islam condemns suicide, and that it is erroneous to glorify such deaths as an expression of religious freedom—especially when that religion specifically prohibits the taking of one's own life. Consequently, the act of self-annihilation can be viewed not only as a rejection of state authority but also a repudiation of the basic doctrines set forth by the Qur'an. Indeed, the truly devout Muslims in Kars are ambivalent about these suicides; the families ultimately disown the deceased and "refuse to arrange the funeral prayer" (406). "Girls who commit suicide are not even Muslims," proclaims one believer, refusing to acknowledge their self-silencing as a cry for help (406).

The rhetorical maneuvers of the Islamists demonstrate that they are less interested in the doctrines of religion and more concerned with the manipulation of the public opinion for political capital. So too the secularists: both sides argue *about* the girls, but the argument only uses them without including them as legitimate political voices. Consider the conversation between an Islamist and the director of a public school. While the subject of this discussion is the hardships endured by the headscarf girls, the girls themselves, who are directly affected by the state's ruling, are absent from the conversation; rather, the two male participants speculate about their agony. In addition to the exclusion of women, the conversation reveals an interesting rhetorical twist: the construction of "secular" and "religious" as contesting categories points not only to their interrelatedness (the secular relies on the presence of the religious), but also to their interchangeability:

- My question is this, sir. Does the word "secular" mean "godless"?
- No.
- In that case, how can you explain why the state is banning so many girls from the classroom in the name of secularism, when all they are doing is obeying the laws of their religion?
- Honestly, my son. Arguing these things will get you nowhere. [...] the real question is how much suffering we've caused our women-folk by turning headscarves into symbols—and using women as pawns in a political game.
- The question I cannot help asking is this: How does all this fit in with what our constitution says about educational and religious freedoms? (40–41)

Note the role swapping: secularism, traditionally associated with free-thinking, is depicted here as an oppressive system of thought that would deny educational and religious rights, therefore moving away from the rational realm. In contrast, religion, which "essentially belongs to the domain of faith and passion," is shown here as a discourse that justifies itself by alluding to "constitutionalism, moral autonomy, democracy, human rights, [and] civil equality."[15] By characterizing these girls as victims of state oppression, the Islamist portrays the state as a repressive regime with no regard for freedom of religion or individual expression. This rhetorical twist is significant: the Islamist, by declaring his belief "in the love of God and the free exchange of ideas," draws on liberal discourse, perhaps shaming his secularist opponent (41). Consequently, the liberal values he invokes in his speech undermine the general stereotype of fundamentalism in which reason is trumped by faith. And yet, when he does not hear what he hopes for, he resorts to aggression; his civility ceases once he takes out the gun from his pocket and pulls the trigger.

Meanwhile, another cluster of headscarf girls emerge as a political group, challenging the traditional meaning of fundamentalism in a different way: by becoming defenders of women's rights. In a series of conversations with them, Ka observes the emergence of a new class of Muslim women who align themselves with feminism in order to protect their right to choose a religious lifestyle. The leader of the girls, Kadife, is well educated and cosmopolitan, originally from Istanbul. She explains to Ka that wearing the headscarf started for her as an experiment, to see how people would react. Her ambivalence toward the ban compels her to come forward as a leader of the headscarf girls, with the agenda of opposing the government's policy of intruding upon women's personal decisions about their bodies. She understands the political implications of her actions: "To play the rebel heroine in Turkey, you don't pull off your scarf. You put it on" (319). She asserts that the headscarf is not a symbol of defeat, but of pride, and views the suicide of the girls as an affirmation of self-respect, a way for the silenced to speak: "A woman doesn't commit suicide because she's *lost* her pride; she does it to *show* her pride" (405). Kadife's decision to side with the headscarf movement can be regarded as her personal challenge to the deafening argument between secularists and believers. By becoming a practicing Muslim with conservative values, despite her secular background and a socialist father, she tries to undermine the stereotypical representations of the Muslim woman as an oppressed subject, devoid of voice or independent mind.

Kadife's friend, Hande, also aligns herself with women's rights, arguing that their protests are less a statement of radical fundamentalism than an articulation of a politically progressive desire to exercise their basic human rights. For Hande, the headscarf is simply an act of asserting the self. She understands the ban as a state policy meant to control the rise of Islamic fundamentalism—which she does not support—but she also feels it would be a personal betrayal if she gave up her individual choice of the headscarf:

> I can't imagine myself without the headscarf. [...] If I could close my eyes just once and imagine myself going bare-headed through the doors of the school, walking down the corridor, and going into class, I'd find the strength to go through with this, and then, God willing, I'd be free. I would have removed the headscarf of my own free will, and not because the police have forced me. But for now, I just can't [...] bring myself to imagine that moment. (125)

Thus, Hande considers the headscarf as a gesture toward independence, rather than a surrender to religious or patriarchal oppression.

Pamuk has a special interest in challenging the stereotypical representation of the Muslim women as lacking political agency. Both Kadife and Hande, by publicly owning their religious practice as a condition of freedom, emerge as political heroines rather than religious ones. Both characters might be recognized as belonging to a category that is an awkward fit for the globalist worldview: Muslim libertarian feminists, a label that complicates the widely held understanding of fundamentalism as essentially "a reaction to the advances of feminism."[16] Through their politicization of the body, they defend women's rights, albeit in ways that dramatically diverge from accepted Western feminist practice; as one girl reveals, "If a lot of girls in our situation are thinking about suicide, you could say it has to do with wanting to control our own bodies" (126). As Leila Ahmed argues, Western feminism has often aligned itself with the colonial portrayal of the veil as a symbol of Islam's "innate and immutabl[e]" oppression of women.[17] While feminism targets the veil as a sign of coercion, Kadife and Hande argue that the absence of the veil is also a symptom of women's victimization in secular societies. In this way, they reclaim the headscarf as a new symbol of freedom: in a conversation with Ka, Hande declares: "After all, when I do take off my head scarf, I won't be doing it of my own free will" (123).

Ultimately, for Pamuk, the emergence of this movement suggests a new type of subjectivity and empowerment: it creates a way of overcoming the silence imposed upon minority positions. Yet, Pamuk also acknowledges that within political and cultural struggles there are also moments where a *respectful* silence might actually help. In particular, he wonders what happens when speech itself blurs into demagoguery, when political and theatrical dialogue becomes indistinguishable, and when rhetoric becomes nothing but a performance. To explore this point, I will focus on a key moment in the novel: an unauthorized military coup headed by a has-been actor, Sunay Zaim, who, framing himself as a follower of Ataturk, declares the beginning of a revolution on a theater stage. Zaim announces that the goal of this revolt is to eradicate religious institutions and to free women from religious oppression: "Those vile beasts with their cobwebbed minds will never be allowed to crawl out of their hole" (158). Zaim's behavior signals the full emergence in the novel of "secular fundamentalism"; Pamuk uses this episode to explore the use of "human" as a prop, and concern for democracy as a form of theater played out by those whose devotion to secularism is merely a form of antagonism.

* * *

Since 1950, there have been three coup d'etats (1960, 1971, and 1980) carried out by the armed forces against the Turkish government for failing to protect the secular structure of the state.[18] These military interventions have established the army as a guarantor of Kemalism and, consequently, a champion of secularism. Although such intrusions were deemed antidemocratic by the West, many Turks approved of the army's stifling of increasingly vicious clashes on the street. The direct outcome of the coups was a reevaluation of Turkey's commitment to democracy and human rights. For Europe, the fear was that the military "rescue" of secular human rights was merely a pretext, a performance meant to mask the army's true interest (solidifying their own power). *Snow* invokes these discussions by reimagining the repercussions of a military coup promising to "tackle [the] parasites" (187).

Thus, Ka watches in amazement as Kars's local municipality is abruptly toppled by the joined forces of the military and the police under the leadership of Zaim. Zaim, once admired for his portrayals of "Che Guevara, Robespierre, and the revolutionary Enver Pasha," has been reduced to traveling in rural Turkey with his theater group. He performs nationalistic plays and promotes the modernization of Turkish women. His signature piece is a bombastic play titled *My Fatherland or My Scarf*, which is intended to indoctrinate girls into a hatred of the veil. The popular response to his highly political plays is not what he had hoped for. Over time, he becomes progressively disillusioned with the rural parts of Turkey, and turns into a cynic who adds belly dancers and football players to appeal to the crowds. Tiring of populism, he eventually devises a drastic plot to "clean up" Kars from fundamentalists. This political agenda coincides with an act of self-fashioning, as he reinvents himself as a revolutionary (modeled after the leaders he had played in the past). On the night of the performance, he appears on the stage "wearing an army uniform from the thirties with the fur hat in the style of Ataturk and the heroes of the War of Independence" (157). Dressed in a full Ataturk costume, he declares his intentions as to punish those who "meddle with freedom" (158).

The setting of the coup points to the blurring of real speech and theatrical speech in the Turkish political debate. Literally staged in an auditorium, the coup is mistakenly viewed at first as a patriotic performance rather than a genuine political intervention. The audience cheerfully applauds, not noticing that soldiers with loaded weapons have been strategically placed in the corners of the hall. When one soldier, unable to restrain his anxiety, accidentally shoots a religious student and leaves him bleeding to death, the audience assumes it is part of the plot: "Nuray Hanim, a literature teacher who attended the

National theater every time she visited Ankara, and who was full of admiration for the beauty of the theatrical effects, rose to her feet [. . .] to applaud the actors" (160). In order to communicate the gravity of the moment, Zaim is forced to announce that "This is not a play—it is the beginning of a revolution" (163). The dumbfounded crowd still cannot grasp the implications of the revelation, and is unable to differentiate between reality and representation until more people are killed and wounded. The public is so used to bellicose rhetoric that they cannot hear the real thing: when dialogue is replaced by constant noise, all meaning is silenced, and fundamentalism is taken first and foremost as mere performance.

Zaim continues to perform the part of a revolutionary even when he leaves the stage and confronts Ka, whom he despises because of his moderate politics. Zaim demands that he testify against the religious students, yet, despite the threat of torture, Ka remains unresponsive. Realizing that Ka cannot be bullied by the threat of physical harm, Zaim tries a different tactic, based on fear and patriotism:

> No one who is slightly Westernized can breathe freely in this country unless they have a secular army protecting them [. . .]—if it weren't for the army, the fanatics would be turning their rusty knives on the lot of them and their painted women, chopping them all into little pieces. [. . .] When we go the way of Iran, do you really think anyone is going to remember how a porridge-hearted liberal like you shed a few tears for the boys from the religious high school? When that day comes, they'll kill you just for being a little Westernized; for being frightened and forgetting the Arabic words of a simple prayer. (207)

Zaim ends up playing a part that is opposite to the one he intended. He invokes Kemalism as the progressive and sophisticated response to simple-minded Islamic fundamentalism—yet his slogans and threats reduce Kemalism to a blunt, antireligious position.[19] He refers to the collapse of democracy in Iran as the future fate of Turkey unless fundamentalists are silenced—yet ironically, it is precisely this militant extremism that marks him as a *new* type of fundamentalist.

The small army under Zaim's authority speaks of liberal values and rights, but they act in a way inconsistent with their rhetoric, declaring a state of emergency, taking complete control of the city, cutting telephone lines, attacking private homes, torturing young students, broadcasting propaganda, and bugging private homes to collect evidence against enemies of the state. Their conduct shows the ironic adaptation of the essential elements of fundamentalist discourse and strategy:

> the sense of danger from the outside, [...] the claim of purity and authenticity; [...] the imposition of social control on members of the collectivity and the drawing of boundaries of legitimacy of the collectivity; and above all, all the use of state media and other resources to capture power or maintain control.[20]

Pamuk's point, perhaps, is that too bitter a battle forces the enemy combatants to grow alike: the binary eventually collapses into one position. Thus Zaim's behavior matches that of the Islamist who kills the director of the public school. Both parties turn to violence to impose their will; neither is able to recognize different shades of identity and in-between positions. We recall the dispute between the Islamist and the director: the Islamist does not believe the director when he repeatedly tries to assure his assailant that he is, in fact, a God-fearing believer. For the Islamist, there is no distinction between the political and the spiritual self: he proclaims the director a misguided sinner participating in a "secret plan to strip the Muslims of the secular Turkish republic of their religion and their honor" (47). In his mind, being secular is synonymous with being an atheist, and this false equation gives him the necessary justification for murder. Pamuk's description of the scene plays up the leitmotif of the novel: "Two more gunshots. Silence. A groan. The Sound of a television. One more gunshot. Silence" (49). The final word of the chapter, "silence," emphasizes Pamuk's concerns about how lack of dialogue eventually begets violence—whether it be self-inflicted (as in the case of headscarf girls) or directed against others (as in the case of the director's murder). For the Islamist, killing a "perpetrator" is justified, a means of avenging those "nameless heroes who have suffered untold while seeking to uphold their religious beliefs in a society that is in thrall to secular materialism" (42). Zaim displays the same type of shallow-mindedness when he declares war against all who are religious, without distinguishing between the private practice of religion and the political use of religion. When he sends the tanks to the dormitory of the religious school, they attack the students indiscriminately. The noise emanating from both sides, in other words, has blurred into one deafening roar. Without any moments of true dialogic interaction, without any opportunity to pause, reflect, and evaluate, there is no chance to distinguish and define. Since *Snow*, the term "secular fundamentalist" has begun to appear regularly in the

Turkish press to describe the increasingly intolerant implementation of secularism.[21] More and more, talk of human rights, of mutual respect, of individual desires and beliefs is drowned out by the sheer volume of accusations, condemnations, and warnings of religious or secular military coups.

* * *

In many ways, *Snow* reflects Pamuk's desire to explore the role of silence in "the possibility of national transformations."[22] Through the excursions of Ka, whose unrewarding journey to Kars leads him to go back to Frankfurt, Pamuk investigates the prospect of starting a dialogue between groups with contesting ideologies to formulate a meaningful way to coexist. But, like the director of the public school, like the headscarf girls, Ka is also silenced; he is murdered by an anonymous terrorist in a Turkish neighborhood in Germany. His friend, the narrator of the story, sees Ka's death as the legacy of a failure to hear one another:

> How much can we hope to understand those who have suffered deeper anguish, greater deprivation and more crushing disappointments than we ourselves have known? Even if the world's rich and powerful should ever try to put themselves in the shoes of the rest, how much would they really understand the wretched millions suffering around them? (266)

Through dialogic exploration, both Pamuk, the author, and Ka, the protagonist, avow their mission to ascertain "the love and the pain in another's heart," including those who oppose the ideology of the secular state (266). This does not suggest that the writer downplays the legitimacy of the secular values that he himself embraces as a Westernized Istanbulite; on the contrary, Pamuk understands the importance of separating the affairs of religion from the affairs of the state, particularly in a country with a long tradition of caliphate. Yet, he is unwilling to expound secularism as a rigid antidote to Islamic fundamentalism, and therefore, he articulates precisely the dilemma—one we have seen played out across North Africa recently—of the modern, progressive Muslim nation attempting to impose secular values upon a religious population.

When I interviewed Pamuk in the summer of 2006, he focused on the headscarf issue as a symbol of the religious and political paradoxes of Turkey, telling me that "I wish that headscarves were something that both secular and political Islamist parties wouldn't be aware of. I wish that this was a country where some people would wear headscarves, some people wouldn't, and no one would notice. But unfortunately it is at the heart of political struggle between political Islamists and secularists."[23] The overt symbolism of the headscarf, its contentious visibility that provokes secularists to pass laws restricting the rights of women, creates only greater furor, contributing to deeper national fragmentation. The alternative to pluralism is fundamentalism—secular and Islamic. By explicating fundamentalism's deeper implications, *Snow* allows us to rethink the state's commitment to democracy and human rights without necessarily choosing one over the other.

What happens finally when two master texts clash, when two textually authorized, fundamentalist identities collide? For Pamuk, it is a paradoxical sort of silence, sound and fury signifying nothing. Literature, he implies, can enter into the conflict, silence the silencers, and restart the vital, nationally necessary dialogue—it alone can undo the damage triggered by silence: "The writer has arrived at the heart of the space of literature when he has established a relationship with the incessant murmur, during which he first listens silently to it. Eventually he interrupts it, reducing it to silence by breaking his own silence."[24] The text ultimately is both the source of and the antidote to fundamentalism.

Notes

1. Pamuk, *Snow*, trans. Maureen Freely (London: Faber and Faber, 2004), p. 21. All future references are to this edition and will be cited parenthetically in the text.

2. The tension between secularism and Islamism in Turkey is as old as the Republic. Article 2 of the Turkish Constitution reads

   The republic of Turkey is a democratic, secular (*laik*) and social State based on the rule of law, respectful of human rights in a spirit of social peace, national solidarity and justice, adhering to the nationalism of Ataturk and resting on the fundamental principles set out in the Preamble. (Qtd. in Dominic McGoldrick, *Human Rights and religion: The Islamic Headscarf Debate in Europe* [Oxford: Hart Publishing, 2006], p. 133)

3. Of course, "Islamism" is itself a problematic term. "Islamists" themselves find this label objectionable, preferring to identify themselves simply as "proper Muslims," invested in restoring "the classical theological tradition by translating it into [a] contemporary political predicament" (Talal Asad, *Formations of the Secular: Christianity, Islam, Modernity* [Stanford: Stanford University Press, 2003], p. 198).

4. Abdelwahab Elmessiri, "Secularism, Immanence and Destruction," in *Islam and Secularism in the Middle East*, ed. Azzam Tamimi and John L. Esposito (New York: New York University Press, 2000), p. 67.

5. Bobby S. Sayyid, *A Fundamental Fear: Eurocentrism and the Emergence of Islamism* (London: Zed Books Ltd., 1997), p. 8.

6. Asad, p. 196.

7. Wendy Smith, "Orhan Pamuk: Outspoken Turk," *Publishers Weekly* 251.34 (2004).

8. Yolande Jansen, "Laïcité or the Politics of Republican Secularism," in *Political Theologies*, ed. Hent de Vries and Lawrence Eugene Sullivan (New York: Fordham University Press, 2006), p. 476.

9. Sayyid, p. 78.

10. The novel is set in 1992 during which time there was a secular, liberal party in power. Currently, there is a conservative, Islamic party in power (AKP), whose views on the headscarf ban differ from those of their predecessors. Any reference to the "state" and "government" in the chapter designates the pre-AKP era.

11. See Menderes Çinar and Burhanettin Duran, "The Specific Evolution of Contemporary Political Islam in Turkey and Its 'Difference,'" in *Secular and Islamic Politics in Turkey: The Making of the Justice and Development Party*, ed. Ümit Cizre (Oxon: Routledge, 2008), 33.

12. In 1925, the constitution imposed a dress code that prohibited any form of religious attire in the public sphere, including *hijab* (the headscarf for women) and *fez* (the traditional hat for men).

13. Qtd. in McGoldrick, p. 135.

14. Sayyid, p. 23.

15. Asad, p. 13.

16. Sayyid, p. 8.

17. "[T]he veil and segregation epitomized that oppression, and that these customs were fundamental for the general and comprehensive backwardness of Islamic societies." Leila Ahmed, "The Discourse of the Veil," in *Postcolonialisms: An Anthology of Cultural Theory and Criticism*, ed. Gaurav Desai and Supriya Nair (New Brunswick, NJ: Rutgers University Press, 2005), pp. 321–322.

18. See İbrahim Kaya's *Social Theory and Later Modernities: The Turkish Experience* (Liverpool: Liverpool University Press, 2004).

19. Matthew Levinger and Paula Franklin Lytle, "Myth and Mobilisation: The Triadic Structure of Nationalist Rhetoric," *Nations and Nationalism* 7 (2003): 178.

20. Sahgal and Yuval-Davis, p. 46.

21. See Mustafa Akyol, "The Threat of Secular Fundamentalism," *The New York Times*, May 04, 2007.

22. Erdağ Göknar, "Orhan Pamuk and the Ottoman Theme," *World Literature Today* 80 (2006): 34.

23. Z. Esra Mirze, "Implementing Disform: An Interview with Orhan Pamuk," *PMLA* 123 (2008): 176–180.

24. John Gregg, *Maurice Blanchot and the Literature of Transgression* (Princeton, NJ: Princeton University Press, 1994), p. 30.

CHAPTER 9

The Spell of the West in Orhan Pamuk's *Snow* and Amitav Ghosh's *In an Antique Land*

Thomas Cartelli

"My Fatherland or My Headscarf"

Ignored amid reports of the 2005 indictment of Orhan Pamuk for holding Turkey accountable for the mass murder of a million Armenians during and after World War I, and for the more recent killing of approximately 30,000 insurgent Kurdish nationalists, were the more serious offenses against Kemalist nationalism that Pamuk arguably commits in his celebrated novel *Snow* (2002).[1] In *Snow* Pamuk not only describes a deadly takeover of the remote borderland city of Kars and violent suppression of the city's Islamists by an unreconstructed Kemalist showman and his henchmen, but also has his expatriate poet-protagonist, Ka, forge sympathetic bonds with religious schoolboys who insist on their complexity and unknowability in ways that Pamuk's narrator (also named Orhan) respects and admires.

The leader of the takeover, Sunay Zaim, attempts to revive the glory days of Kemalist orthodoxy by making the performance of an old piece of secularist agitprop, *My Fatherland or My Head Scarf,* the occasion for an armed coup while a seemingly never-ending blizzard isolates the city from the rest of the country. Pamuk initially presents Sunay's plans to perform *Head Scarf* in the ironically deflationary manner that Eastern European filmmakers have perfected over the course of the last 50 years. But the satiric tone abruptly changes when Sunay calls for soldiers to open fire on the Islamist schoolboys as they protest the play's climactic moment in which a young woman proclaims her independence by removing her headscarf and, upon being attacked by her family and angry traditionalists, responds by burning it. The power of this scene is enhanced both by its unexpectedness and by the sympathy for the religious schoolboys that Pamuk has carefully cultivated. In its recounting, the scene gains added dimension from its contextual surround: a city that is geographically remote from cosmopolitan Istanbul, which has historically been the site of violent conflicts among Russians, Turks, and Armenians, and more lately, of bitter political struggles between and among secular nationalists; nationalist, Marxist, and Islamic Kurds; and, especially, political Islamists, who have cast the creeping shadow of "a second Iran" over the region.[2] Recent witness to the murder of its mayor, and almost certain to witness the election of a political Islamist as his successor, the city is already at such a pitch of tension and anxiety that "even the most westernized secularists in [the National Theater] were frightened by the sight of their own dreams coming true" when the young woman burns her headscarf in Sunay's play.[3]

However, neither sympathy for the religious schoolboys nor anxiety about the shooting's aftermath is allowed to sustain itself in the following pages, which are largely devoted to Ka's characterization as a supremely self-involved poet who has not, as he has claimed, come to Kars to investigate the suicides committed by the city's latter-day headscarf girls, but to reestablish a lost connection with Ipek, a former schoolmate, whom he hopes to persuade to share his heretofore solitary expatriate life in Frankfurt. Stubbornly fixated on Ipek's embodiment as his last chance for personal happiness, Ka is more than willing to sacrifice whatever misgivings he might once have harbored about jeopardizing the lives of others in order to possess her. To his credit, Ka initially sustains being bullied and beaten by the not-so-secret police for his sympathies toward the schoolboys and his association with Blue, the leader of the city's political Islamists. But presented with only one way out of this impasse, and motivated as well by jealousy of Blue's past relationship with Ipek, Ka opportunistically betrays Blue in exchange for safe passage to Frankfurt for himself and Ipek. Rejected in turn by the more principled Ipek, Ka ultimately becomes the victim of a payback-killing for his betrayal of Blue after his return to Frankfurt, which our narrator, Orhan, explores and comments on in the last movement of the novel.

The book's closing pages are haunted by an unusual request that the author conveys from Fazil, one of the surviving schoolboys, to the effect that Orhan's readers—tempted as they might be to "sympathize with the way we are and even love us"—shouldn't "believe anything" Orhan has to say "about any of us," and by a last tearstained vision of "shabby rooms full of people watching television" that the author recalls seeing as his train departs from the city.[4] Both request and vision echo an earlier perception of Ka's about the impoverished city, its "sweet and funny" schoolboys, and the struggle of its suicide girls—who "saw at once that the heart of the matter was shame"—"to find a private moment to kill themselves."[5]

"The Spell of the West"

A novelist whose past work variously trafficked in Nabokovian meta-fictions and the painstaking historical miniaturism anatomized in his 1998 novel *My Name Is Red*, Pamuk had, before *Snow*, shown little interest in addressing recent developments in Turkey, which include the increasing movement of social and religious conservatives from the countryside to the city, the ascent of Islamist parties that represent them to parliamentary majorities, and the predictably strident reaction to these developments of the largely right-wing secularist opposition. In *Snow*, Pamuk not only addresses such developments, but positions both his protagonist, Ka, and the narrator, conspicuously named Orhan, as characters who inadvertently make the same discoveries he has apparently already arrived at. In this respect, among others, *Snow* operates as a sustained, self-reflexive meditation on authorial responsibility that is all the more honest for its refusal, on the one hand, to make Ka a self-effacing, magnanimous hero and, on the other, to forgive the commitment to vengeful violence of the radical Islamists who murder Ka after his return to Frankfurt. Like the Turkish government, which has been engaging in an on-again, off-again courtship of Europe, the pursuit of stronger economic ties to Russia, a closer embrace of traditional Islam, and a strategic rethinking of its long-established partnership with Israel, in order to elevate its regional standing in relation to Iran and the Arab states of the Middle East, *Snow* forges a fitful and indeterminate path of its own between its Western and Eastern-oriented tendencies. Yet despite giving unusually sympathetic space, voice, and time to representatives of political Islam, the book paints a picture of a culture in which not only Ka, a child of the Westernized ruling elite, but the Islamists themselves feel the "mocking devil" of the West inside them.[6]

In the economy of the novel, the fates of the bourgeois expatriate Ka and the would-be celebrity-radical Blue are twinned in more ways than one, Ipek having been Blue's mistress before ceding that position to her sister Kadife, who is the most public face of the town's headscarf girls. Though he portrays with greater sympathy the charmingly sincere musings of the religious schoolboys—one of whom wants to claim a space for Muslims who read and write science fiction—Pamuk devotes more sustained time to Blue, whose critiques of the West and insistence that Turkish Muslims should work with and within their own cultural traditions and heritage are variably privileged and qualified. At one point, for example, he has Blue deliver an eloquent commentary on the neglected story of Suhrab and Rustem—drawn from Ferdowsi's *Shanameh*, the Persian "book of kings"—to support the claim that "we've fallen under the spell of the West, we've forgotten our own stories."[7] At another, he has him parry the Western critique of the embrace of fundamentalism in the Islamic world, claiming that "it is not poverty that brings us close to God [...] no one is more curious than we are to find out why we are here on earth and what will happen to us in the next world," while offering incisive critiques of the ideological inflexibility of the West, among which the rhetorical question, "Can the West endure any democracy achieved by enemies who in no way resemble them?" is the most penetrating.[8] By contrast, virtually all actions associated with resurgent Kemalism in the novel are presented as unqualifiedly crude, regressive, violent, vulgar, and authoritarian.

Yet it's exactly when Blue's ability to surprise Ka and the reader alike with the thoughtfulness of his positions is most pronounced that Pamuk chooses to display Blue's credulity, jealousy, and egotism in ways that predictably accord with prevailing Western views of political Islam.[9] Pretending that he really is the cosmopolitan Westernized intellectual the provincial residents of Kars take him for (instead of the timid exile he is in fact, who has virtually no interactions with the German residents of Frankfurt), Ka pointedly baits Blue with the fabricated story of his friendship with one Hans Hansen, whom he presents as an editor of a Frankfurt newspaper that might be willing to publish a "statement" by Blue. (Hans Hansen, we learn, is actually the name of the Frankfurt salesman who sold Ka his beautiful charcoal woolen overcoat: the most conspicuous signifier of Ka's European otherness during his stay in Kars.) Ka starts by claiming that the consummately enlightened Hans Hansen "takes offense when people discuss the West as if it's a single person with a single point of view." But Blue is too tied to his Occidentalist ideology to be persuaded out of his belief that "that's how it is [...] There is, after all, only one West and only one Western point of view," adding, "And we take the opposite point of view."[10] Intent on contesting Blue's unexamined beliefs about "the West," Ka persists, painting an impossibly rosy picture of a Europe in which "Everyone, even the most ordinary grocer, feels compelled to boast of having his own personal views." Ka then takes a different tack, flattering Blue into thinking that his remarks could constitute a "proclamation" and that some "biographical details" about their author might be desirable, to which Blue pompously responds: "'I've prepared those already [...] All they need say is that I'm one of the most prominent Islamists in Turkey and perhaps the entire Middle East."[11]

At this point in their interview, Ka becomes boldly opportunistic. Trying to turn Blue's desire for notoriety into an occasion to get Ipek's father out of his hotel so that he, Ka, can make love to Ipek in his absence, Ka concocts a plan that requires a Kurdish nationalist and an ex-communist (Ipek's father) to co-sign Blue's proclamation in order to improve its chances of being accepted for publication by Hans Hansen. Then, to win Blue's trust in Ka's friendship with the German, Ka fabricates the story of being invited to a family dinner at Hans Hansen's house in which he also seeks to arouse Blue's envy at the comforts and equanimity of the Hansen household. Initially, Blue's confidence in his Occidentalist views of the West would appear stronger than any "facts" to the contrary Ka can fabricate, as evinced by the following exchange prompted by Blue's question, "Did you see a cross on the wall?"

"I don't remember. I don't think so" [said Ka].

"There was a cross, but you probably didn't notice," said Blue. "Contrary to what our own Europe-admiring atheists assume, all European intellectuals take their religion and their crosses very seriously. But when our guys return to Turkey, they never mention this, because all they want to do is use the technological supremacy of the West to prove the superiority of atheism."[12]

The next question Blue asks is possibly more indicative of what Pamuk wants to reveal about his character than is the misguided certainty with which Blue speaks of European intellectuals: "Did they pity you? Did their hearts go out to you because you were a miserable Turk, a lonely destitute political exile, the sort of Turkish nobody that drunken German youths beat up just for the fun of it?"[13] Although Blue is clearly taking pleasure in baiting Ka, one cannot fail to notice how much Blue's construction of the "Turkish nobody's" perceived inferiority to his German host embeds assumptions about his own perceived inferiority that emerge during his first interview with Ka. Blue tells

Ka in this earlier encounter that wherever he walked when he was in Germany

> there was always one German who stood out of the crowd as an object of fascination for me. The important thing was not what I thought of him but what I thought he might be thinking about me; I'd try to see myself through his eyes and imagine what he might be thinking about my appearance, my clothes, the way I moved, my history, where I had just been and where I was going, who I was. It made me feel terrible but it became a habit; I became used to feeling degraded, and I came to understand how my brothers felt.[14]

The nuances of this exercise in transference are hardly lost on Ka who rather perversely proceeds to paint a picture of the increasing comfort he was made to feel in the company of the graciously hospitable Hansens, which he knows will exacerbate Blue's envy and self-pity while contradicting Blue's belief that Ka's pride was crushed in the transaction:

> They were a happy family, but that didn't mean they were flashing smiles every other minute, as we do here even when there's nothing to smile about. Maybe this is why they were happy. For them life was a serious business to be dealt with responsibly. It wasn't a dead-end struggle or a painful ordeal the way it is here. But their gravity of purpose permeated every aspect of their lives. Just as the moons and fishes and suchlike on their curtains helped lift their spirits.[15]

For good measure, Ka closes his account of his lovely evening by returning to the earlier point of contention, "There were no crosses on the walls, just beautiful scenes from the Alps. I would have given anything to see this all again," a remark that elicits Blue's "open revulsion."[16]

Among the many objectionable moves Ka makes in the sequence, one may wonder which one exactly prompts so open a display of contempt on Blue's part. Does Blue simply not credit Ka's cruelly fabricated account? Does he know that he is being toyed with and resent it? Or is his revulsion directed more toward Ka's fawning admiration for the Hansen household than to the content of Ka's story—which, if it were true, would effectively contradict Blue's claim to know all about European intellectuals? In a section of *Violence*, Slavoj Zizek writes:

> The problem with fundamentalists is not that we consider them inferior to us, but rather that they themselves secretly consider themselves inferior. [...] The problem is not cultural difference (their effort to preserve

their identity), but the opposite fact that the fundamentalists are already like us, that secretly they have already internalized our standards and measure themselves by them.[17]

Zizek's formulation is, of course, hardly as original as he seems to assume. It is, moreover, motivated by his dubious (and consoling) assumption that the Western cultural imaginary is so universally influential that it has penetrated the collective unconscious of those who say they hate "us" the most. Indeed, how can Zizek presume to know that the same standards "we" measure ourselves by have been internalized by "the fundamentalists," as if either "we" or "they" can be construed in the same inclusive generalization Blue seeks to apply to European intellectuals in *Snow*? What space does such a formulation allow for other, more penetrating and less easily assimilable observations made by Blue or by the religious schoolboys in the course of the novel? (Could Zizek, for example, imagine a religious schoolboy whose sincerest aim is to write Islamic science fiction?) In the event, it is the obsequious way in which Ka mimes his devotion to the European liberal-humanist dream, with its "gravity of purpose" that can still make room for the "moons and fishes" of childlike optimism, and that seems best designed to prompt Blue's "revulsion," though Blue surely must know that Ka's happy evening with his good Germans has been ramped up (if not invented) for his benefit. And the fact that Blue *is* repelled, either by Ka's performance of inferiority, or by Hans Hansen's perfectly ordered commonwealth, speaks well for Blue's capacity to exercise standards of measurement that are arguably his own.

Blue is, however, hardly a predictable character as Pamuk writes him; he is as much a "pretender" as we assume others might be in his position, and far from orthodox either in his professions or behavior. Indeed, his dialogues with Ka often make him seem more intent on enjoying notoriety than on effecting radical social change. But for a self-styled political Islamist, Blue is more eloquent, perceptive, and penetrating than Zizek might care to imagine, and also more of a true believer. In this respect, among others, Blue resists another of the established theses about fundamentalist radicalism that Zizek recirculates in *Violence*: that it is a "shield" erected "in panic" against the too sudden, and insufficiently mediated, onrush of modernization. Lacking the "new social narratives and myths [that] slowly came into being" over the course of several centuries in the West, Muslim societies," Zizek claims, "were exposed to this impact without a protective screen or temporal delay, so their symbolic universe was perturbed much more brutally."[18] The problem with this thesis is the extent to which it flatters the West into thinking it has a veritable monopoly both on what is thought or thinkable in the rest of the world and on keeping pace with the "onrush of modernization" it has set into motion. (How, one wonders, does "the West" explain to itself the regressive belief of tens of millions of modern Americans in apocalyptic religious fantasies and collateral disbelief in evolution?) Pamuk resists this thesis not only by presenting the spiritual content of Islam in compelling ways, and by advancing the counterthesis that poverty and irresponsible governance are the truer breeding ground of political Islam, but also by asserting the thinkability of different thoughts in the Islamic world. As noted earlier, Blue is allowed to make this point himself when he movingly recounts the "thousand-year-old story" of Suhrab and Rustem and concludes:

> Once upon a time, millions of people knew it by heart—from Tabriz to Istanbul from Bosnia to Trabzon—and when they recalled it they found the meaning in their lives. The story spoke to them in just the same way that Oedipus' murder of his father and Macbeth's obsession with power and death speak to people throughout the Western world. But now, because we've fallen under the spell of the West, we've forgotten our old stories. They've removed all the old stories from our children's textbooks. These days, you can't find a single bookseller who stocks the *Shehname* in all of Istanbul! How do you explain this?[19]

At the same time, of course, the displacement of such books by "the spell of the West," which this passage both laments and confirms, leads us back, inexorably, to a second reckoning with Zizek's thesis concerning the Islamist's alleged internalization of a sense of inferiority. It also intriguingly resonates with Edward Said's discussion of "the troubling, disabling, destabilizing secular wound," which he considers "the essence of the cosmopolitan, from which there can be no recovery, no state of resolved or Stoic calm," but which Blue seeks to seal with the imprint of a religion whose provenance is, as Said confirms, profoundly syncretic.[20]

How would Pamuk—or Blue—explain how things have reached this pass? Is it primarily the fault of the imperializing force, or the technological superiority, of the West? Is it mainly attributable to the alleged weakness, inferiority, or backwardness of Islamic religious cultures and civilizations? Are powerful outposts of global capitalism like Saudi Arabia and a history of authoritarian governments like those of Kemalist Turkey, Mubarak's Egypt, and Saddam's Iraq also to blame? Or could it rather be owing to the powerfully repressive counterforce of political Islam, and its puritanical suppression of traditional music, dance, art, and literature? Although Blue doesn't mention it, while high-culture markers like the *Shehname* may have become conspicuously absent from the bookstalls of the Middle East, the *Koran* has never been so ubiquitous. How would Blue explain *this*? He would likely beg the question, and take the tact he pursues in his last interview with Ka, stressing the difference between the communitarian basis of Islamic practice and belief, and the incapacity of so Europeanized an "individual" as Ka is to comprehend the love of God:

> "I don't want to destroy your illusions, but your love for God comes out of Western romantic novels," said Blue. "In a place like this, if you worship God as a European, you're bound to be a laughing stock. Then you cannot even believe you believe. You don't belong to this country; you're not even a Turk anymore. First try to be like everyone else. Then try to believe in God."[21]

As other moments in Blue's interactions with Ka make clear, a distinct leveling impulse informs Blue's take on political Islam, which specifically precludes a "typical little European from Nisantas" like Ka from even claiming identification as a Turk. Although the West has cast its spell over Ka and the privileged class he represents, it has not presumably had its way with Blue who, in the same interview, also claims, "I refuse to be a European, and I won't ape their ways. I'm going to live out my own history and be no one but myself. I for one believe it's possible to be happy without becoming a mock European, without becoming their slave."[22]

"The Explosive Barrier of Symbols"

The process of his evolution from "godless leftist" to religious militant that Blue describes in the autobiographical remarks he passes on to Ka in their final interview is described as being mediated by his "hatred of the West," his admiration for Iran's Islamic revolution, and the inspiration of "Frantz Fanon's work on violence," among other things.[23] Though it has its basis in an unexplained feeling of hatred, Blue's transformation is otherwise logical and coherent. And it has sustained itself over the course of Blue's service in the wars in Chechnya and Bosnia, in which he pointedly claims never to have killed anyone, thereby establishing his commitment to his professed ideals while avoiding being easily assigned the role of wild-eyed terrorist. The transformation of workaday

Egyptian *fellaheen* into observant Muslims, described by Amitav Ghosh in his 1992 book, *In an Antique Land*, is a very different process and far less romantic than the fictional Blue's passage through post–Cold War hotspots, political exile in Germany, and the development of a self-styled notorious identity in Turkey. But it too appears to have its basis in a specific relationship of inferiority to the West.

Ghosh weaves two narratives through a work of nonfiction that starts by recounting a period of anthropological fieldwork in Egypt in 1980, ends by describing return visits to Egypt made in 1988 and 1990 (at the beginning of the first Gulf War), and in between involves Ghosh's reconstruction of the movements of a twelfth-century Jewish merchant and his Muslim slave from Egypt through Aden to the western coast of India and back. By the time of Ghosh's second visit, "All the brightest young men had beards, and many more wore white robes as well," but according to Jabir, one of Ghosh's more articulate interlocutors, it was no longer "safe to look like a Muslim" given the government's fears about political Islam's threat to its authority.[24] In Ghosh's version of Zizek's thesis, the path Jabir takes to orthodox Islam can be contextualized by what Ghosh calls "the real and desperate seriousness of [the *fellaheen's*] engagement with modernism," their seeing "the material circumstances of their lives in exactly the same way that a university economist would: as a situation that was shamefully anachronistic, a warp upon time." What prompts Ghosh's articulation of this thesis is the refusal of a group of fellaheen to believe that Ghosh's India, a place they associate with the manufacture of diesel water pumps, hence, as far above them on the "ladder of 'Development.'" could possibly house peasants "in adobe villages [who] turned the earth with cattle-drawn ploughs" as they still did in Egypt.[25]

In 1980, the 17-year-old Jabir was prouder than any other of his fellow villagers at having a man from such an advanced country in their midst. The Jabir that Ghosh meets in 1988, however, is more conflicted by his recent experiences with "modernism." Their first conversation begins when Jabir does what to Ghosh seems an astonishing thing given all the time he has spent in the two Egyptian villages in question, that is, lock the door to his room, thereby shutting out the boys who have been following them through the village as well as the rest of Jabir's family, for whom the closing off of private space is (allegedly) a new concept. Jabir then recounts his years at a nearby university, the camaraderie of friends made there, his learning "the real meaning of Islam," a summer job spent working construction in Iraq, a stint in the army, and his present job as a bricklayer while he waits for a "government job to which he is entitled by virtue of his college degree."[26] But the optimistic narrative is broken by Jabir's implied certainty that the government job won't materialize, and that if he wants to marry and achieve the level of self-respect his younger brother has already achieved, he will have to return to Iraq soon.

None of Ghosh's interlocutors are as sweet, funny, or as pure of heart as Pamuk's fictional religious schoolboys. Like Jabir, they pragmatically attempt to reckon with lives in which "the relations between different kinds of people [...] had been upturned and rearranged" in the space of six years, largely because of the Iran-Iraq war, which, according to Ghosh, placed Iraq in desperate "need of labour to sustain its economy."[27] While many better-off young men stayed at home for college and fell under the spell of Islam, their poorer neighbors went off to Iraq and returned with televisions, refrigerators, and enough money to marry and add additional floors to their parents' homes.

When Ghosh returns for a last time in 1990, at the beginning of the Gulf War, everything has changed again. In the last page of the book, he recounts watching the news on a color TV that another of his young interlocutors has brought back from Iraq. What they saw was

> footage of the epic exodus: thousands and thousands of men, some in trousers, some in jallabeyyas, some carrying their TV sets on their backs, some crying out for a drink of water, stretching all the way from the horizon to the Red Sea, standing on the beach as though waiting for the water to part.[28]

In addition to alluding to the reverse exodus across the Red Sea on which Moses led the Jews (which Said explores in his book *Freud and the non-European*), this passage speaks to the deeper theme that links *In an Antique Land* to *Snow*, and, by extension, to the role played by the *other* in narratives of national self-definition set in North Africa and the Middle East (see, for another example, Tayeb al-Salih's *Season of Migration to the North*).[29] For Ghosh as for Pamuk, that *other* is *the modernist West* broadly considered, the always already apparent elephant in the room around which Ka's debates with Blue pivot, which makes its intrusive presence felt even more in an earlier exchange between Ghosh and a deeply ethnocentric Imam. This conversation gets off to a bad start when the Imam speaks of Hindus as knowingly as Blue speaks of European intellectuals—claiming that "They worship cows" and "burn their dead" and will never progress if they "carry on doing these things."[30] But it turns positively surreal when the Imam and

Ghosh—"delegates from two superseded civilizations, vying with each other to establish a prior claim to the technology of modern violence"— get into a quarrel about whether India or Egypt has better bombs and guns, which is ignited by what Ghosh terms "the explosive barrier of symbols"[31] that has been erected far from the purview of Egypt or India alike. As Ghosh concludes: "Despite the vast gap that lay between us, we understood each other perfectly. We were both travelling he and I: we were travelling in the West."[32]

Coda

A chapter in *Fragments of Culture: the Everyday of Modern Turkey* (2002) begins by remarking an incident in February, 1998, in Istanbul when a small plane commissioned by the Turkish national postal service (or PTT) showered thousands of leaflets on a large-scale demonstration of "thousands of students from different universities holding different ideological views ranging from leftist to nationalist rightist, and Islamist to liberal democrat" who rallied to protest "a new circular from the Ministry of Education banning headscarves and beards in universities." Unusual as it already was to have generally opposed parties unite in defense of a cause so closely identified with political Islam, the scene became odder still when the message of the leaflets was made plain, that being the PTT's offer to provide "free service for people to send faxes to the English-language weekly *Time* in order to elevate Ataturk from second to first in their survey of the most influential people of the twentieth century" (a standing that had already been inflated by an energetic get-out-the-vote effort conducted over the Internet).[33] The author of the chapter, Ayse Saktanber, interprets "both the content and the image of this episode as a graphic depiction of Turkey's predicament, which can be formulated as 'modernisation from above, Islamisation from below,'" while being careful to note that "in this demonstration these Islamist students [...] were not against the Turkish state as such, but rather Kemalism as the official ideology of the republic and its westernizing project," and were engaged in an effort "both to build an identity and represent their 'otherness.'"[34]

Roughly 13 years after this collision between resurgent Kemalism and headscarf demonstrators, with Recep Tayyip Erdogan, the head of Turkey's Islamic Justice and Development Party (AKP), serving a second successive term as prime minister, it would appear that some of the wider gaps between modernization and Islamization have been bridged. Indeed, Ghosh's "explosive barrier of symbols" may itself be in the process of dissolution as the spell of anxiety and emulation the West has long cast over Turkey and the rest of the Middle East also begins to lift. Pamuk himself has recently remarked "the fading" of the "rose-colored dream of Europe," which was "once so powerful that even our most anti-Western thinkers and politicians secretly believed in it," either "because Turkey is no longer as poor as it once was," or "because it is no longer a peasant society ruled by its army, but a dynamic nation with a strong civil society of its own." More pointedly, Pamuk contends that "Turkey and other non-Western countries [have become] disenchanted with Europe" because of its "callousness toward the sufferings of immigrants and minorities, and the castigation of Asians, Africans, and Muslims now leading difficult lives in [its] peripheries." Such attitudes and behaviors indicate Europe's lack of faith in its own "fundamental values," while retrospectively confirming Blue's suspicion that the evening Ka spent with Hans Hansen's family was nothing but a tall tale.[35]

Notes

1. According to *Spiegel Online International*, January 23, 2006, Pamuk "was charged with the criminal offense following an interview he gave the Swiss newspaper *Tages Anzeiger* in February 2005. In the interview he said that 30,000 people had died in the conflict between the Turkish security forces and Kurdish nationalists, and that 1 million Armenians had died in Turkey during World War I, and [that] 'nobody but me dares to talk about it.' Official Turkish policy is to deny that there was any genocidal campaign against the Armenians, claiming that they died along with many ethnic Turks during the collapse of the Ottoman Empire. Pamuk's comments provoked outrage amongst right-wing nationalists in Turkey. The writer was then charged under Article 301, which makes it illegal to insult the republic, parliament or any organs of state." http://www.spiegel.de/international/0,1518,396786,00.html

2. As Pamuk writes, "Fear of the political Islamists was so great that [. . .] not even in their sleep could [the National Theater audience] have imagined the state forcing women to remove their head scarves as it had done in the early years of the Republic" (148). All quotations from *Snow* are drawn from Orhan Pamuk, *Snow*, trans. Maureen Freely (New York: Vintage, 2004). Orig. *Kar* (Istanbul: Iletism, 2002).

3. Pamuk, p. 148.

4. Ibid., p. 425.

5. Ibid., pp. 15–16, 25.

6. Ibid., p. 98. Ka refers to this "mocking devil inside him" as he unsuccessfully tries to purge himself of such "Western" tendencies as his "need

for solitude" (97) and habitual skepticism during his interview with Sheikh Efendi in chapter 11. Islamists like Blue feel it more projectively, anticipating that they will be perceived as inferiors in interchanges with Europeans.

7. Ibid., pp. 77, 78–79.
8. Ibid., p. 228.
9. These views have been rearticulated in Slavoj Zizek's recent diagnosis of Islamic *ressentiment*. According to Zizek, "What [terrorist fundamentalists] lack is a feature that is easy to discern in all authentic fundamentalists, from Tibetan Buddhists to the Amish in the U.S.: the absence of resentment and envy, the deep indifference towards the non-believers' way of life. If today's so-called fundamentalists really believe they have found their way to truth, why should they feel threatened by non-believers, why should they envy them?" He adds that "Deep in themselves, terrorist fundamentalists also lack true conviction—their violent outbursts are proof of it. How fragile the belief of a Muslim must be, if he feels threatened by a stupid caricature in a low-circulation Danish newspaper." In Slavoj Zizek, *Violence* (New York: Picador, 2008), pp. 85–86.
10. Pamuk, p. 228. Cf. Zizek: "Those who propose the term 'Occidentalism' as the counterpart to Edward Said's 'Orientalism' are right up to a point: what we get in Muslim countries is a certain ideological vision of the West which distorts Western reality no less, though in a different way, than the Orientalist vision distorts the Orient," *Violence*, p. 60.
11. Pamuk, pp. 228–229.
12. Ibid., p. 230.
13. Ibid., p. 231.
14. Ibid., p. 73.
15. Ibid., p. 232.
16. Ibid., p. 232.
17. Zizek, p. 86.
18. Ibid., p. 82.
19. Ibid., p. 78.
20. See Edward Said, *Freud and the Non-European* (London: Verso, 2003), 54. While the fictional Blue would likely be happy to approve Freud's assignment of an Egyptian origin to Moses, he would be less keen about having to concede the European provenance of many of his political ideas: this despite his own Orientalist valorization of what is, after all, a classic *Persian*—as opposed to a Turkish—text. The sixteenth-century assimilation of other Persian cultural artifacts and artistic practices by the Ottomans is one of the principal stories embedded in Pamuk's earlier novel *My Name is Red*, trans., Erdağ M. Göknar (New York: Vintage, 2001). Orig. *Benim Adim Kirmizi* (Istanbul: Iletisim, 1998).
21. Pamuk, p. 327.
22. Ibid., p. 324.
23. Ibid., pp. 321–323.

24. Amitav Ghosh, *In an Antique Land* (New York: Vintage 1992), p. 295.
25. Ibid., p. 200.
26. Ibid., pp. 308, 311.
27. Ibid., pp. 321, 293.
28. Ibid., p. 353.
29. In particular, see the chapter entitled "'Like Othello': Tayeb Salih's *Season of Migration* and Postcolonial Self-Fashioning" in my book, Thomas Cartelli, *Repositioning Shakespeare: National Formations, Postcolonial Appropriations* (London: Routledge, 1999), pp. 147–168.
30. Ghosh pp. 234–235.
31. Ibid., p. 210.
32. Ibid., p. 236.
33. Ayse Saktanber, "'We Pray Like You Have Fun': New Islamic Youth in Turkey: Between Intellectualism and Popular Culture," in *Fragments of Culture: The Everyday of Modern Turkey*, ed. Deniz Kandiyoti and Ayse Saktanber (New Brunswick, NJ: Rutgers University Press, 2002), pp. 254–255.
34. Saktanber, p. 255.
35. Orhan Pamuk, "The Fading Dream of Europe," *NYR* Blog, December 25, 2010. http://www.nybooks.com/blogs/nyrblog/2010/dec/25/fading-dream-europe/

PART IV

Pamuk and Translation/Untranslation

CHAPTER 10

Orhan Pamuk's *Kara Kitap* [*The Black Book*]: A Double Life in English

Sevinç Türkkan

> No translation would be possible if in its essence it strove for likeness to the original. For in its afterlife—which could not be called that if it were not a transformation and a renewal of something living—the original undergoes a change.
>
> —Walter Benjamin, "The Task of the Translator"[1]

Since its publication in 1990, Orhan Pamuk's *Kara Kitap* [*The Black Book*] has generated volumes of critical essays, which read it as a theory of the postmodern novel,[2] a bildungsroman,[3] a picaresque novel,[4] a detective novel, an encyclopedic novel, an experiment in innovation of the Turkish language and syntax,[5] a cultural history of Istanbul,[6] a quest in the tradition of mystical Islam,[7] and an elaborate mediation on identity.[8] Moving beyond these readings of the book, I turn my eye to its English translators. Taking my cue from Walter Benjamin's words above, I investigate the "afterlife" of *Kara Kitap* in English translations and illuminate how they have informed the reception and interpretation of the novel away from the language of its origin.

Pamuk belongs to a generation of Turkish writers who emerged after the 1980s. After the 1980s, Turkish politics and culture radically transitioned from leftist-socialist to neoliberal worldviews. The writers of the earlier era preoccupied themselves with political realism. Writers of Pamuk's generation have been reworking Ottoman cultural and historical themes while also engaging with "Ottamanesque" style and experimenting with Turkish language in ways that is no longer "threatening" to readers concerned with representations of national identity.[9] Strikingly different from the language of his previous novels, in *Kara Kitap*, Pamuk writes in a dense and elaborate Turkish, brings in culturally resonant idiom and colloquialisms, and at times switches to lofty language and formal decorousness. He uses new and old language registers, experiments with language and syntax, and creates a complex narrative rich in allusions, sound, and meaning. He transforms formal and syntactical aspects of the language to reveal his mastery in traditional storytelling and journalistic writing. While some chapters in the novel provide insights into the talk of the commoner and the everyday spoken dialects of Turkish, others use elevated tone and archaic vocabulary to echo forgotten histories and erased languages. The author boldly experiments with language, mixes styles, and even pushes the standards of Turkish grammar. *Kara Kitap* is rich in postmodern literary tricks, intertextual and metatextual allusions, and stretches the limits of the genre, the novel.

Pamuk's cosmopolitan image at home and abroad depends heavily on the work of his translators. He became well known in the English-speaking world with his sixth novel *My Name is Red*[10] [*Benim Adım Kırmızı*] in Erdağ Göknar's award-winning translation.[11] However, by that time, Pamuk had already had two other translators, Victoria Holbrook, who translated *The White Castle*[12] [*Beyaz Kale*] and Güneli Gün, who translated two of his novels, *The Black Book*[13] [*Kara Kitap*] and *The New Life*[14] [*Yeni Hayat*]. At present Maureen Freely is known as his "definitive" translator.[15] It is important to note that Pamuk was introduced to English readership with *The White Castle* in Holbrook's straightforward and unadorned British English. This is significant since for English readers Holbrook's translation came to represent Pamuk's style and set the context in which subsequent translations were going to be read and received.

Gün's translation of *The Black Book* and *The New Life* received harsh criticism especially from British reviewers who complained that her use of idiomatic American English was inappropriate. Reviewing the novel for the *Times Literary Supplement*, Ronald Wright wrote, "I suspect the grace notes have suffered in translation. Pamuk is known as a stylist, but the slangy AmerEnglish offered here does not suit the setting."[16] Another reviewer, the novelist and poet Donald M. Thomas found Gün's language to be "polished if slightly stilted English,"[17] and the British novelist and critic Adam Mars-Jones commented that the text is "hardly a pleasure to read...and here the blame seems to lie squarely with the translator Güneli Gün. Her familiarity with Turkish is not in question, it is her familiarity with English that seems so debatable."[18] Most book reviewers have neither the time nor the inclination, nor the language skills necessary to compare the original and the translation or to consider the validity of their opinion. Nevertheless, their comments can break a book, a translator, and a fine writer. They attack Gün's language, but they do not read the original Turkish text; how do they know what Pamuk's prose is really like?

This case of translation and reviews becomes especially striking when we consider the context in which it is taking place. There is an enormous imbalance between the vast and versatile literary output of the literature written in Turkish and Ottoman languages and what is published in English translation from this significant yet overlooked literary canon. The 2008 PEN/IRL report on literary translation surveys the current condition of the literary trade around the world, providing dramatic data on its imbalance.[19] The United States ranks very low in the number of translated books published each year. Only 2.6 percent of all the books published in the United States are translations. This number gains particular significance when compared to 72.5 percent, which is the average for translated books in Turkey every year.[20] The pervasive monolingualism of the United States, exacerbated by its traditional disregard for foreign-language study, has resulted in enervating insularity, leading to increased isolation within the world community. This lamentable situation has resulted in a serious imbalance and disconnect to the point where all literatures of the world are assumed to have been written in English since they "exist" only when and as long as they are translated into English. In publishing and academic circles, there has been a significant effort in bringing recognition to the invaluable place of translations as well as to translators as creative writers. Yet, there is still much to be accomplished in educating the common reader and the book reviewer and critic. Bibliographies of Turkish literature in English translation reveal that every year an average of only ten literary works (novels and short stories and poetry anthologies) originally written in Turkish are made available to English readers.[21] In this context and given this dire translational scene and imbalance between literatures in translation, Pamuk's *Kara Kitap* appeared in a new English translation in 2006, thus becoming the only Turkish novel to receive two English translations.

Gün's initial translation of *The Black Book* (1994), its negative reception in the *Times Literary Supplement* and in other London publications, Pamuk's Nobel Prize (2006), and the eventual new translation of *The Black Book* (2006) by Freely present an interesting case study. It raises a multiplicity of questions: although both *The Black Book* and *The New Life* in Gün's translation were harshly criticized, why is it that only *The Black Book* appears in a new translation? Why is it that Pamuk's first two novels *Cevdet Bey ve Oğullari*[22] [*Cevdet Bey and Sons*] and *Sessiz Ev*[23] [*Silent House*] haven't been translated into English yet? How has Pamuk's image as an international writer evolved and is supported by the translations since the Nobel Prize? How can we account for the differences between Gün's and Freely's translations when both versions tell the same story but stylistically in two entirely different ways?

At the heart of *The Black Book* lies a search, a search for a beloved, for an ideal, and for an authentic self. The plot is deliberately simple. A young lawyer, Galip, returns home one evening to find out that his beautiful wife Rüya has left him. He then embarks on a literal journey to search for his runaway wife in the backstreets of Istanbul. Rüya's disappearance coincides with that of Celâl's, Galip's cousin and the famous newspaper columnist. When Galip's physical search proves futile, he embarks on a more intellectual journey. He moves into Celâl's apartment to read his archive, literally to acquire his memory banks, and find clues as to where Rüya and Celâl might be hiding. Eventually, he loses Rüya and Celâl—they are murdered—which is a necessary stage in his bildung in order to assert his self and emerge as a writer. Pamuk inserts this simple plot into a complex structure: he writes a polyphonic, polyvalent, allusive, obscurantist, and an unstable narrative in which chapters of storytelling alternate with chapters of Celâl's newspaper columns. The novel is a labyrinthine quest through the city of Istanbul, encompassing an encyclopedia of Turkish life past and present with its cultural delights and historical shames.

The opening of *The Black Book* as well as the entire novel suggests a double plane of illusion and reality, which is the major concern of the book. Every story, allusion, pun, and even color connects with this double plane. The title of the first chapter reads "Galip Rüya'yi İlk Gördüğünde" ["When Galip saw Rüya for the First Time"]. For the Turkish reader the pun on the name Rüya, which also means "dream" is obvious. In Turkish, the title of this chapter reads "when Galip saw *Rüya* for the first time" and "when Galip saw *the dream* for the first time" (emphasis mine). This is also justified by the fact that the character Rüya does not have a physical presence in the text, and the question of whether she belongs to the world of reality or that of illusion remains unclear throughout the novel. Similar to the writings of postmodernist writers, Pamuk denies us anything that might read as a clear clue to an unequivocal reading. The narrative point of view is unreliable. The search is circular and multilayered. The frame story is Galip's search for his lost wife, which merges with the search for a lost older cousin, Celâl, Galip's alterego, second-self, double, and his literary father. These two searches run parallel to merge with a more existential one, that of Galip's search for his self. The multiple acts of storytelling make the novel a metafiction, and all the stories merge into one to make the novel an allegorical tale of Platonic search.

Gün's translation gave Pamuk's *Kara Kitap* a living voice in idiomatic American language, which is at times irreverently colloquial and at times intensely erudite, as is the original. She met the demand of Pamuk's impressionistic use of Perso-Arabic, Turkic, and pure Turkish language registers with Latinate, Anglo-Saxon, and contemporary words and expressions. As a creative writer herself,[24] she interprets the novel by emphasizing its intertextual and metatextual aspects, thereby attracting attention to language, rewriting, and translation as mediation. Her translation highlights the novel's intertextuality with Western and Christian canonical texts, prioritizing them to political, social, language- and culture-specific references in the original. In this sense, she is a visible translator, which is precisely what was disquieting for British reviewers. As Lawrence Venuti points out, translation is acceptable

> when it reads fluently, when the absence of any linguistic or stylistic peculiarities makes it seem transparent, giving the appearance that it reflects the foreign writer's personality or intention or the essential meaning of the foreign text—the appearance, in other words, that the translation is not in fact a translation, but the "original."[25]

Venuti traces the covert existence of the translator in texts that conform to the British canon of fluency and transparency, which is the practice of concealing the translator under the illusion that it was originally written in English. The illusion of transparency is shattered, however, if a translator uses a language other than the standard English, which was the case with Gün's translation. Gün's colloquial and idiomatic American English disquieted British reviewers. What they would have perceived as a transparent translation is not at all transparent but mediated, the kind of translation that subsumes all authors from various cultures into the dominant voice, thereby domesticating the foreign element. Although logically a translation is the work of two authors, we trick ourselves into thinking that we are reading the original words of the first author. However, the translator's text is a work of her own creativity, an interpretation, a construct, and a reflection of her own worldview and not simply a revelation of that of the first author. The other major translation strategy that Venuti identifies besides "domesticating" is "foreignizing," that is, making the text opaque, which calls attention to itself by using archaisms that distance the text both from the original and also from the prevailing values of the target culture. Rightfully, Venuti's agenda is to call attention to and recognition for the work of the translator as creative art, thus championing the foreignizing strategy. However, when discussing these strategies it is necessary to make concrete the context in which translation takes place. Venuti works with the Italian language and culture, which are readily available to the Anglo-American world. When translating from Turkish into English, the strategy of foreignizing would not serve the same end. As Marilyn Booth, an eminent translator and scholar who works with the Arabic language and literature, has pointed out, some cultures are already considered foreign, distant, and unavailable to the Anglo-American world that rather than foreignizing, "the task of creating sympathy and identification with a work and its characters is a particularly urgent one."[26] Similarly, translating from Turkish into English entails careful ethical and translational strategies. When Gün translated Pamuk's novel, he did not have the Nobel Prize, *The Black Book* was only his second novel to be translated into English,[27] and the world of the Turk was (and is still) considered foreign, distant, and unavailable. Further "foreignizing" of that world would be keeping alive the myth of the "unspeakable Turk." Gün's translation needs to be understood in this context. Reducing her translation as "domesticating" because it is rendered predominantly in American idiom or as "foreignizing" as it reads to British reviewers would be homogenizing her work, which otherwise crosses a multiplicity of linguistic registers and styles.

Gün is not only a translator but also a creative writer who, although born and raised in Turkey, now lives in the United States and writes in English. Her two novels, *Book of Trances*[28] and *On the Road to Baghdad*,[29] were well received even in the pages of the *Times Literary Supplement*, where her translations were condemned. It would be limiting to study her translation without closely considering the translator's work as a creative writer. There are similarities between Gün's idiosyncrasies as a creative writer and the way she translated Pamuk's *Kara Kitap* into English. In her own novels, Gün comes across as a postmodern writer, who exposes history as a myth. In line with her affinity for postmodern literary devices and ransacking archival material, Gün translates

The Black Book by emphasizing its intertextual and metatextual aspects, thereby attracting attention to the mediated nature of the act of writing and rewriting. The translation reveals her concerns with her own image as an immigrant writer in the United States, who writes in English, a nonnative tongue, and employs Turkish and Ottoman historical and cultural themes. She reveals sensitivity to the mainstream American reading and writing public's lack of interest in "other" literatures and themes. Her translational strategies demonstrate her concern with how the text and the literature it represents are going to be received by the target audience.[30] Her translation is significant as a case study of a specific moment in the history of translation from Turkish into English, when the target audience's interest in Turkish literature and culture was limited. Interest in Turkish literature and in literary translation from Turkish into English has increased after Pamuk received the Nobel Prize in 2006. Gün's translation needs to be situated and understood within this specific context. In her attempt to create an audience for the translation and for Turkish literature in general, she avoids focusing on the "unintelligible" aspects of the source text, those aspects that do not translate into English or require the immersion of the reader in the specificities of the Turkish literary and cultural history. Rather, she focuses on the text's allusions to Western literary and cultural narratives, thereby facilitating the Western reader's identification with the Turkish text.

Herein, I give one characteristic example[31] of Gün's translation before I proceed to my analysis of Freely's new translation of *The Black Book*. I identify one crucial difference between the original *Kara Kitap* and Gün's translation: the original emphasizes a specific Turkish context and makes strong allusions to Arab and Persian literary traditions while the translation recontextualizes the original Turkish setting, situates the novel within a Judeo-Christian understanding, and emphasizes the novel's intertextual references to Western literary narratives. The most important implication of this difference is that the English text acquires a clear redemptive element, which allows for a positive interpretation of the ending. The original *Kara Kitap* though, is a rather black book, stressed by the author's harsh criticism of the contradictions of modern-day Turkey.

Although in her translation Gün retains the names of the characters as they are (except that she spells "Celal" as "Jelal," the implications of which I discuss here), she has the protagonist Galip look up the meaning of the names in a dictionary of Ottoman Turkish:

Galip has read Rüya's name for the first time on one of the postcards that grandma stuck into the frame of the mirror on the buffet where the liqueur sets were kept. *It hadn't surprised him that Rüya meant "dream"; but later, when they began figuring out the secondary meanings of the names, they were astonished to find in a dictionary of Ottoman Turkish that Galip meant "victor" and Jelal "fury."*[32]

Gün adds the entire last sentence above at a strategic moment in the first chapter, thereby ensuring that the target reader understands, in a subtle way, the meaning of the names and their metaphorical implications. While her creative intervention changes the content, it does not deviate from the plot line. A more literal translation of the first chapter would not have retained the intertextual and metatextual aspects of the source text. The sentence above not only reveals the meaning of the names but also directs the reader's attention to specific historical and linguistic concerns of the original novel, such as the Turkish language reforms, the legacy of the Ottoman Empire, and their implications for modern-day Turkey. Gün's intervention both attracts attention to the fact that the reader is reading a translation from Turkish into English and subtly points to the roots of the original language, which might not be known even to modern Turkish readers of today. The characters looking up their names in a dictionary of Ottoman Turkish is also in line with the typical characteristics of the protagonist Galip, who, later in the novel, in a similar manner, consults Jelal's newspaper columns in an attempt to understand the meaning of what he considers to be "clues," that might lead him to Rüya and Jelal.

In addition to meaning "fury," "Jelal" also means "divine" and is one of the 99 names of "Allah" in Islam. Jelal's family name, "Salik," connects with this secondary meaning, since it means "the traveler on Sufi Road."[33] Gün translates the text in such a way that the meaning she does not reveal at the beginning, that is, "divine," gradually reveals itself as the identification between Jelal and Mevlana Celalledin Rumi becomes more apparent. Gün transliterates the original "Celal" as "Jelal," a strategy she follows closely in the rest of her translation. There is an obvious similarity between Gün's "Jelal" and the biblical Jesus figure. Not only the letter "J" but also the characteristics of that character as a savior figure, whom his readers read and follow devoutly and who is murdered at the end, support this interpretation. In one of his columns, Jelal develops an interest in Hurufism, a mystical kabalistic Sufi doctrine based on the belief that things are embodied in letters. The word "hurûf" in Arabic literally means "letters of the Alphabet," and Jelal's study of letters and faces achieves prophetic proportions in the text.[34]

Gün's transliteration of the name "Celal" as "Jelal" adds a Christian point of view to the source text's Sufi overtones. While Islamic mysticism in the form of Sufism might not be intelligible for the English reader, the Christian overtones in the translation function as a moment of identification for Western readers. This translational strategy creates a bridge between otherwise seemingly incompatible religious understandings, the Christian and the Islamic. It is significant that in his review of the novel, Robert Irwin points to the Christian point of view in the novel and comments on the Dantean aspects of Galip's journey.[35] Joan Smith, who reviews the translation for *The Nation*, comments that it is the author Pamuk, who, at a certain point in the text, reveals the meaning of the names.[36] As I demonstrated earlier, it is not Pamuk but Gün's creative intervention and recontextualization of the text that give rise to these comments. These reviews are important in that they reveal how much the translation has shaped the English readers' understanding of the novel. They testify to how reviewers assume textual transparency and ignore the translator's creative agency.

Being situated between two languages and cultures and writing in American English for an American audience have an enormous impact on how Gün writes and translates. This aspect of the writer translator resulted in a unique style and subject matter, which have added a welcoming creativity to Pamuk's novels in English. Her translation of *The Black Book* made the world of the "unspeakable" Turk familiar by highlighting references and allusions to the Western and Judeo-Christian literary and cultural canon. Her primary purpose as a translator was to perform a bridging role between Turkish and American literatures and cultures and to introduce Pamuk to Western readers before he reached international fame. Nevertheless, discouraged by negative reviews and criticism, Pamuk changed his English translator to Erdağ Göknar and eventually to Maureen Freely.

The new translation of *The Black Book* appeared in 2006. The most significant impact of the new translation is that it draws attention to the translator, to translation as an act of mediation and interpretation, and to Turkish literature in general. Most reviews of Gün's translation did not mention at all that they address a text in translation, and negative reviews only served to marginalize the text and its translator. Reviews of Freely's translation almost uniformly hail the text as a "new translation" and acknowledge the translator, albeit in problematic ways, which I discuss herein.

In this part of the chapter, I focus on Freely's translation and analyze it in light of the afterword she wrote to the translation.[37] I draw on other texts, such as her novels, journalistic writing, and interviews, to understand and explain her position as a translator. Freely's translation reveals that she opted to create a clear and a readable text in English. She accomplished this by restructuring the text, adding italics and parentheses where she deemed appropriate, cutting down long sentences and paragraphs, and avoiding transliteration of names. Although her textual editing results in a clear and seemingly transparent and readable text, it also ends up clarifying the literary ambiguities of the original. Her intention to clarify and render the text readable, however, do not explain why she left many words such as, "Istanbullus" [citizens of Istanbul], "hamams" [baths], "meyhanes" [dives], "saz" [stringed musical instrument], "medrese" [seminary], "Istiklal caddesi" [Istiklal avenue or Liberty avenue], the proper name "Alaaddin"[38] [Aladdin] without translating them when they translate into English unproblematically. In particular, in this new translation, the image of the city of Istanbul stands out, supporting the image on the cover of the translation I discussed above.

The new translation, when analyzed carefully in relation to Freely's other writings, reveals the translator's nostalgic attitude to the city and its culture in which she grew up in the 1970s. The special emphasis placed on the city in this new translation also functions to bolster Pamuk's late image as "the writer of the City." Among the Turkish and world writers who have referenced Istanbul as their source of poetic imagination, Pamuk is one whose life and works are most intensely connected with the city's history and textual representations. Pamuk's international fame largely depends on his untiring rewriting and reproducing of the city of Istanbul, of its literary, historical, and architectural archives. Pamuk's personal and professional preoccupation with the city intensified and culminated in 2006 when he was awarded the Nobel Prize for Literature. The announcement of the Swedish Academy cited Pamuk as a writer who in the quest for the melancholic soul of his native city has found symbols for the clash and interweaving of cultures.[39] Since then, Pamuk has seen himself as the Istanbul novelist and has claimed to be the first novelist who has seen the city in its full depth, through its history and geography. He prides himself to have represented the city as part biography and part autobiography. In retrospect, he views *Kara Kitap* as "a personal encyclopedia of Istanbul":

> In *The Black Book*, I finally did something I've been wanting to do for years, a sort of collage, bits of history, bits of future, the present, stories that seem unrelated... To juxtapose [all these] is a good technique

for signifying a meaning that should [only] be intimated, indirectly alluded to.[40]

That is, Pamuk's Istanbul is a text and not a verifiable reality. It is a stage of stories and histories that are projected to the present only in retrospect. The novel and the city represented in it are archives of remembrance and recollection, which, like memory, almost always entail a certain lack or loss.

The trope of the city is one key element that makes this novel "translatable." In his study of national languages of developing nations, Ferguson writes that the language of "minor" cultures at some point of their history is regarded by their own native speakers as "backward" and "inadequate" and believed to require "modernizing" among other aspects.[41] In an effort toward language, literature, and culture modernization, the ultimate criterion is to bring the allegedly "backward" nation to a stage of "translatability" among the "modern" nations of the world. As Ferguson writes, the modernization of a language is the process of its becoming "the equal of other developed languages as medium of communication."[42] It requires the process of joining the world community of increasingly "intertranslatable languages recognized as appropriate vehicles of modern forms of discourse."[43] However, languages do not become "intertranslatable" through equal processes of transformation. "Weaker" languages and literatures are expected to "achieve" one-to-one correspondence with "stronger" ones. Implicitly, translatability is sought by the former and demanded by the latter. This "achievement" or, in other contexts, "modernization" more often than not means serious language, social, and cultural engineering for "developing" countries. The city of Istanbul as an image and literary trope achieves this translatability in Pamuk. It connects him to other international authors such as James Joyce, who capitalizes on the city of Dublin, and the modern flaneur, Charles Baudelaire. As one scholar has pointed out, being a novelist of Istanbul involves making the city readable for the globalized culture of the West.[44] This also explains why Pamuk's first two novels, *Cevdet Bey ve Oğulları* [Cevdet Bey and Sons][45] and *Sessiz Ev* [Silent House],[46] have not been translated into English. The former is an extremely long family saga written in modernist style, and the latter is Pamuk's first experiment with unreliable narration, both of which thematize culture-specific concerns. They do not fit with the author's projected image and therefore "do not translate" into the West.

There is no doubt that Pamuk's position as a Nobel Laureate plays a significant role in the willingness of publishers to issue a new translation. Otherwise, publishing a translation of any book written originally in Turkish is a matter of serious negotiation between the publisher, translator, and author. For publishers, who almost always make decisions based on profit, translations of Turkish literature do not rank high unless the author is award winning or a best seller at home or unless the publisher caters to an academic audience. Pamuk's increased authority also allowed him to supervise the English translations of his novels after the Nobel Prize. The centrality of the city of Istanbul in *Kara Kitap* is another reason why Pamuk pushed for *The Black Book* to appear in a new translation although both *The Black Book* and *The New Life* translated by Gün were harshly criticized. The new translation cannot be studied outside such a socioeconomic and historical context. Yet, relying strictly on a social-causal model to explain the translation runs the risk of overlooking the human element, the translator's creative impact on the final product. It is crucial therefore to study the new translation not only from a diachronic but also from a synchronic perspective.

Before translating *The Black Book*, Maureen Freely already established herself as Pamuk's authoritative translator and has translated his novel *Snow* (2005), his memoir *Istanbul: Memories and the City* (2004), and his essay collection *The Other Colors* (2007). She had the advantage of translating *The Black Book* in retrospect and in light of later developments related to Pamuk's image as an international writer. In the new translation, she tones down Pamuk's exuberance in *Kara Kitap* and simplifies the style to make it compatible with the style of his later books. She highlights the image of the city while the original resonates with the masterpieces of Persian and Arabic literary traditions. The original *Kara Kitap* is a dense and opaque text. Turning it into a clear, readable, and fluent narrative is a mistake. That is, the new translation strongly contributes to the consolidation of Pamuk's late image as the writer of a specific trope—the city—and the master of a specific style—straightforward and unadorned.

In the afterword to the translation, Freely writes:

> We all used Omo detergent, Ipana toothpaste, Job shaving cream, and Sana margarine. I remember a man on a donkey delivering milk straight from the farm. Another man with a horse-drawn cart delivered water. We bought glassware from Pasabahce, Turkey's only glassmaker. Our shoes came from the dozen or so shops lining Istklal caddesi, and our silk scarves from Vakko, Turkey's only department store.[47]

The most significant aspect of this afterword is that it is heavily marked by Freely's nostalgia related to the city of Istanbul. Nostalgia (from *nostos*, meaning to return home, and *algia*, meaning longing) is longing for home that no longer exists or has never existed (*OED*). It is not only a sentiment of loss and displacement but also a "romance" with one's own fantasy.[48] The word "nostalgia" does not appear in the Index of Freud's *Standard Collected Works* although Freud comes close to discussing the concept when he analyzes the psychology of grief in his essay "Mourning and Melancholia." In this essay, Freud writes that melancholia develops in a form of grief for a lost object or for a loss of any kind, a situation in which "one cannot see clearly what has been lost" and which Freud relates to "an unconscious loss."[49] That is, in melancholia the loss is of an ideal kind. Although, like Freud, Goethe never uses the word "nostalgia," he offers a connection between the two concepts: nostalgia is "reviv[ing] an innocent past with sweet melancholy."[50] In her book *The Future of Nostalgia*, Svetlana Boym offers a useful distinction between the two concepts. While melancholia confines itself to the planes of individual consciousness, nostalgia is about the relationship between individual biography and that of a group or nations, between the personal and the collective.[51]

What interests me in Freely's nostalgia is not the impossibility of reviving a home, real or imaginary, but the sentiment itself, the melancholy, and its stylization. In other words, I use the term "nostalgia" to point to Freely's specific situation with regard to the city of Istanbul and how her idealization and recollection of the place explains the translation and represents her response to the present. Nostalgia, creative and stylized, is an artistic device and a strategy of survival, a way of making sense of the impossibility of going back. Translating *The Black Book* gave Freely an opportunity to revisit and explore an imagined homeland. Similarly, in *Enlightenment*[52], the novel she wrote after translating *The Black Book*, Freely develops an aesthetic of "having been there" and longing for a distant home. She cherishes Istanbul's distance but does not consider going back there. She remains attached to where she is now, which allows her to reimagine and aestheticize the city from afar.

In the first chapter of the book, when Galip's grandparents discuss Celal's writings and complain that he disgraces them by revealing family secrets in his newspaper column, the grandfather says "Apartman yazısında bizim apartmandan sözettiğini kim bilmiyor ki allahaşkına!" [For Heaven's sake, who doesn't know that the building he writes about in his column is our apartment building!][53] Freely's "For love of God, can there be anyone *in this city* who does not know that the apartment he mentions in that column is the one in which we sit?"[54] Here as well as throughout the novel, Freely inserts references to the city when in the original there are none. This also connects to how Freely translates another very central image in the novel, the name of the apartment building: Şehrikalp Apartmentı. Here, Pamuk draws on Şeyh Galip's Ottoman Turkish romance *Hüsn Aşk* [*Beauty and Love*], where Aşk [Love] is banished to "Diyar-ı Kalp" or to the "Land of the Hearts"[55] to conjure the alchemy in order to be worthy of Hüsn's hand. One has to understand this allegory in light of the Sufi understanding of unity-of-being ontology. In this allegory Aşk's journey to "Diyar-ı Kalp" stands for the inner journey and the path of the dervish undertaken in order to realize the true nature of existence. On the path to Diyar-ı Kalp, Aşk overcomes obstacles, which symbolizes his completion of "the journey through the levels of the soul at the point where it connects with spirit."[56] He enters the Land of the Heart, which he never actually left, only that now his soul is purified, and his heart can see clearly, and he sees that Beauty is there, in his heart. He comes to an understanding that thus far his perception was awry, and that, in fact, he has never been separated from her. In reality, Love is Beauty and Beauty is Love. This realization takes place in Aşk's heart and "Diyar-ı Kalp" stands for the heart.

In *Kara Kitap*, Pamuk alludes to "Diyar-ı Kalp" by naming the apartment building "Şehrikalp" and adopts the theme of an inward journey. In the beginning, Galip literally searches for Rüya and Celal on the streets of Istanbul until he ends up at Celal's apartment in "Şehrikalp Apartmanı." Here, he embarks on an intellectual journey through Celal's writings in order to acquire "his memory banks" and to find out where they might be hiding. In analogy with Şeyh Galip's allegory, Pamuk's Galip fails literally to find them. Rather, he undergoes a journey inward and eventually realizes his potential as a writer in Celal's apartment, in Şehrikalp Apartmanı.

Freely translates the name of the building as "the City-of-Hearts Apartment."[57] However, "the City of Hearts" carries a completely different meaning from what Pamuk's original intention was. This turns out to be the central image in the translation and connects with the setting of the novel, the city of Istanbul. This might be the reason why many of the reviews of the new translation read the texts as a "city novel." Also, Freely's translation, "the City-of-Hearts Apartment," brings attention to the theme of human love in the novel (Galip's search for his beloved wife) and the multiple love stories inserted and narrated in the text. It is possible to conclude that her interpretation highlights the setting and the plot at the expense of silencing the literary allusions and subtleties involved in the noun phrase "Şehr-i Kalp."

Finally, this case study demonstrates the need for sensitive and symptomatic reading of translated literature. Translations are not transparent copies of originals. Literary translation is a creative act, the study and critique of which needs to be anchored within a specific historical, geographical, and temporal horizon. Translations address a different audience and emerge under different conditions and in contexts distinct from those of the original. Nevertheless, today, book reviewers and critics still write about translations as if they were transparent copies of the original works. Literary translation in a largely monolingual public sphere is thus overlooked. Gün and Freely's translations of *The Black Book* narrate the same plot and follow closely the formal aspects of the original text. Nevertheless, there are differences in stylistics and emphasis, which need to be understood not in comparison to the original text but in relation to the translators' intended audience and agenda. Today, translation is not an option. It is a necessity. Aesthetic appreciation of translations can powerfully illuminate literary and cultural similarities that connect us and differences that give any text or culture a unique character. The importance of translation is even more pronounced for works in less widely spoken languages. Without the creative contribution of his translators, Orhan Pamuk would be unknown outside Turkey. It is the translations that paved the way for Pamuk to win the 2006 Nobel Prize in Literature. It is because of the existence of translations that one can read his *Kara Kitap* as *The Black Book* in English, as *Das schwarze Buch* in German, as Черна книга in Bulgarian, and in many other languages. Following Benjamin's words in the quote that precedes this essay, a successful translation is an expansive transformation of the original, a concrete manifestation of cultural exchange, and a new stage in a work's life as it moves from its first home out into the world beyond.

Notes

1. Walter Benjamin, "The Task of the Translator: An Introduction to the Translation of Baudelaire's *Tableaux Parisiens*," in *The Translation Studies Reader*, ed. Lawrence Venuti. 2nd ed. (London and New York: Routledge, 2002), pp. 75–85.

2. Berna Moran, *Türk romanına eleştirel bir bakış*, vol. 3 (Cağaloğlu, Istanbul: Iletişim Yayınları, 1994), p. 3.

3. Azade Seyhan, *Tales of Crossed Destinies; The Modern Turkish Novel in a Comparative Context: World Literatures Reimagined* (New York: Modern Language Association of America, 2008), p. 150.

4. Jale Parla, "Why *The Black Book* Is Black," *The World and I* 6.4–6 (1991): 447–453, 447.

5. Brent Brendemoen, "Orhan Pamuk-Bir Türkçe sözdizimi yenilikçisi," *Kara Kitap Üzerine Yazılar*, ed. Nüket Esen (Istanbul: İletişim Yayınları, 1996), pp. 128–141, 129.

6. Sibel Irzık, "Istanbul (*The Black Book*, Orhan Pamuk, 1990)," in *The Novel; volume 2: Forms and Themes*, ed. Franco Moretti (Princeton, NJ: Princeton University Press, 2006), pp. 728–735, 728.

7. Kim Sooyong, "Master and Disciple: Sufi Mysticism as an Interpretive Framework for Orhan Pamuk's *Kara Kitap*," *Turkish Studies Association Bulletin* 17.2 (1993): 23–42, 23.

8. Sevinç Türkkan, "Orhan Pamuk's *Kara Kitap*: (British) Reception vs. (American) Translation," *Making Connections: Interdisciplinary Approaches to Cultural Diversity* (Spring, 2010): 39–58, 45.

9. Erdağ Göknar, "Orhan Pamuk and the 'ottoman' theme," *World Literature Today: A Literary Quarterly of the University of Oklahoma* 80.6(11) (2006): 34–38, 34.

10. First published in the United States by Alfred A. Knopf in 2001.

11. In 2003, Göknar received the prestigious international IMPAC Dublin Literary award for his translation of *My Name is Red*.

12. First published in the United Kingdom by Carcanet Press in 1990.

13. First published in the United States by Farrar, Straus & Giroux in 1994, and in the United Kingdom by Farber and Farber in 1995. Gün's translation is out of print. It is replaced by Maureen Freely's new translation published in 2006 by Vintage International.

14. First published in the United States by Farrar, Straus & Giroux in 1997.

15. Scott McLemee, "The Black Book," *Newsday* (July 23, 2006).

16. Ronald Wright, "From a Breeze-Block Istanbul," *Times Literary Supplement* 4932 (October 10, 1997): 23.

17. D. M. Thomas, "Crash," *Times Literary Supplement* (April 6, 1997).

18. Adam Mars-Jones, "The West Has Eaten Our Underpants," *The Observer* (October 5, 1997): 18.

19. Esther Allen, ed., *To Be Translated or Not to Be* (Barcelona: Institut Ramon Llull, 2008), p. 24.

20. Erol Burçin, İngilizce'den Türkçe'ye film çevirileri üzerine bazı gözlemler. *Metis Çeviri* 3 (Summer 1988): 148–150.

21. Saliha Paker and Melike Yilmaz. "A Chronological Bibliography of Turkish Literature in English Translation: 1949–2004," *Translation Review, Special Issue: Turkish Literature and its Translation* 68 (2004): 15–8.

22. First published in Istanbul, Turkey, by Karacan Yayınları in 1986.

23. First published in Istanbul, Turkey, by Can Yayınları in 1983.

24. She is the author of *Book of Trances: A Novel of Magic Recitals* (1979), and *On the Road to Baghdad : A Picaresque Novel of Magical Adventures, Begged, Borrowed, and Stolen from the Thousand and One Nights* (1991).

25. Lawrence Venuti, *The Translator's Invisibility : A History of Translation* (London and New York: Routledge, 2008), p. 1.

26. Marilyn Booth, "Translator v. Author (2007)," *Girls of Riyadh Go to New York*. *Translation Studies* 1.2 (2008): 198–212, 199.

27. At present, six of Pamuk's eight novels circulate in English translations in addition to his memoir *Istanbul: Memories and the City* and the essay collection *Other Colors*.

28. Güneli Gün, *Book of Trances: A Novel of Magic Recitals* (London: J. Friedmann, 1979).

29. Güneli Gün, *On the Road to Baghdad: A Picaresque Novel of Magical Adventures, Begged, Borrowed, and Stolen from the Thousand and One Nights* (Claremont, CA: Hunter House, 1991).

30. Güneli Gün, "Something Wrong with the Language," *Times Literary Supplement* (March 12, 1999).

31. For a detailed discussion and close reading of specific images in Gün's translation, Cf. Türkkan, 2010.

32. Orhan Pamuk, *The Black Book*, trans. Güneli Gün (New York: Farrar, Straus, Giroux, 1994), pp. 9–10 (Italics mine).

33. Ibid., p. 303.

34. It is interesting to note that one of the meanings of the word "celal" is "divine," and when transliterated as "Jelal," the name recalls the Christian savior figure. This is an example of a phonetic approximation of two languages that otherwise are very distinct. What is more significant is that, only through the practice of translation such approximation becomes apparent.

35. Robert Irwin, "Tales of the City," *The Times Literary Supplement* 4814 (July 7, 1995): 21.

36. Joan Smith, "Three Authors in Search of Body," *The Independent* (August 13, 1995).

37. It is well known that, since the Nobel Prize, Pamuk has been closely scrutinizing the English translations of his novels. At times, it is difficult to tell whose decision a particular translational choice is, the translator's, the author's, or even the copyeditor's. In this chapter, I focus on the translators as creative and constrained rewriters. I aim to throw light on their role in the circulation of Pamuk's image as a "cosmopolitan" author. There is no doubt that any study of the process and product of translation illuminates the multiplicity of agents who control the production, reproduction, and circulation of literary texts and images that circulate with them.

38. "Alaaddin" is the Turkish spelling for the Aladdin character in *The Thousand and One Nights*. In the original text this character is an obvious allusion to its namesake in the *Nights* while the *Nights* is an intertext in the novel.

39. http://www.nobelprize.org/mediaplayer/index.php?id=102.

40. Orhan Pamuk, *Other Colors: Essays and a Story*, trans. Maureen Freely (New York: Alfred A. Knopf, 2007), p. 139.

41. Charles A. Ferguson, "Language Development." *Language Problems of Developing Nations*, ed. J. A. Fishman, C. A. Ferguson, and J. Dasgupta (New York: Wiley, 1968), p. 27.

176 • Sevinç Türkkan

42. Ibid., p. 32.
43. Ibid., p. 32.
44. Irzık, p. 735.
45. Orhan Pamuk, *Cedet bey ve oğullar* (Istanbul: İletişim Yayınları, 1982).
46. Orhan Pamuk, *Sessiz ev* (Istanbul: Can Yayınları, 1983).
47. Maureen Freely, Afterword, in Orhan Pamuk, *The Black Book*, trans. Maureen Freely (New York: Vintage International, 2006), p. 465.
48. Svetlana Boym, *The Future of Nostalgia* (New York: Basic Books, 2001), p. xiii.
49. Sigmund Freud, *General Psychological Theory: Papers on Metapsychology* (New York: Collier Books, 1963), p. 166.
50. Quoted in Aaron Santesso, *A Careful Longing: The Poetics and Problems of Nostalgia* (Newark, NJ: University of Delaware Press, 2006), p. 13.
51. Boym, p. xvi.
52. Maureen Freely, *Enlightenment* (Woodstock, NY: Overlook Press, 2008).
53. Orhan Pamuk, *The Black Book*, trans. Maureen Freely (New York: Vintage International, 2006), p. 15.
54. Ibid., p. 7 (emphasis mine).
55. As translated by Victoria Holbrook in Victoria R Holbrook, In Şeyh Galip. *Beauty and Love* (New York: Modern Language Association of America, 2005).
56. Ibid., p. xiii.
57. Orhan Pamuk, *The Black Book*, trans. Maureen Freely (New York: Vintage International, 2006), p. 8.

CHAPTER 11

Occulted Texts: Pamuk's Untranslated Novels

Erdağ Göknar

Orhan Pamuk's mature fiction belongs to the post-1980 "Third Republic," a period characterized by Turkey's gradual neoliberal integration into global networks.[1] In terms of the Turkish novel, this was a profound period of literary innovation under the influence of international postmodernism. Nevertheless, Pamuk began writing in the early 1970s, in a Cold War era marked by social realism known as the "Second Republic" (between the 1960 and 1980 military coups). His novels consequently developed through layers of literary modernity, establishing a catalogue or a palimpsest of genres, techniques, and styles. Extraordinary in its breadth, Pamuk's oeuvre moves from the social realism of *Cevdet Bey and Sons* to the multiperspectival modernism of the *Silent House*; from the Ottoman historical allegory of *The White Castle* to the cosmopolitan intertext of Eastern and Western forms in *The Black Book*; from the mystical Sufi metafiction of *The New Life* to the historiographic postmodernism of *My Name is Red*; and from the violent ideological conversions of *Snow* to the unrequited love and Istanbul material culture of *The Museum of Innocence*. His eight novels published between 1982 and 2008 (in Turkish) trace his development from national litterateur to global author, redefining dominant literary tropes in the process.[2]

This chapter begins with the observation that Pamuk's fiction both embodies and rehistoricizes the major tropes of the modern Turkish novel. These tropes repeatedly appear in a symbolic complex that maps Republican literary culture through an inscription of contexts of *devlet*, or "state" (such as cultural revolution, modernization history, and military coup); *din*, or "religion" (such as Turkish Islam, Ottoman cultural memory and material culture); or a combination of the two including (ideological) conversion, (Muslim) cosmopolitanism, and (secular) Sufism. Pamuk constructs his mature novels over the cartography of these paradoxical cultural contexts.

However, the first literary mode of Pamuk's authorship, as conveyed in his early, untranslated novels, is historical, or, more accurately, historiographic. In keeping with the Republican imperative of devlet, these novels follow an Empire-to-Republic structure with a telos of secularization. Furthermore, they are inaccessible to most readers because they remain untranslated into English and other major languages by the will of the author. The absence of these texts in translation presents critics not literate in Turkish with a pervasive problem leading to misreadings and inaccuracies in the interpretation of Pamuk's literary modernity.[3] The "untranslated Pamuk," including important nonfiction articles and essays, serves to establish the vital point that Pamuk's literary modernity emerges from a genealogy that is tied to social realism and even the historiography of secular modernization.[4]

Pamuk began writing about bourgeois Istanbul families during the Second Republic (1960–1980), posing something of a challenge to the dominant mode of literature on Anatolia. His first two novels, *Cevdet Bey and Sons* (*CBS, Cevdet Bey ve Oğulları*, written 1979, published 1982) and *The Silent House* (*SH, Sessiz Ev*, 1984), are historically grounded in the Turkish literary tradition and trace out the Empire-to-Republic bildungsroman. Drawing on narratives of Ottoman and Republican modernization, Pamuk's first two untranslated novels are multigenerational treatments of social and political history written at a time when Pamuk openly described himself as a "leftist." Between these two books, Pamuk began writing a novel of "bourgeois leftism" that remained incomplete because of publishing restrictions enacted after the 1980 coup.[5] Pamuk's third published novel, and the first to be translated into English, is *The White Castle* (*WC, Beyaz Kale*, 1985). This novel is structured around an Ottoman manuscript discovered in a forgotten Ottoman archive by a Republican intellectual, a common figure in modern Turkish literature. Faruk Darvınoğlu is the selfsame historian of *The Silent House* who has lost his faith in the discipline of history. As a framing device, Darvınoğlu's translation, transliteration, and publication of the manuscript in the wake of the 1980 coup functions, among other things, as a metaphor for the reintroduction of Ottoman cultural memory into the Republican present.

The Empire-to-Republic Bildungsroman: *Cevdet Bey and Sons*

Cevdet Bey and Sons–originally titled *Darkness and Light* (*Karanlık ve Işık*)–represents the dialectic of enlightened forces of progress versus "dark" forces of tradition.[6] This Empire-to-Republic bildungsroman and European-influenced family novel tells the story of Cevdet Işıkçı, a Muslim business pioneer in a sector dominated by Levantines, Greeks, and Armenians. (Işıkçı literally means "light-seller" or "proponent of light" and is an allusion to the Enlightenment.) In describing three generations of the Işıkçı family the novel summarizes twentieth-century Turkish cultural and social history according to an "Empire to Republic" metanarrative from 1905 to 1970—and concludes just months before the 1971 military coup.[7] The novel features scenes of Anatolia (Erzincan and Ankara) that address the conflict between elite Istanbul cosmopolitanism and regional culture.[8]

Cevdet Bey and Sons is a classic manifestation of the Empire-to-Republic bildungsroman, which depicts the rise of a Turkish national bourgeoisie. The novel is divided into three parts that juxtapose three revolutionary eras in late Ottoman and Republican history between 1905 and 1970.[9] In a dialectical "secularization thesis" framework, each part portrays a distinct social force of "light" (enlightenment) opposed to an "Eastern/Oriental" backdrop of political "darkness" (Islamic tradition).[10] A triptych of revolutions (the 1908 constitutional revolution, the Kemalist cultural revolution of the 1920s and '30s, and the military coup of 1971) structures the novel, corresponding to three generations of the Işıkçı family. The setting moves among cosmopolitan Istanbul (as the imperial Ottoman capital and later peripheralized Republican city), rural Anatolian Kemah, and the new "modern" capital of Ankara. Part One ("Foreword") and the Part Three ("Afterword") each recounts a single day. Narrative weight is given to Part Two, set during the three years of the Kemalist cultural revolution, including the death of Atatürk and the transition to İsmet İnönü's rule.[11] In its form and content the novel corresponds to a realist Lukácsian understanding of the historical novel.[12] Throughout the novel, Pamuk relies on a dramatic "oppositional dialogue" technique to reflect the dialectic from Empire-of-Faith to Republic-of-Reason. The oppositions of "darkness" and "light" reveal the influence of the secularization thesis.

Late Ottoman Modernity

The "Young Turk" revolution is the first of the historical revolutions and coups that punctuate the Empire-to-Republic bildungsroman. Part

One of *CBS* describes a day in the life of Cevdet Bey in 1905 and represents the late Ottoman era, during the rule of Ottoman Sultan and Islamic Caliph Abdülhamid II just three years before the 1908 constitutional revolution.[13]

There are two measures of time that persistently affect Pamuk's characters: the Muslim time of din and the revolutionary time of secular devlet. The Republican secular masterplot demands unidirectional development and progress from the former to the latter, which Pamuk codes as "darkness" and "light" in *CBS*.[14] For Pamuk, whose historical understanding is informed by Republican (and by extension, European) historiography, the dialectic follows the secular masterplot. "Light" rests squarely with devlet and revolution, social engineering, and the leftist coup.

CBS begins with an anxiety dream sequence. Cevdet, the "merchant of light," wakes up agitated. He is late, literally, and figuratively "belated."[15] To underscore this point, Cevdet Bey first looks out of the window to determine the time by the location of the sun. What is known as *alaturka* or "ezani" (related to the call to prayer) time is based on a system whereby midnight is always at sundown. The day, divided into two segments of darkness and light, is ordered around the call to prayer, the first beginning at sunrise and the fifth at sunset. (This orientation determines the times of the five daily prayers.) Next, annoyed at himself for using a traditional method of telling time, Cevdet looks at his wristwatch, a tool of synchronization with the modern, which tells him that it is "*yarım*" according to Muslim time (just after sunrise).[16] Throughout his day, Cevdet Bey continually tells time in the old-fashioned way and has yet to adopt the new revolutionary "time" of modernity represented by his older brother Nusret.[17]

Nusret, a "Young Turk" and physician who has fallen ill and has recently returned to Istanbul from Paris, advocates revolutionary social change under the model of the French Revolution. He belittles Cevdet and is dismissive of his work and ambitions. For Nusret, Istanbul and the empire are sunken in the "darkness" of what is portrayed as Sultan Abdülhamit's rule as an "Oriental despot."[18] Pamuk's coding of Muslim time as "darkness" and revolutionary European modernity as "light" reflects the accepted ideology of the secularization thesis.[19]

The novel's first section is dominated by a sense of belated modernity for Ottoman Muslims in cosmopolitan Istanbul as reflected in the economic and the political aspirations of Cevdet and Nusret, respectively.[20] The cosmopolitan Islam Pamuk depicts here is set in direct contrast to the secular modernity focusing on Ankara and Anatolia as conveyed in Part Two. The novel separates contexts of din and devlet in keeping with the secularization thesis. As he develops his literary modernity in subsequent novels, Pamuk will return to contexts of "sacred" Muslim time with increasing frequency, a return that will allow him to recuperate the enchantment of story ("*hikâye*") from the secular disenchantment of the Empire-to-Republic bildungsroman.

Engineers of the Revolution

The cultural revolution is the second historical revolution that structures the Empire-to-Republic bildungsroman. Part Two of *CBS* is set during the three-year period of the cultural revolution (1936–1939) and constitutes the longest section of the novel. Here, Pamuk focuses on the generation of Cevdet Bey's sons who represent the educated secular elite during the monoparty era (1923–1950) of Mustafa Kemal Atatürk's Republican People's Party. As opposed to the cosmopolitan Ottoman businessmen and pashas that are depicted in the novel's first section, the second section centers on Refik, Muhittin, and Ömer, three longtime friends who are literally engineers and figuratively "engineers of the nation."[21] These three ambivalent characters meet in various contexts and reflect on their changing aspirations, their disappointments, and successes and failures set against the backdrop of the Kemalist cultural revolution.[22]

For the sake of "secular conversion," the cultural revolution abolished the Ottoman sultanate (1922); abandoned the cosmopolitan Ottoman capital, Istanbul, for rural Ankara (1923); abolished the Islamic Caliphate and religious courts (1924); outlawed Sufi orders and adopted European-style dress (1925); adopted the European calendar, criminal, civil, and commercial codes (1926); changed the alphabet from Ottoman script to Latin letters (1928); struck the declaration identifying Islam as state religion from the constitution (1929); granted women the right to vote (1934); and enshrined secularism, revolution, and statism as constitutional principles (1937). The positivist social engineering produced by these changes had a number of sources including ethnonationalism, Soviet-socialism, and Anglo-French Orientalism/colonialism. Progress occurred, Republican historiography argued, when Turks moved through revolutionary stages from the darkness of din to the enlightenment of devlet. Indeed, urban elites, intellectuals, and teachers were expected to take the revolution to the people of Anatolia, creating a symbiosis between urban Republican intellectual and Anatolian peasant. The crisis that arose in this confrontation between the Republican enlightenment ideals of devlet and the religious tradition of din became a recurring theme in Republican novels such as Halide Edib's *Vurun Kahpeye* (*Strike the Whore*, 1926), Reşat Nuri Güntekin's *Yeşil Gece* (*Green Night*, 1928), Yakup Kadri's *Yaban* (*The Outsider*, 1932), and A. H. Tanpınar's *Sahnenin Dışındakiler* (*Waiting in the Wings*, 1950). In *CBS*, Pamuk develops this theme with his engineer protagonists in scenes that are set in rural Kemah near Erzincan, implying, like these earlier authors, that the divide between modernity and the masses is a crisis that the "revolution" has yet to resolve.

Retracing the logic of the secularization thesis in *CBS*, Pamuk sets the Ottoman Muslim context of din (Part One) in contrast to the secular state, or devlet dominance of the Kemalist cultural revolution (Part Two).[23] Part Two focuses on forces of "darkness" and "light" during the cultural revolution that separated the time and contexts of din from those of devlet through a sustained period of political and social engineering. The novel depicts contexts of din that are subordinated and pushed into the private sphere while traces of its social memory are repressed. For example, the scene where the secular engineer, Refik, a typical Pamuk character of ambivalence, must perform the ritual *namaz* prayer at his father Cevdet Bey's funeral captures the estrangement of this secularized generation, for whom religion is a relic. Refik must be prodded by his brother Osman (*Osmanlı*, lit. "Ottoman") to participate in the prayer:

> "*Namaz?*" thought Refik . . . . He thought about how he would remove his shoes . . . . In the past, he'd come here with servants and also during Bairam holidays with his father . . . . "I should have performed my ablution first!" he thought, but it seemed Osman hadn't either . . . . Refik turned to look behind him: the stocking feet of the gardeners and doormen standing in the back weren't so peculiar. "This place [the mosque] becomes them!" he thought . . . . Refik thought, "my father's dead," and staring at the nape of the man before him, he imitated his movements. He thought that it wasn't right that he was making these movements, bowing and rising, despite not believing.[24]

The alienation, uncanniness, and displacement Refik senses in the setting of a mosque where he must pray is a striking indication of the broken unity of din and devlet. The "father" here might be read allegorically as the figure of the Muslim Ottoman. The Islamic rituals of his obsequies all belong to the realm of din. However, in the national context of a "Turkishness" of sublated Islam, the mosque becomes a liminal social space. Cultural ambiguity arises from the lack of legibility between the two cultural spheres as represented by the mass of praying Muslims and engineer Refik, respectively. The secular conversion of the cultural revolution is conveyed through Refik (who later states, "If only I could believe in Allah"[25]). Though a distinction between public (secular) and private (religious) comes to mark modern Republican spaces, these distinctions have been revealingly blurred in this mosque scene. Furthermore, class disparity is emphasized, with Islam being associated with the lower classes and secularism with the enfranchised secular elite. An enforced temporality between din and devlet is also quite clear: din is presented as a primitive past time and devlet as the civilized present and future. As such, the Muslim namaz prayer preformed by the ritually impure Refik is nothing but a sacrilege. He mimics the movements of prayer during a ritual emptied of meaning. The act of worship is reduced to one of faded memory in the museum of a mosque during his reluctant commemoration of the death of the (Ottoman Islamic) father. Pamuk reveals in Part Two that modernity is a project of epistemic and cultural violence coded as social revolution. In Part Three, the trope of revolution is developed and revised in yet another iteration, this time as a socialist project for the overthrow of the bourgeoisie.

The Leftist Coup

The coup appears as final legacy of revolutionary change, and as such is an echo of the cultural revolution writ small. Part Three (the "Afterword") is centered on a day in the life of Cevdet Bey's grandson, Ahmet, an aspiring artist and Galatasaray Lycée graduate educated in French. Ahmet is in the compromised position of being a revolutionary, bourgeois youth focused on his own artwork before an imminent military coup, which he hopes will bring about a socialist revolution. (In actual Republican history, the hopes for such a coup are forestalled by a nationalist coup in 1971.) The debate that defines this autobiographical section is the relevance of art to revolutionary political change. The section marks the period of Pamuk's own coming of age as a novelist, when Turkey, then a "third world" country caught between socialism and capitalism in the Cold War, was torn by the civil violence between leftist and rightist political factions.[26] Much of the action takes place in Ahmet's apartment-cum-studio, as if in a one-act play, where he is visited first by his older sister Melek, next by the revolutionary youth Hasan, and finally by his girlfriend İlknur (lit. "first light") who is completing a doctorate in Ottoman art history. İlknur, a character with access to the dismissed Ottoman past, gives us an indication of the direction Pamuk's fiction will take in its subsequent critique of the Empire-to-Republic bildungsroman.

As with the first two sections, Part Three reveals anticipation and anxiety about the possibility of revolutionary change ("light"), in this case, about an impending leftist coup like "Torrez in Bolivia."[27] The main tension between art and revolution is revealed in this exchange between Ahmet and Hasan, a member of TİP, the communist Turkish Workers Party:

> Hasan gazed at Ahmet's paintings for a moment. Then his cheerful face hardened as he returned from dreamy reverie to reality: "Look, you've depicted some cats here... and you've depicted some bourgeois, or whatever, you know these people here, now when I look at it I feel something!" He was on the verge of embarrassment: "I really do sense something but... But, brother, you know as well as I do that you can't instigate a revolution with these things!" As if a feeling of guilt were upon him, he grew timid.[28]

Both characters accept revolutionary potential as the measure of artistic representation. For Ahmet (and Pamuk), this realism is in keeping with modern secular progress inflected by a Marxist aesthetic that puts art in the service of socialism. In this section, furthermore, Hasan makes an allusion to the dissident poet Nâzım Hikmet (1901–1962) by reciting a line of verse: "What you seek is not in your room but outside." The reference is twice repeated (in CBS, p. 568 and 587). This is from a strident Marxist-Leninist poem entitled "What You Seek" ("Aradıkların," 1962) by Hikmet while he was in exile in Moscow.[29] The poem ends with the line, "What you seek is in you."[30] The poem, verging on agitprop, is not representative of Hikmet's best work, but is an ideological "poem of duty" that calls both for transnational connection to revolutionary social engagement and for individual (in this scene, artistic) agency in social change. The "outside" might be any number of contexts, including what lies beyond the horizon of the nation-state or the present time. In his poem, Hikmet foregrounds the role of the individual, a role that finds its corollary in Pamuk's later figuration of the author or the "writing subject."[31] In the "Afterword," the revolutionary force of history is thus sublimated through art, in this case painting, but by extension, through writing as well.

In subsequent novels, I argue, a number of things begin to occur: 1) the narrative form, rather than the historical content, of Pamuk's literary modernity begins to change; 2) historical secular authority gives way to literary authority such that contexts of din begin to become legible to and coexist with those of devlet; and 3) the Turkish novel, in transcending the secularization thesis, becomes legible as a form of world literature through tropes that can be read as both secular and sacred.

The Silent House of Republican Modernity

Pamuk's first novel stands in agreement with scholars of Turkish literary history that the very history of Ottoman and Republican modernization gives rise to the modern Ottoman and Turkish novel, which as a mimetic form is a symptom of that history.[32] However, Pamuk's second novel, SH, is a cynical reexamination of the Republican secularization thesis. It is through narrative techniques of first-person multiperspectivalism and stream-of-consciousness memory that Pamuk begins the revision of the social realist mode of Turkish literary modernity so faithfully performed in CBS.[33]

The Silent House maintains the same three-generation "Empire to Republic" periodization as CBS. In contrast to the generational saga of the Işıkçı family, however, SH portrays the dysfunctions of the Darvınoğlus (lit., "Son-of-Darwin"), often in a mode of black humor. The three main time periods in CBS (late Ottoman, early Republican, and 1970s Istanbul), covering a period from 1905 to 1970, are again represented, this time extended to the eve of the 1980 coup. However, Pamuk's second novel makes use of a Faulknerian style that revises these periods so they appear synchronically through limited first-person points of view. Instead of providing the dominant scaffolding for the novel, the Empire–to-Republic framework in SH is appropriated and fragmented through a retrospective focus on memory (both personal and Ottoman archival). The novel tells the story of three grandchildren who make a weeklong summer's visit to their grandmother's house near Istanbul, which proves to be the empty abode of the imagined community. The weeklong narrative-present opens to 70 years of late Ottoman and Republican history through a multiperspectival technique that gives prominence to subjective notions of time.[34] Fatma Hanım, the matron and grandmother, stews in bitter memories of her husband, Selahattin, a deluded European-educated modernizer and atheist who aspired to write an encyclopedia that would close the gap between "East" and "West." The traditions of the pre-Republican past, no longer the basis for social change through the secularization thesis, persist forcefully as an indictment of revolution through the narration of five characters: Recep, the illegitimate and "dwarfed" child of modernizer Selahittin Darvınoğlu; Fatma Hanım, Selahittin's bitter wife and devout matron of the Darvınoğlu family; Hasan, the young, ideological convert to extreme Turkism who harbors ill-fated love for Nilgün, the young socialist; Faruk, the Republican intellectual and a professor of history at the state university; and Metin, the young entrepreneur who wants to leave Turkey to live out the American dream. All of these characters suffer from social alienation and are involved in relationships of unequal affection or unrequited love. As a novel that intertwines the legacy of revolutions with articulations of cultural memory, SH focuses on the third Republican generation, represented by Selahattin's three grandchildren, Metin, Nilgün, and Faruk, and an "illegitimate" fourth grandchild, Hasan.[35] Allegorically, they each represent ideological aspects of contemporary Turkish society and politics.

The Silent House irreversibly breaks down the omniscient voice of Republican social history. Multiperspectivalism interrupts the progressive narrative by making the value to be derived from progress contingent on social position and point of view. The appearance of the satiric figure of "the historian," Faruk Darvınoğlu ("Truth-Seeker Son-of-Darwin"), is only the first indication of the derisive black humor that will dominate Pamuk's later novels.[36] The Silent House ends only weeks away from the 1980 military coup in a context of alienation and community fragmentation. Of the three grandchildren, one is a lonely alcoholic (and parody of the Republican intellectual), another dies after a politically motivated beating by ultranationalists, and the third dreams of leaving for the United States in pursuit of the American dream. Unmistakably, Pamuk's second novel declares the bankruptcy of any unified vision of national or social progress.

In SH, Pamuk has abandoned his earnest portrayal of revolution as part of a dialectic of social progress to initiate changes in the novel form itself. Here, the revolution as a trope has become a narrative artifact open to various manipulations.[37] Represented by three generations, the revolution is parodied through Selahattin's obsessive mania for progress, diminished through an absent second generation represented by Doğan and his illegitimate half-brothers, and figuratively "killed off" in the death of the leftist student Nilgün. This is a symptom of larger formal changes in Pamuk's aesthetics of the novel, developments that begin to push the boundaries of Republican literature and modernity. No longer does Pamuk allow the novel to be a social representation of historical contexts. In SH, the dialectic of oppositional dialogue has been replaced by internal monologue and stream-of-consciousness narration, the omniscient third-person point of view has become limited, first-person, and multiperspectival, and realism has been distorted by modernist subjective time. In transcending Republican history, Pamuk introduces a new narrative perspective. This perspective structures the novel itself: *SH* is constructed out of discrete versions of personal and archival memory rather than an overarching dialectical tension of opposites ("darkness" and "light") as in *CBS*.

Allah Is Dead

In contrast to *CBS*, *SH* presents the positivism of the cultural revolution and its present-day legacy in modes of the tragic and the grotesque. The first generation of late Ottoman revolutionary enlightenment is represented by Selahattin Darvınoğlu, a medical doctor.[38] Around 1912, Selahattin (born in 1881, the same year as Atatürk) is exiled by Talat Pasha of the "Young Turk" Union and Progress Party from Istanbul for his involvement in politics. He settles with his wife Fatma in nearby Gebze. The temporary exile becomes permanent as Selahattin grows increasingly obsessed with authoring an encyclopedia that will prove "Allah is dead" and bring the ideals of the scientific revolution and Enlightenment to Turkey, enabling it to "catch up with Europe." He spends 30 years writing the encyclopedia but is unable to complete it, in part, he complains, due to the 1928 Alphabet Reform that changed the Ottoman script to Latin letters.

Fatma is persecuted then haunted by her atheist, modernizer husband, a symbol of authoritarian positivism. Selahattin, an inquisitor figure, attempts to force the ideological conversion of those around him, in particular, his wife. She resists his arguments and logic, later claiming at his grave that she has succeeded in avoiding the brave new world of his future "atheist state."[39] Through her interior monologue, which becomes a confessional testimony, Fatma ridicules him as an obsessed alcoholic. Meanwhile, Selahattin claims that Fatma is frigid, demonstrates the nonexistence of Allah, fathers two illegitimate children with the maidservant, and determines that the fear of death (and nothingness) is the vital element that separates "East" from "West." In short, Pamuk has begun a multilayered parody of the revolution trope. In a night of retaliation for her husband's transgressions, Fatma severely beats both of his illegitimate children, leaving one (Ismail) crippled and the other (Recep) stunted.

Cultural Memory

Cultural memory, in personal and archival contexts, is clearly conveyed through the stream-of-consciousness narrations of Fatma and Faruk. Pamuk contrasts Fatma Hanım's powerful memory of the past in *SH* to Nigan Hanım's dementia and amnesia (the symbol of an inaccessible past). The former despises her husband's patrimonial legacy and the latter adores that of her husband. Cevdet Bey leaves a prosperous family living in a Nisantaşı apartment in his wake whereas Selahattin Bey leaves only a dilapidated, tragic, and empty house. The two novels present divergent commentaries on the Empire-to-Republic bildungsroman. This discrepancy is revelatory in terms of understanding Pamuk's engagement (and disengagement) with Republican literary modernity. By using memory as a vehicle to return from the future-oriented time of devlet to a retrospective time of memory, Pamuk is preparing the reader for a reinscription of the redemptive contexts of din. The reforms of the cultural revolution targeted the collective memory of the nation including Ottoman Islam, Sufism, and Istanbul cosmopolitism. Thus, Pamuk's transformations in narrative form are both literary techniques and political gestures directed toward changing dominant Republican epistemologies.

Dwarfing the Cultural Revolution

The second Republican generation is represented through Doğan Darvınoglu and his two illegitimate half-brothers, Recep and Ismail. Doğan retires from his position as district governor (*kaymakam*) in Kemah and returns to Gebze, falling into a family pattern of alcoholism and idiosyncratic projects of social idealism. His half-brothers, Recep and İsmail, are the children of Selahattin and the maidservant. They are parodic figures of the Republican principle of folk modernization: enlightenment ideals introduced to "modernize" the Anatolian people or *halk* (known as *halkçılık*). These three characters sit in striking contrast to the three secular elite engineers (Ömer, Refik, and Muhittin) who represented the ideals of the same generation in *CBS*. Recep is literally and figuratively a "dwarfed" product of the cultural revolution, signifying its underdevelopment and alienating effect. İsmail works as a state lottery-ticket vendor, whose occupation carries obvious metaphorical commentary on secular devlet. The entire revolutionary generation has been peripheralized, derided, and dismissed in a way that is a reflection of changes in form between Pamuk's first and second novel.

The Ottoman Archive

To encourage the reassessment of din, Pamuk articulates another trope in *SH* related to memory: the archive. The archive (of cultural memory) counterbalances the trope of revolution (and ideological conversion). Pamuk mounts a sustained critique of Republican ideology through the archive, a repository of textual objects and their memories. In *SH* (and later in *The White Castle*) this unknown archive, a space that is located "underground," is described as follows:

> I find it much more agreeable to work in a place whose very existence is denied by specialists than to work with my jealous and envious colleagues in the Prime Minister's Archives . . . . And as I work my way through them [these papers], I can almost see the men who dictated them, wrote them down, or whose life has been in one way or another linked to the contexts of these documents . . . . As I read along, the piles of yellow papers slowly give way, just as at the end of a long sea voyage, when the fog that has hung over you throughout the trip clears up, suddenly you see a stretch of land, with its trees, its rocks and its birds, which fills you with admiration—in the very same way, millions of existences and stories contained haphazardly in these documents, becoming somewhat less hermetic as I read them, suddenly take shape in my mind.[40]

The passage alludes to a journey taken in the discovery of a new world through the medium of archival texts. This signifies the birth of a new literary imagination that had been circumscribed by the parochial discipline of Republican history. It is in the space of a forgotten archive in Gebze, a town that used to be the seat of an Ottoman kadiship, that Faruk confronts the crisis of history and the historian. This space represents something of a cell, and Faruk is incarcerated as he contemplates the possibility of new authorial projects. Faruk's meditations on history are significant to revealing Pamuk's own transformations as an author. Faruk admits early in the novel that he is "afraid of losing his faith in what's known as history."[41] This is a dilemma of history and authorship that unfolds throughout Faruk's experiences in the archive. The archive, furthermore, is an intertextual space where documents and manuscript pages reside side by side in an uncatalogued fragmentary state.

Faruk believes that history is distorted by the stories used to link disparate events in a causal chain. He is preoccupied by a question of form, of confounding versions of history, and of representing history as it "truly" exists in ruins and fragments. Conceptually, he is slowly gaining consciousness of another narrative level of historical understanding focusing on narrative that is, to use Hayden White's term, "metahistorical". This is also an authorial level that enables the development of literary modernity through the transcendence of the telos of Republican modernization history.

Faruk discovers that he cannot avoid the temptation of story (i.e., metanarrative) as a medium for causality and emplotment: "Returning to its old habit, my brain stubbornly demands, as always, that I come up with a short story summarizing all these facts, a convincing narrative."[42] This gives rise to an epistemological problem that he resolves through experimentation in narrative form. "This insane longing to hear a story fools us all, pulling us into a dream universe when we live in a real world of flesh and blood." The ambivalence between a materialist, realist perspective and a romantic, literary one is evident. Faruk believes that the archive itself can be a model for such a new history of noncausal "endless description." His thinking applies to a revision of literary modernity as well, that is, one based on a model of intertextuality and an innovation in literary form that moves away from the realist dialectic of social history that dominated Republican literature between 1960 and 1980. Faruk is convinced that the work of a historian is "that of a storyteller,"[43] and that "history is nothing but stories."[44] Later, he thinks that breaking the chain of causality will enable him to "get rid of the moral motive and of everything that is apodictic/true,"[45] which will allow him to attain freedom and potential in his work. It is not hard to read this historical debate as one about the liberation from confinements of Republican discursive space. The dilemma, predicated on narrative, is both historical and literary, with the site of authority moving from the historiographic to the literary.

Through Faruk, Pamuk exposes the potential for a new aesthetics of literary modernity. The Ottoman archive, the Republic's wildly signifying collective unconscious, provides the perfect laboratory for such narrative experimentation with texts that will lead to historiographic, and, in turn, identity-based transformations. Clues in SH reveal that this new narrative aesthetic will be fragmentary, multiperspectival, metahistorical, and open to interpretation (this is borne out in The White Castle and Pamuk's subsequent postmodern works). Faruk's meditation approaches a treatise on the theory of the novel that emerges from the heteroglossia of countless archive stories. The type of novel Pamuk produces, again through the vehicle of the historian-cum-author Faruk, in WC, is reflected in Faruk's "historian's dilemma" regarding narrative and disciplinary method. By distinguishing story (emplotment) from historical fact, Pamuk is able to transcend the confines of the national tradition. This type of deconstruction in the Republican literary field, in turn, leads to an international, intertextual space—an archive of world literature.

Faruk's concern is nothing but a literary one. Finally, he settles on a Calvino-esque "deck of cards" metaphor: events are the cards and among them are, like jokers, a number of "story" ("*hikâye*") cards that meaningfully assemble and organize the textual events.[46] It is in this process of breaking down history that Pamuk, through Faruk, is attempting to transcend Republican ideology.

Of course, in a telling inversion, Faruk's archival research will not produce a history at all, but rather, a story, a captive's tale, an account about himself, among other things, for *he* is the captive, like Pamuk, incarcerated in the ideological space of national discourse. Though the "house" of Republican history has fallen silent for Pamuk, the "castle" of the Ottoman past reemerges as a blank text waiting to be interpreted and overwritten. His next novel will thrust him back into the cosmopolitan context of imperial Istanbul. This manipulation will involve a monumental reintroduction of discursive contexts of cosmopolitan din into those of secular devlet.

Thus, in *SH*, the Empire-to-Republic framework of *CBS* has given way to formal literary innovations and new narrative aesthetics. As such, Pamuk has begun inscripting a challenge to the cultural revolution and its anticosmopolitan foundations. As a character that combines the authority of the Ottoman historian, the subversive archivist, and the translator-author, Faruk mediates between the history of devlet and the redemptive story of din, eventually targeting the former through the symbols and discourses of the latter. In *SH*, Pamuk brings us from a traditional monolithic understanding of history into a theoretical understanding of versions of history, or historiography, before finally arriving in a new world of literary aesthetics. Whereas *SH* alludes to the possibility of narrative redemption, *WC* demonstrates this redemption through the mystical emergence of "Him," a secular-sacred literary formation embedded in the narrative structure of the novel.

Conclusion: From Occulted Texts to Occulted Literary Traditions

Pamuk is something of a scholar of the modern Turkish literature, and his fiction works through Republican literary conventions, forging new literary idioms and new understandings of the Turkish novel as a secular-sacred form emanating from Istanbul. His determination to situate himself as the culmination of a tradition that he had to learn and study, to emulate and to surpass, generated something like a love-hate relationship. Begrudgingly, when pressed, Pamuk names only a few authors who have influenced him: A. H. Tanpınar, Kemal Tâhir, Yusuf Atılgan, and Oğuz Atay. Rather, he is more likely to be represented as a dissident of the state (the experience of many Turkish authors of the Second Republic). Or he is far more likely to present himself as a student and practitioner of an international canon, as he does in the edited and abridged 2007 English version of the belles-lettres collection, *Other Colors* (*Öteki Renkler*, 1999), and in his 2010 Charles Eliot Norton Lectures, *The Naïve and the Sentimental Novelist*.

As I have argued, Pamuk's early novels—the first in a realist and the second in a modernist style—can be grouped together as faithful appropriations of Empire-to-Republic historiography. In content, they cannot be called "politically engaged" in any obvious way. But his modifications in form alone in *The Silent House* begin to mount sweeping arguments for recuperating the elisions and repressions of Republican modernization. Pamuk deepens his "argumentation through form" in subsequent novels. As Pamuk's early fiction moves from omniscient historical realism (*CBS*) to modernist stream-of-consciousness memory (*SH*) and to historiographic postmodernism (*WC*), the reader is moved through a recapitulation of modes of literary modernity that grow increasingly more layered, cosmopolitan, and intertextual.[47] Over the course of these three novels, Pamuk's literary authority tentatively challenges and then overwrites historical realism as a mode of representation. Gradually, in Pamuk's novels, the figure of the "historian-in-crisis" will be replaced by the figure of the "author-in-crisis." Archival texts will be replaced by missing or absent texts—narrative spaces that prefigure the mystical return of Sufism (outlawed during the cultural revolution). Pamuk's narratives will become multilayered and synchronic in an attempt to overwrite these lacks, lacunae, and absences.

The fact that, as of this writing, Pamuk does not want his first two novels translated (into English and other major languages) is revelatory, for these are the novels that squarely place him in the Turkish Republican literary tradition. By preventing their translation, he is editing his position in the canon and dehistoricizing his literary genealogy. This enables him to foreground Istanbul cosmopolitanism and world literature as the *sole* contexts of his literary production. The contrast between the Turkish (1999) and English (2007) versions of his collection of belles letters, *Other Colors*, confirms this anxiety of literary positioning: the post-Nobel English version emphasizes a canon of world literature whereas the individual sections on the influence of modern Turkish authors A. H. Tanpınar, Kemal Tâhir, Orhan Kemal, Aziz Nesin, Yaşar Kemal, and Oğuz Atay have all been deleted from the volume. These are literary influences that are formative to Pamuk's mature fiction and vital to an informed understanding of the function and development of his novels.

Notes

1. For more on the division of twentieth-century Turkish history into first, second, and third republics, see Erik J. Zürcher, *Turkey: A Modern History* (London: I. B. Tauris & Co. Ltd., 1993).

2. In English translation, this periodization is slightly shorter, from 1990 to 2010, as his first two novels have not been translated.

3. Paul de Man makes an early theorization of the term "literary modernity" in a way that is illuminating to the Turkish context. In opposing "modernity" to "literature," De Man postulates an antinomy: "Modernity and history seem condemned to being linked together in a self-destroying union that threatens the survival of both. If we see in this paradoxical condition a diagnosis of our own modernity, then literature has always been essentially modern." See Paul De Man, "Literary History and Literary Modernity," *Daedalus* 99.2 (1970). In the Turkish context, "literary modernity" manifests as the contestation between the novel and Republican modernity.

4. Early influential texts on Turkish modernization history in English that espouse the "secularization thesis" include Niyazi Berkes, *The Development of Secularism in Turkey* (London: Hurst & Co, 1998/1964); Bernard Lewis, *The Emergence of Modern Turkey* (London, New York: Oxford University Press, 1961); and Serif Mardin, *The Genesis of Young Ottoman Thought: A Study in the Modernization of Turkish Political Ideas* (Princeton, NJ: Princeton University Press, 1962). These texts accepted the Eurocentric assumption that state secularization (or "Westernization") equated to modernization.

5. Personal conversation with the author. Pamuk read me a scene from his notebooks of this incomplete political novel that described the thoughts and feelings of the bourgeois protagonist who has decided to "liberate" (i.e., steal) a book from an Istanbul bookstore. The novel focuses on youths from well-to-do Istanbul families who have ideological convictions in Marxist socialism and want to engage in acts of civil unrest (stealing property or tossing a bomb at the prime minister, for example) yet come from the middle classes. About 250 pages of this novel exist in long-hand form.

6. *Cevdet Bey and Sons* was awarded the Orhan Kemal Novel Award in 1983. Orhan Kemal (1914–1970) was one of the main proponents of social realism along with Kemal Tâhir and Yaşar Kemal. The guidelines of the award

explicitly state that the award recognizes novels "written with realist and socialist intent and under the condition that they do not oppose or counter Orhan Kemal's artistic vision and worldview." See "Orhan Kemal Roman Armağını: Yönetmelik" accessed May 3, 2011: http://orhankemal.org/v04 /yonet_tr.htm.

7. Pamuk alludes to the Turkish novel canon through references to prominent revolutionary figures in late Ottoman and Republican literary history. Part One contains direct allusions to Namık Kemal (1840–1888) and Tevfik Fikret (1867–1915), intellectual authors known for their opposition to Sultan Abdülhamit. Part Two refers to Yakup Kadri's iconic national-utopia novel, *Ankara*: This is also a novel in three parts that depicts (1) Istanbul during the late Ottoman Allied occupation, (2) Ankara during the cultural revolution, and (3) a future time of Anatolian village utopia. Part Three alludes to the renowned dissident-socialist poet Nâzım Hikmet (1902–1963). Pamuk also references an international canon: Holderlin, Balzac, and Rousseau, for example.

8. Pamuk revisits Anatolia in his fourth and sixth novels, *The New Life* and *Snow*, respectively. Both novels mostly take place outside of Istanbul and contain strong parodies of modernization history and national ideology. See Orhan Pamuk, *Yeni Hayat (The New Life)* (Istanbul/New York: İletişim/Farrar Straus Giroux, 1994/1998); and *Kar (Snow)* (Istanbul/New York: İletişim/Knopf, 2002/2003).

9. *CBS* is a social and economic history of the establishment of the Republic and the rise of a Muslim bourgeoisie who will later constitute the Republican elite. The transformation from Ottoman Muslim to Republican Turk will give rise to dilemmas of definition regarding "Turkishness." We can summarize this dilemma by stating that manifestations of "Turkishness" are predicated on various cultural iterations of *din* and *devlet* that emphasize or deny the antinomy. Pamuk's experimentation with the contexts of this literary-cultural script leads both to new notions of literary modernity as well as a redefinition of Turkishness.

10. For each of the three periods, these oppositions are (1) constitutional rule versus sultanic autocracy, (2) cultural revolution versus Anatolian-Islamic tradition, and (3) leftist versus nationalist coup. The three constitutional, cultural, and socialist revolutionary phases are referred to in Turkish as *meşrutiyet, inkılap,* and *devrim,* respectively.

11. Characters in the first two sections of the novel are authors of incomplete or poorly received book projects: Cevdet Bey pens an unfinished memoir, *My Half-Century in Business (Yarım Asırlık Ticaret Hayatım)*; Refik writes a utopian vision of Anatolian progress entitled *The Development of the Village (Köy Kalkınması)* as well as keeps a journal; Muhittin writes a collection of poems. All of these characters have failed aspirations as authors. The theme of the writer manqué in Turkish literature has been addressed by Jale Parla, "The Writer-Manqué : Orhan Pamuk and His Predecessors," paper presented at the Turkey: Political and Literary Intersections conference, Duke University November 3, 2007.

12. See Georg Lukács, *The Historical Novel* (London: Merlin Press, 1962).

13. By simply portraying the cosmopolitan, multilingual, and multiethnic context of late Ottoman Istanbul, Pamuk is arguing for the legibility of the era's society rather than dismissing it as simply antimodern. Part One depicts characters that are Armenian (Mari Çuhaciyan), Jewish (Eskinaz), and converts to Islam (Fuat Bey, a *dönme*). As a Muslim, Cevdet Bey is a minority in the business circles of Istanbul's Jews, Greeks, and Armenians. French is the lingua franca of elite culture. In short, Pamuk has provided a historically realistic literary description of fin de siècle Istanbul. Cevdet Bey will marry the daughter of an Ottoman pasha, loyal to the sultanate, to increase his social standing. The context of Part One is of cosmopolitan Ottoman *din*. See Orhan Pamuk, *Cevdet Bey Ve Oğulları (Cevdet Bey and Sons)* (Istanbul: Karacan Yayınları, 1979/1982).

14. In the standard Empire-to-Republic narrative, "Empire" represents tradition and darkness whereas "Republic" represents modernity and light. Pamuk's first two novels accept this trajectory and the Eurocentric underpinnings of secularization thesis. However, the unilinear (diachronic) and omniscient history of *CBS* becomes multivalent (synchronic) and multiperspectival in *SH*—a change that signifies a political challenge to the secularization thesis. After his second novel, Pamuk never returns to modernization historiography as a formative component of literary modernity.

15. For more on belated modernity and national literary traditions, see Gregory Jusdanis, *Belated Modernity and Aesthetic Culture: Inventing National Literature* (Minneapolis: University of Minnesota Press, 1991).

16. In bringing together technology (the chronograph) and Muslim time, the scene describes Ottoman Muslim modernity. The historical reality of an Ottoman Muslim modernity is completely denied in the dominant Republican Empire-to-Republic narrative.

17. The themes of dream and time reveal the influence of Ahmet Hamdi Tanpınar's work. See Ahmet Hamdi Tanpınar, *Saatleri Ayarlama Enstitüsü (the Time-Regulation Institute)* (Istanbul: Dergah, 1962); and *A Mind at Peace*, trans. Erdağ Göknar (New York: Archipelago Books, 2009).

18. For an alternative history of Abdülhamit's rule see Selim Deringil, *The Well-Protected Domains: Ideology and the Legitimation of Power in the Ottoman Empire 1876–1909* (London: I. B. Tauris, 1998).

19. This perspective conflates nationalism, socialism, as well as Orientalism since it reflects the cultural logic of an internalized Turkish version of top-down national-, colonial- or Soviet-style modernization.

20. Pamuk consistently draws attention to identity formation. His characters are often drawn with an uneasy sense of self. Cevdet Bey, for example, muses, "Why am I this way?" This retort finds parallel expression by other characters in each part of the novel.

21. For more on the relationship between engineers and ideology in the Turkish modernizing context, see Nilüfer Göle, *Mühendisler Ve İdeoloj: Öncü Devrimcilerden Yenilikçi Seçkinlere (Engineers and Ideology: From Vanguard Revolutionaries to Modernizing Elites)* (Istanbul: İletişim, 1986).

22. The Turkish term *inkılap* ("revolution") describes the social engineering of this period. In *CBS*, the character Süleyman Ayçelik ironically defines *inkılap* as follows: "*İnkılap* is the project of providing what's in the best interest of the people (*halk*) to

the people, despite the people but for the people" (*CBS*, p. 409). This succinctly summarizes one of the major overarching dilemmas of Republican secular modernity.

23. In the intervening years, a series of wars have occurred that culminated in the partition of Ottoman territory and the rise of the modern Middle East. The influx of refugees from the Balkans and the Caucasus and the expulsion of Armenians and Greeks ("*Rum*") have resulted in vast demographic changes making Anatolia more Sunni Muslim, preparing the way for the establishment of a predominantly Muslim Republic. Ironically, this transformation in the religious identity of the population is diminished and concealed by state secularism.

24. Pamuk, *Cevdet Bey Ve Oğulları (Cevdet Bey and Sons)*, p. 213.

25. Ibid., p. 237.

26. In the plot, a French revolutionary cultural influence can be discerned in Part One, a German national-socialist influence in Part Two, and a Soviet socialist Russian influence in Part Three. British and American high literary modernism (e.g., the works of Virginia Woolf and William Faulkner) is evident in *SH*.

27. A number of texts, earlier written by characters, appear in the last section. Refik's journal, sections of which are excerpted in Part Two, reappears as Ahmet has İlknur read the Ottoman text aloud. Cevdet Bey's memoirs also appear. These accounts of the two preceding historical periods are literally and figuratively in the hands of the third generation.

28. Pamuk, *Cevdet Bey Ve Oğulları (Cevdet Bey and Sons)*, p. 564.

29. For an introductory analysis of Hikmet and his work, see Saime Göksu and Edward Timms, *Romantic Communist: The Life and Work of Nazım Hikmet* (London: Hurst & Co., 1999).

30. What You Seek (Nazım Hikmet, 1962, my translation)

what you seek is not in your room but outside
trucks are carrying what you seek
cranes with cement blocks hoist it
what you seek is in the trees of Leningrad street
and in the escalators of metros
what you seek is in stations of separations and reunions
and in the food sack of the tall
woman in a red headscarf
what you seek is in the frescoes of Rubliov
you can ask two bronze figures what you seek
one stands before the Russian cinema
the other before the Moscow cinema
in Sverdlov Square a full-bearded stone figure stands
he knows best what you seek
what you seek is in the red brick structure in Revolution Square
what you seek is in the people on the streets
what you seek is in you

31. For an overview of theorizations of this category, see Sean Burke, *The Death and Return of the Author: Criticism and Subjectivity in Barthes, Foucault, and Derrida* (Edinburgh: Edinburgh University Press, 1998).

32. See for example Ahmet Evin, *Origins and Development of the Turkish Novel* (Minneapolis, MN: Bibliotheca Islamica, 1983); Robert P Finn, *The Early Turkish Novel, 1872–1900* (Istanbul: Isis Press, 1984); Jale Parla, *Don Kişot'tan Bugüne Roman (The Novel from Don Quijote to Today)* (Istanbul: İletişim, 2000); Azade Seyhan, *Tales of Crossed Destinies: The Turkish Novel in a Comparative Context* (New York: Modern Language Association, 2008).

33. The allusions to canonized author intellectuals of the Ottoman/Turkish tradition with a revolutionary bent emphasize Pamuk's acceptance of a Turkish literary history that echoes the Empire-to-Republic dialectic: Namık Kemal and Tevfik Fikret (Part One), Yakup Kadri (Part Two), and Nâzım Hikmet (Part Three) all advocated revolutionary change and were persecuted by the state. Here, literary history follows the revolutionary dialectic from Empire to Republic. This body of work is contrasted to European authors (or their characters) of revolutionary bent including Balzac (Rastignac), Dostoyevsky, Voltaire, Rousseau, and Hölderlin. The two contrasting "archives" are presented in the expected "East" versus "West" opposition.

34. There is an obvious Faulknerian influence in the novel. In particular, the characters, themes, structure, and style of *As I Lay Dying* are prominent. Southern gothic and grotesque themes are conveyed to the Turkish context and inflect the Empire-to-Republic narrative.

35. Metin is the depoliticized figure of future neoliberalism, Nilgün is an aspiring engaged leftist studying sociology, and Faruk is the figure of the Republican intellectual-in-crisis. Hasan is an ideological convert and a victim of ultranationalist Turkism, a favorite Pamuk character (and an updated version of Muhittin in *CBS*).

36. The nuances of irony and parody present in Pamuk's novels do not often convey in translation. This is another source of misinterpretation, especially when Pamuk uses satire with physical or verbal scenes of violence: The violence conveys, the satirical nuance does not. See, for example, Sibel Erol, "Reading Orhan Pamuk's *Snow* as Parody: Difference as Sameness," *Comparative Critical Studies* 4.3 (2007). During a personal conversation with Pamuk, he repeatedly interrupted himself with bouts of laughter while reading a draft version of the "theater coup" scene from *Snow*. The humor in this scene is clearly lost on Anglophone readers based on reviews of the novel.

37. However, the novel ends with an allusion to *Robinson Crusoe*. Not only does this conjure a master-slave relationship that will be developed in *The White Castle, Crusoe* was one of the first novels translated into Ottoman Turkish in the 1860s, establishing a precedent for the modern Turkish novel. Of course, the cultural revolution is also parodied in the relationship between Crusoe/Fatma and Friday/Recep.

38. Dr. Selahattin is similar in character to his contemporary, Dr. Nusret of *CBS*.

39. Orhan Pamuk, *Sessiz Ev (the Silent House)* (Istanbul: Can, 1983), p. 24.

40. Ibid., p. 56.

41. Ibid., p. 41.

42. Ibid., p. 161.

43. Ibid., p. 113.

44. Ibid., p. 115.

45. Ibid., p. 161.

46. See for example *The Castle of Crossed Destinies,* a novel that prefigures Pamuk's *WC*: Italo Calvino, *The Castle of Crossed Destinies,* trans. William Weaver (New York: Harcourt, 1977).

47. The term "historiographic postmodernism" is identified and defined by Linda Hutcheon, *A Poetics of Postmodernism: History, Theory, Fiction* (New York: Routledge, 1988).

Contributors

Mehnaz M. Afridi, PhD, University of South Africa, is an assistant professor of religious studies, and director of The Holocaust, Genocide, and Interfaith Education Center at Manhattan College. She is currently writing a book entitled *Shoah through Muslim Eyes* and has published in *Sacred Tropes: Tanakh, New Testament, and the Qur'an as Literature and Culture* (Brill), and in *Not Your Father's Antisemitism: Hatred of the Jews in the Twenty-First Century* (Paragon House).

Esra Almas is an assistant professor in English literature and humanities at Doğuş University, Istanbul. She completed her PhD at the Amsterdam School for Cultural Analysis, University of Amsterdam, where she also taught in the department of literary studies. Her dissertation explored the links between literary capital and Istanbul's literary cityscape in Orhan Pamuk's work. Her research interests include critical theory, world literature, Turkish diaspora, and urban studies.

David M. Buyze, PhD, University of Toronto, teaches at the University of Vermont as online faculty. He has most recently published "Carmen Boullosa's *Duerme*, & the Inventing of Difference in Race and Religion," *Journal of Race, Ethnicity, and Religion*, April 2011, and "Identity, Interiority, & *Snow*," *Spiritual Identities: Literature and the Post-Secular Imagination*, 2010. He was until recently a fellow at the Schusterman Institute for Israel Studies at Brandeis University in summer 2011, and was previously an NEH Summer Institute fellow in Venice, Italy, in 2008.

Thomas Cartelli is professor of English and film studies at Muhlenberg College in Allentown, Pennsylvania, where he teaches courses on Shakespeare, postcolonial literatures, and North African and Middle Eastern literature and film. He is the author (most recently) of *New Wave Shakespeare on Screen* (Polity, 2007) and *Repositioning Shakespeare: National Formations, Postcolonial Appropriations* (Routledge, 1999).

Sander L. Gilman is a distinguished professor of the liberal arts and sciences as well as professor of psychiatry at Emory University. A cultural and literary historian, he is the author or editor of over 80 books. His *Obesity: The Biography* appeared with Oxford University Press in 2010; his most recent edited volume, *Wagner and Cinema* (with Jeongwon Joe), was published in that same year. He is the author of the basic study of the visual stereotyping of the mentally ill, *Seeing the Insane*, published by John Wiley and Sons in 1982 (reprinted: 1996) as well as the standard study of *Jewish Self-Hatred*, the title of his Johns Hopkins University Press monograph of 1986. For 25 years he was a member of the humanities and medical faculties at Cornell University where he held the Goldwin Smith Professorship of Humane Studies. For six years he held the Henry R. Luce Distinguished Service Professorship of the Liberal Arts in Human Biology at the University of Chicago, and for four years he was a distinguished professor of the liberal arts and medicine and creator of the Humanities Laboratory at the University of Illinois at Chicago. During 1990–1991 he served as the visiting historical scholar at the National Library of Medicine, Bethesda, MD; 1996–1997 as a fellow of the Center for Advanced Study in the Behavioral Sciences, Stanford, CA; 2000–2001 as a Berlin prize fellow at the American Academy in Berlin; 2004–2005 as the Weidenfeld Visiting Professor of European Comparative Literature at Oxford University; 2007 to the present as professor at the Institute in the Humanities, Birkbeck College; 2010 to 2013 as a visiting research professor at the University of Hong Kong. He has been a visiting professor at numerous universities in North America, South Africa, the United Kingdom, Germany, Israel, China, and New Zealand. He was president of the Modern Language Association in 1995. He has been awarded a Doctor of Laws (*honoris causa*) at the University of Toronto in 1997, was elected an honorary professor of the Free University in Berlin (2000), and was elected an honorary member of the American Psychoanalytic Association (2007).

Erdağ Göknar is assistant professor of Turkish studies at Duke University and an award-winning literary translator. He holds a PhD in Near and Middle Eastern Studies and has published articles on Turkish literature and culture as well as three book-length translations (most recent editions listed): Orhan Pamuk's *My Name is Red* (Everyman's Library, 2010), Atiq Rahimi's *Earth and Ashes* (from Dari, Other Press, 2010), and A. H. Tanpınar's *A Mind at Peace* (Archipelago, 2011). He is the coeditor of *Mediterranean Passages: Readings from Dido to Derrida* (UNC Press, 2008) and his analysis of Orhan Pamuk and the modern Turkish novel,

Orhan Pamuk and the Politics of Turkish Identity from Islam to Istanbul, is forthcoming from Routledge. He is the recipient of a Fulbright fellowship, an NEA translation fellowship, and the Dublin IMPAC Literary Award (jointly with Pamuk).

Hande Gurses holds a BA in English language and literature (Bogazici University, Istanbul, 2005) and an MA in cultural studies (Goldsmiths College, University of London, 2006). She is currently completing her PhD at the French Department, University College, London. Drawing on the theoretical background provided by the writings of Jacques Derrida, her study focuses on the role of displacement in the works of Orhan Pamuk. Her thesis analyzes the different strategies used in Pamuk's writings to undermine the old and tired dichotomies that include East/West, word/image, reality/fiction, original/copy.

Fran Hassencahl, PhD, associate professor of communication and director of the Middle Eastern Studies Minor, at Old Dominion University in Norfolk, Virginia, teaches courses in rhetoric, intercultural communication, and political communication. She was a Fulbright scholar in Morocco and an exchange faculty at the University of Aleppo in Syria. Her research interests include the political uses of metaphor and the intersection of tradition and modernity in the Middle East. Her published research focuses on political cartoons, which address issues concerning 9/11, the Iraq War, Yasser Arafat, and swine flu. Her other publications examine magazines read by Turkish women and Pamuk's *The White Castle.*

Michael Pittman, PhD, is currently associate professor of humanities and religion at Albany College of Pharmacy and Health Sciences in Albany, New York. His areas of research interest include Sufism, Turkish literature, Iranian cinema, and the work of G. I. Gurdjieff. Pittman is editor of and contributor to *G. I. Gurdjieff: Armenian Roots, Global Branches,* based on selections from the Armenia-Gurdjieff Conferences he organized in Yerevan, Armenia, from 2004 to 2007. His current work, *Classical Spirituality in Contemporary America: The Confluence and Contribution of Gurdjieff and Sufism,* is forthcoming from Continuum Press in 2012.

Esra Mirze Santesso is assistant professor of English at the University of Georgia. She received her BA from Boğaziçi University in Istanbul, Turkey, and her PhD from the University of Nevada in Reno. She specializes in postcolonial literature and teaches courses on British imperialism and the South-Asian diasporic identity. Her current project, entitled *Disorientations: Muslim Identity in Anglophone Literature*, investigates the extent to which the questions and theories of postcolonial identity can be applied to Muslim subjects living in the West. She has also published articles on Turkish literature and film; her interview with Orhan Pamuk appeared in *PMLA* (2008).

Sevinç Türkkan is a visiting assistant professor at State University of New York—College at Brockport. She is completing her PhD degree at the University of Illinois-Urbana with a dissertation on the English and German translations of Orhan Pamuk's novels. She has published articles on Orhan Pamuk, translation reception, and cinema. Her translations from German appeared in the Best European Fiction 2010, published by Dalkey Archive Press. Her most recent scholarly presentations address issues of translation and ethics, global book markets, and modern Turkish literature and cinema.

Hülya Yılmaz, PhD, is senior lecturer in German, Comparative Literature, and Turkish Studies at the Pennsylvania State University. She authored a book on the influence of Sufism on the nineteenth- and twentieth-century German literatures. Her book reviews and presentations at national and international conferences stress her research on transnational and migrational literatures, literary reflections of the Turkish diaspora, gender and identity issues within the context of Turkish Islam, the Orientalistic representation of women in contemporary Turkish German literature and cinema, Germany's ghazal writers, and the discourse of Occidentalism in the writings of Islamist women of Turkey.

Index